The Winding Dirt Road

by

Jiu Da

HISTORIUM PRESS

With great power comes great responsibility.
François-Marie Arouet

All stories are fictional.

Table of Contents

PROLOGUE

The minute Paisan Sima awoke that morning, he caught a whiff of a sulfur-like odor akin to that of rotting cabbage. He had trouble catching on to the source where it might have come from, but he somehow got this niggling feeling that something awful was afoot. Without delay, he went straight to the bathroom and showered.

After getting dressed, he served himself a cup of tea while gazing out the window. It was a misty morning. Rivulets of rain were running down the window, blurring the view outside.

As he stood absentmindedly while gawking at streams of rain running down on the windowpanes, he briefly thought this was an important day. Just then, the phone rang.

A call from one of his assistants, Ms. Aihan Song, told him that the exam results were ready for him to review. He told her he would be there in an hour.

Having recently finished his doctorate, Paisan Sima begun teaching at a university in a northeastern Chinese capital. Following his appointment, he promptly organized a critical exam to select the best among the socialist elite.

Along with Ms. Aihan Song as his long-time assistant, the government assigned Mr. Mingtao Cai a little while back to help Professor Sima handle the exams.

Yet, despite everything proceeding according to plan, a colleague vehemently objected to it earlier and voiced his concerns that his fellow might have overstepped the mark and overreached himself. He argued nothing could start anew without antecedent reform or transformation. He concluded this exam could be an inevitable prelude to something inauspicious, an apple of frightful discord.

Professor Sima stuck to his position in the teeth of his colleague's critical remarks. Speaking persuasively and with vehemence, he asserted that this was the most relevant and accurate evaluation ever. It was a touchstone for future elites; he insisted.

The exam comprised two parts. The first gauged the test-taker's competency on social and cultural awareness and language skills. It also evaluated how they fared in Chinese literature, calligraphy, poetry, songs, and interpersonal skills.

The most intimidating and challenging part, however, was the second one. Unlike the first part, which allowed a time slot of two hours to complete, the second part could take up to six hours.

The second part of the test covered many significant topics, ranging from political discourse, economics, moral discourse, philosophy, social order, psychology, sociology, and natural laws to human evolution. Primarily open-ended, the questions demanded thorough answers to show the test-taker's skills. It assessed their knowledge of

unique topics or areas, how they reacted to a particular situation, and how they applied their expertise.

Not long after arriving at the institution, Professor Sima settled in and reviewed the test results.

Despite his positive impression of the first exam part, Professor Sima recognized the greater significance of the second. How the test-takers did in the first part was irrelevant; the second part truly counted.

However, the exam results for the second part turned out to be so bungling that they were causing Professor Sima alarm and disquiet. All the while, he clucked his tongue with a disappointing 'tsk, tsk, tsk' while shaking his head now and then.

Only after he patiently went through all the tests one by one did he notice the answers more or less followed the same pattern.

In the political narrative, they failed to explain the meaningful relationship between the masses and the political elites.

Regarding topics on social order, they all derived their views from the conflict theory perspective. Therefore, they were all favorably disposed toward policies that relied heavily on cruelty and inhumanity.

In philosophy, being heavily predisposed by socialist ideologies, none could effectively apply the basic fundamental theory of causes and effects or evoke objectivity and rationality to account for certain phenomena.

In psychology, all were eagerly looking for ways to alter human nature.

In sociology, they carelessly tied up sociology with psychology and needed help in understanding the primary functions of a group or those of individuals.

In history, they all provided distorted accounts or events of the historical past.

In moral discourse, they could explain an independent, isolated virtue well, but provided hysterical and incoherent explanations of how this virtue would be so negative when it mingled with socialist ideologies.

As a result, all the test-takers failed their exams. Once Professor Sima realized the potential consequences of these results, the uncertainty riveted him to the spot. He never knew it was that bad, but this was bad. If he ever made the test results public, that could spell the end of his career or his ending up in the back of the beyond.

As Professor Sima continued to delve into the consequences of the results, it was slowly getting dark outside. The day was overcast, marked by showers that came and went. The sun must have set an hour ago. Street lamps had switched on, casting their amber glow on the pathways around the adjacent buildings.

At this time, Professor Sima dismissed Mingtao, telling him he would handle the exams alone from that point on. For unknown reasons, Mingtao had stayed behind after Aihan took leave an hour ago.

By now, the room had slowly descended into darkness. Professor Sima turned on his desk lamp to banish the gloom around his table and continued to meditate on the results.

But the more he thought about them, the more panicky he became. He briefly deliberated reversing the test results to forestall catastrophe, like turning the list upside down.

Those who achieved satisfactory marks, or the mediocre, in the middle of the list, did not pose any actual problems. That was because whichever way he turned, those in the middle would remain in the middle, anyway.

The genuine issue was those at the rear of the list, which inevitably posed an inextricable dilemma for Professor Sima. Violence, indifference, aggression, and ruthless tactics characterized those at the bottom, who exhibited conspicuous yet disturbing patterns.

Reversing the list or turning it upside down would end up putting those with disturbing patterns as the best. That was another kind of calamity altogether.

The only good thing about that was that, since none of the best were on the original list, none of the worst were after he turned it upside down.

Just as Professor Sima was wracking his brain to devise a solution fast while clucking his tongue 'tsk, tsk, tsk' nervously, he seemed to hear a faint squeaking sound coming from someone's shoes.

Unsure it came from the hallway or inside the room, he stood up and turned around to look. Just then, he saw five or six dark figures standing merely a few yards behind him in complete silence.

The instant when Professor Sima came into visual contact with these unexpected guests, they scared him silly. He stepped back unexpectedly and bumped into his table, causing it to move a few inches while the table legs screeched against the concrete floor.

Holding his breath, he glanced through his dimly lit room, eyes fixed in a squint. He now clearly perceived they were men, all in black. Just as he continued to study these men silently with great dread, the lead man broke the eerie silence by demanding Professor Sima to come with them at once.

Professor Sima demanded to know, "Why? Did I break any law?" "No." came a terse, icy reply.

Professor Sima knew well that it was too dark for anyone to detect his countenance, which now might turn pale, a betrayal of his panic-stricken state. But beads of cold sweat gathered around his forehead attested he was so.

Professor Sima asked again, "Am I under arrest?" "No, just talk," came another brief, stiff response.

The speaker barely finished when Professor Sima barged in impatiently. "Then talk!" But his demand did not elicit any response from the seemingly unbudging dark figure.

It was futile to resist, Professor Sima reasoned. Having decided not to choose the greater of the two evils, he elected to keep his dignified manner in any way possible. Of medium height and about 150 pounds, he could hardly bear seeing the image of him being dragged out of the building like a rag doll by these roughnecks while they pushed his head down.

Professor Sima then flung a batch of papers on his desk, quietly leaving the building with them and entering the waiting black sedan.

While sitting inside the vehicle, he casually gazed out the car window at his office on the second floor. He then spotted a looker-on whose eyes remained fixed upon him. As Professor Sima raised his eyes to get a good look, there was no other but Mingtao himself.

As Professor Sima wondered why Mingtao was still there, the car momentarily started moving and slowly vanished quietly into that rainy night.

No one knew what happened to Professor Sima afterward or his whereabouts until a month later.

Down below, in the right corner of a daily newspaper, a small section devoted to some insignificant announcements said that Professor Paisan Sima was 'removed' for reasons of bribery and corruption, but not in so many words.

That was the last time anyone saw or heard anything related to him.

RITE OF PASSAGE

Fabin sat quietly outside after school in a sullen silence. Not far behind him, a boy with plump, rosy cheeks was lollygagging around. He took a step closer and closer and poked Fabin in his back. Fabin twisted around to check behind when he met eyes with his friend, Lucas Wong.

With a sheepish grin, his friend quizzed, "You look so gloomy. What's the matter?" Fabin told him he had lost the award for best student to Xia Chen.

Upon hearing that, Lucas looked at his friend with detached amusement. The award was just a nominal recognition rather than anything substantial for him. He found it hard to understand why his friend took the matter seriously. But just as nosy about everything as he always was, Lucas followed. "How did he get that?"

Fabin did not answer the question but confided. "My mom's going to get mad at me."

"Oh, your mom!" Lucas suddenly realized the source of his friend's anxiety and asked,

"So, did you ask Ms. Qui why?" "No."

Both were silent for a while, quietly watching students spill out of the school in their exuberant mood and onto the waiting buses or sedans outside.

It was another scorching afternoon that day, with no breath of wind to ease. Fabin was fanning himself with a leaflet while he and Lucas continued to watch their lackadaisical watch as people came and went.

As the stream of students gradually slowed to a trickle, Lucas suddenly realized something. He shifted his attention to

Fabin and asked, "Oh, I just remembered something. The last time Ms. Qui was sick, did your mom help her out?"

Fabin became intrigued by the unexpected topic his friend brought up. That was at least six months ago when Ms. Qui fell ill.

Fabin replied halfheartedly, "Yes, my Mon helped her with a gift card." Lucas asked offhandedly, "How much?"

Fabin frowned and hit back, "Does that matter? It was just a kind gesture."

Being so eager to find out what the amount was, to the point of being rude, Lucas kept at it. "Yeah, yeah, but how much?"

Fabin became annoyed and replied, "Worth 100 bucks. Why?"

Upon hearing this, Lucas seemed unsure of what he had heard, so he asked again, "100 HKD?"

Fabin appeared offended by the remark and retorted, "So?"

Lucas finally showed self-satisfaction and replied, "You know what I know? I found out Xia Chen's parents gave Ms. Qui 1000."

Fabin cried out, "What! 1000?"

"Yes, one thousand. Xia Chen told me personally. You could hear a trace of smugness in his voice because it was not in Hong Kong dollars. It's in US dollars."

Upon hearing this, Fabin was dumbstruck, mouth agape with disbelief.

At that point, Lucas sneaked a look at his friend and scoffed. "Looks like it's going to take more than being smart to stay competitive, my friend."

Lucas did not hide his belittlement of his friend for being naïve and clueless. Born and raised in Kowloon, he boasted, "I hear more, know more."

Ms. Qui was once an idealistic educator. Motivated by her desire to become a teacher while still in high school, she believed education was the cornerstone of a better society. Once she began her teaching career, she worked tirelessly to make her aspirations a reality, never shying away from her responsibilities.

However, as years went by, she noticed that the atmosphere in the teaching environment deteriorated. She witnessed hands exchanging gifts, favors delivered, and even outlandish recommendations demanding cash. She saw it all as this insidious atmosphere slowly crept into the school she once held sacred. Even though she remained silent and kept it all to herself, she could not ignore the fact that she had to work twice as hard to meet her needs, while others had made twice as much with little effort.

Eventually, by her late twenties, she slowly came to accept that one had to be a

bold-faced grabber or a thin-skinned loser. When that moment of realization came, she chose the middle way.

Even knowing Fabin was originally from the mainland, Lucas went on without reservation. "Your people are warped! You know that? That's what my parents said. All the time, your government blames corruption on human nature. When corruption sprouts up like wild weeds, they do not know how to deal with them. So, what do they do? They treated them collectively, razing them to the ground, flattening the entire field..."

As he spoke, he swept his hand across where the buildings stood and continued. "Then what? Like before, corruption grows again, and they flatten it again. They keep doing this without knowing the party is the source of this corruption. Absolute power starts at the very top and spreads to all the posts branching off below. When dogs and chickens have absolute power, too, all hell breaks loose. You understand? That's what my parents told me. They also said, once in a while..."

As Lucas continued spieling out a rap of beef about this and that, Fabin exhibited signs of increasing discomfiture. Then, words abruptly burst from him in a rush, "Wait a minute! Wait a minute! This is all about what? What weeds? What dogs and chickens?"

Wallowing in the excitement brought about by his discovery, Lucas ranted and raved non-stop. Seeing his friend look discomfited, he realized he might have babbled too much.

In an about-face, he stopped, put up his right hand as a conciliatory gesture, and said,

"Take it easy, pal! Don't overthink it. Things will be fine. Yeah, everything will be OK..."

Lucas then took a hesitant step away from Fabin while waving his hand at him and saying, "See you!"

The minute Lucas took off, Fabin found himself deep in thought. If that was all about the gift card, he seemed strangely relieved.

But as he walked down the path, he realized he was not the one to share the blame.

* * * * *

When Mrs. Eng saw Fabin, she did a double-take before asking him inquisitively,

"How did you get that broken lip?"

"Oh, it's nothing," Fabin replied, still focusing on a jigsaw puzzle half done on a table.

Mrs. Eng seemed unrelenting about what had happened and kept asking, "What's wrong?"

At this moment, Fabin glanced up from the jigsaw puzzle and replied, "Anping and James got into a fight."

Mrs. Eng knew Anping Huang and James Chan were Fabin's classmates. James was living with his family in a flat below.

Suspiciously, she asked, "Did you get into a fight?" "No, I didn't."

Her eyes popped in displeasure as she continued her grilling. "Then how did you get a bruised lip?"

"I didn't know how it all got started... Well, they both are touchy and defensive. They always cause a scene whenever they bump into each other."

Running out of patience, Mrs. Eng pressed on. "Then what?"

"All I knew was that Anping mentioned his parents would cast votes in the election before taking him to a mall. Then, suddenly, James hit back, saying something like, 'Cast vote for appointed candidates? Democratic dictatorship? Look like your parents find the pleasure of getting a good sniff whenever leaders do a fart.'"

Mrs. Eng's complexion turned grim; her mouth twisted a little.

Fabin continued, "James's slurring of his parents enraged Anping. Without saying another word, he swung a punch at James. As the two were trading blows at each other, I tried to break it up when I got hit by Anping."

Fabin finished telling the brawl with a giggle.

Mrs. Eng was unsure whether Fabin giggled at the punch or something about the fart. For the entire duration, she stood there with her arms folded across her chest. With a scowl on her face, she looked deadly serious. Immediately after, she pointed the finger at Fabin while anchoring her left hand on her hip and shouted, "That is not funny!"

Fabin frowned, unsure what Mrs. Eng referred to. But he remained quiet, knowing that she was prone to mood swings, and there was no telling how she would react.

Fixing her gaze on Fabin, she chided him. "It is not something you spoiled brats bumming around can ridicule about. You don't know a thing about the world."

Fabin blinked, thinking he was not the one who intended to bring up this subject. He just remained silent, fixing Mrs. Eng with a stare.

Once from a rural backwater in China, Mrs. Eng endured all kinds of ill-treatment, from the hands of affluent locals to local officials. Trapped in a place where she had no control over her life, she learned to stoop low, fawn, and obey ever since she was young. But as long as her abusers did not remove the mantel of abuse, she knew she would never straighten her back.

Over the decades, while dwelling on how best to weather the vicissitudes of tomorrow, she understood the only way to gain protection against mistreatment and abuse was to possess that very abusive power to protect herself from abuse.

Absolute power rendered all things tyrannical; abuse begot abuse.

To her, it thus stood to reason that the goal of absolute power was to preserve that same power to eradicate abuses. As years wore on, she slowly gained a bizarre, superstitious belief that her faith in communism was the only way to fight for justice and to safeguard her security and protection. Without it, she would bear an eternal wound of indignity and abuse.

Mrs. Eng continued to clarify her position while her eyes bulged. "Let me tell you why you should never disagree with the authorities. First, you donated but failed to meet other expectations, and the party involved accused you of bribery. Or, you made a profit but were short of sharing an adequate amount with others, and they charged you for staging an insurrection. Worst still, if you hold protests or anti-government views, they will treat you with Aripiprazole, which makes you feel weenie and wacky that you can not even tell who is your dad and who is your mom."

Then, with a frown, she snarled. "You dare say it smells bad..."

At that moment, while holding out her right hand, she pressed the tip of her index finger against her thumb and mimed something like squeezing a wedge of lemon in front of Fabin's nose while her face contorted in a grimace with the effort. She then burst out. "They're going to snuff out all your three generations!"

She raised her voice, as if James had deliberately targeted her with his nasty putdown, launching her into an unhinged meltdown in which she squealed, "I say it smells good. So what!"

Fabin cringed at her suggestion, his mouth twitching slightly while his eyes rolled. He felt she had somehow taken the term too literally, and now it ended up having to decide whether it smelled good or bad. That was not what James meant at all.

After collecting a fraction of a second, Fabin made a pantomime of checking his watch. He then hauled himself to his feet in one slow motion, as if any unprovoked movement might incur Mrs. Eng's other wrath.

Standing with the height below her shoulders, Fabin felt even smaller at her rousing ire. He hesitantly nodded while avoiding eye contact and replied in a mumble, "All right, all right, I've got it. I've got it."

He then tippytoed quietly out of the room, still feeling her intense glare of contempt behind his back.

He barely took a few steps toward the door when a warning came from behind. "Watch your back, you hear!"

$$* \quad * \quad * \quad * \quad *$$

Mr. Ngo came holding a laundry basket with freshly washed clothes and asked Fabin to help him. Fabin felt annoyed by the request.

Most residents in his area hung their clothes on bamboo poles that haphazardly protruded from their windows. Because of the unfurled colorful garments flapping in the breeze in public spaces, local folks dubbed them "international flags." Even though Fabin knew the job was easy, it required time and patience.

Once, a powerful gust blew away a pair of red Victoria's Secret underwear with noticeable white trim. Shortly thereafter, someone spotted it hanging from a flat window a block away. Fabin was tasked with getting it back, as it was a prize in someone's wardrobe. But the boy found the errand extremely nerve-racking as much as nail-biting.

Fabin laid down his pen and came over halfheartedly.

Seeing Fabin's languid movements, Mr. Ngo chided him. "Don't be too slack." "I'm not. My homework is due tomorrow."

"I thought you told me you did."

"No, it turned out to be somebody's work."

"That's OK."

Fabin found Mr. Ngo's remark jarring. He wanted to make sure he heard it right. "You think it's OK?"

Mr. Ngo told him, straight-faced, "It's not the right thing, but it is never wrong to get things done."

Fabin murmured, "Only if you have no pangs."

Mr. Ngo scoffed, "Pangs? Do you mean conscience? How much do you think it weighs? How much does it cost?"

As Fabin tried to figure out what Mr. Ngo was getting at, Mr. Ngo continued, "Try not too daft."

Mr. Ngo resumed, "Have you heard what our former Party member said before? If we don't have the thing we need, we buy it. If we know how to build something, we produce it. But what do we do with things we can't buy or produce? Tell me!"

Unsure what the answer was, Fabin kept quiet. But Ngo kept pressuring him. "So, what are we going to do?"

Ngo's parents sought refuge in China during the Sino-Vietnamese War. As a child of two different ethnicities and backgrounds, Ngo embodied the traditional values inherited from both cultures. But as he grew older, he relinquished all of his previous generation's long-standing honesty and goodness. When the man came to Hong Kong seeking better recognition, Ngo overtook the threshold of the ordinary and became a propaganda carrier for the country the man had now adopted.

As he became more audacious and reckless, the locals deemed this unabashed drumbeater cursed, because the curving of his mouth conjured up an Asian carp devouring everything.

Fabin made a wild guess. "If we can't buy, can't build... just grab it?"

Suddenly, Mr. Ngo realized there was little choice for the answer, even though the question seemed tricky enough.

Mr. Ngo intended to refer to a sharing pool based on collectivism, which spurred collective minds. According to his definition derived from the communal concept, he suggested nothing was personal; it was a free-for-all everyone could be part of. However, since he wanted to avoid being associated with a socialist ideology, he was vague about his views.

Mr. Ngo attempted to correct it. "No, no. Of course, not like that. Not like that. Ah... It's a kind of exchange and cooperation among different people."

After a brief pause, Mr. Ngo seemed reluctant to give up his attempt despite what had transpired. He kept at it. "But just think about it. Just tell yourself what you need to do. I need not answer."

With that, he cut off their conversation.

Fabin was slow to respond. When he wanted to ask a question, Mr. Ngo was gone.

Once in a while, Fabin would visit Mr. Ho Wing to practice Chinese calligraphy. Mere happenstance one afternoon bonded their acquaintance when Mr. Wing came to

Fabin's flat to collect a fee for delivering newspapers. Seeing Fabin practicing calligraphy while waiting, Mr. Wing took over the brush and produced two beautiful characters with great delicacy and force in each stroke. His handsome writing left a lasting impression on Fabin but, defied his bias. Had Fabin not seen it with his own eyes, he would not have swallowed that a man with a heedless appearance could write such beautiful characters. That attested to the saying he often heard that looks should not judge a man, as appearances could be deceiving.

From that day on, Fabin would now and again come to Mr. Wing's flat to practice calligraphy.

Just like any other evening, Mr. Wing would let Fabin practice independently and offer advice on his strokes on and off while pacing back and forth.

Halfway through, Fabin broke the silence by asking, "You told me you have been to England before, didn't you?"

"Yeah."

"Do priests there raise a flag every morning?"

That question came as a surprise, as it was facetious. Mr. Wing snickered and asked,

"Why did you ask that?"

"Well, before I moved here, every morning when I passed a temple near my house, there were always some Buddhist monks lining outside and performing flag ceremonies in their orange robes. After that, they saluted and cited some patriot slogans."

Upon hearing this, Mr. Wing barely refrained from sniggering, shaking his head contemptuously. Unexpectedly, he raised his voice, apparently agitated. "No, they would not do silly things like that."

After briefly pausing, he murmured, "That is a disgrace."

"Why do you think it is silly? I thought these monks were merely doing that for a show."

Fabin replied with an insouciant shrug.

Mr. Wing exploded, "Don't be smart-aleck. No one does that for fun. You're still young, like sloppy jello, wiggling from right to left, from left to right. You are malleable at best."

His taunt took Fabin aback. With medium height and heavy build, Mr. Wing was not the man who observed social niceties. He had the rugged countenance and a stiff upper lip of a man who brooked no-nonsense and could be blunt and direct.

Mr. Wing pulled over a chair and sat down. Pointing the finger at Fabin, he said, "Listen! You are still too young to understand things around you. I'm going to tell you this once. You might not understand it now. But keep it to yourself, and one day it will come to you."

He then started, "Out there, you might find something funny to laugh your head off. But know this. Since the early days of the Republic, there has been a faint, blurry line between right or wrong, good or bad, moral or immoral, decent or indecent, justice or injustice, legal or illegal, friendly or hostile, empathy or apathy, honesty or dishonesty, fairness or favoritism, and so on. Between two opposite entities, this blurry line, functioning as an arbitrary scale, allows them to determine your standing and reputation.

"The movement of the scale determines the state of one's worthlessness or worthiness. From this, it instinctively leads to a prevalent attitude of admitting nothing and denying everything."

Mr. Wing paused as if he was running out of breath after having spouted all the virtues the world offered.

He then continued, "However, if you care to dig deeper, that typical attitude may have shared a common root, as it would later grow into the prevailing personification that sees everything as neither good nor cruel or the perception of good mingled with cruelty."

All the while, Fabin was sitting there, wide-eyed, with his brush poised over his worksheet. Mr. Wing did not know why he acted like that, but he finished his loquacity, anyway. "Those monks, just like any people, when they blur the line between what is decent and what is indecent, nothing will be too obscene for them to commit. When the time comes, we shall reassess the course that led us here and how it weighs upon our experience."

Without giving Fabin time to reflect on what he had just gone through, Mr. Wing stood up abruptly and announced, "You have learned enough today. Pack up and go home!"

Fabin felt like something dinned into his head, and without ceremony, he found himself nudged out of the house and into the street. He could not understand why adults talked in that way - things that were bizarre and incomprehensible. The boy was unsure whether his newly gained experience with people around him would be helpful down the road. And in no uncertain terms, their expressions, whatever he chose or whichever direction he was going to take, he would face a choppy, turbulent transition ahead.

With a sullen mood, he slowly left under the cover of darkness.

Fabin, eleven going on twelve, attended a middle school where the school assigned Ms. Gui, a lead teacher, to Hong Kong many years ago. A native of the mainland, Ms. Gui was in her early fifties. Mr. Ngo was Fabin's father, Mrs. Eng, his mother, and Mr. Wing, a retiree who lived with his wife in a flat a block from Fabin's apartment.

I Am Going Home

Xintai Chin was lying in bed, awake, even though the sun was high. Every morning he woke up, he would feel faint with hunger, followed by a wave of despair sweeping over him. If the man got up, the bitterness of life awaited. Instead of facing it, he remained motionless, and a semblance of peace would prevail. But moments of peace seldom last.

Every night he went to bed, he always wished he would never wake up again. That thought comforted him but never came. But if he had gotten his wish to depart from the affliction that tormented him, he thought, what would happen to his children?

When he thought of that, his anguish deepened. For him, the liminal state between life and death was the undead of the living. But if he lived while plagued with the relentless onslaught of hunger, it beggared hope for a better tomorrow.

In the months following the drought during the Arduous March, which desolated farmland, food supplies gradually dwindled, and livestock died. Soon, famine set in. Day in and day out, people craned forward. Nothing came.

As desperation grew, people resorted to eating whatever they could find - grass, roots, tree bark, live worms, or even scraps for pigs. Some got swollen faces from eating grass, diarrhea from the soil, or indigestion from tree bark. One of the teenage sons from a neighboring family poisoned himself by eating mushrooms.

Initially, his parents thought his symptoms of nausea, abdominal pain, and sweating would pass. Instead, he died the following day. Xintai helped wrap the boy's body in a plastic bag. Together, they dug a shallow hole near a hill and buried him with a layer of earth.

A few days later, while Xintai was foraging near the burial site with his children, he noticed disturbances in the soil over the grave. Concerned, he covered it with more earth. The next day, to his horror, a pack of hungry, stray dogs scratched away the soil and dragged the body out. They devoured everything. The boy's parents cried their hearts out.

That night, Xintai dreamt of himself lying on the ground. A dog was looming over him, tearing his torso apart and seizing his guts with its baring teeth. Xintai woke up with a start, soaked in a cold sweat.

Xintai was still lying in bed, paralyzed by the numbness of hunger. As he continued to be consumed by hopelessness, he vaguely heard two people conversing in Mandarin. He regained his attention and listened. The house was quiet, the air still. He heard two people speaking outside his home anew. He hurled himself up to a seating position and got off the bed.

Slowly, Xintai shuffled with fatigued steps toward the door. Then, in glaring daylight, he saw one individual heading back to the main road. The one still nearby was a young man in his early 20s. He wore brownish-green casual pants with a black puffer jacket without sleeves over his white t-shirt. He was holding a long pole.

"Eh! eh!..." Xintai waved his hand to get the young man's attention. The young man raised his head and looked at Xintai momentarily.

"Anything to spare?" Xintai implored in Mandarin in a subtle northern accent while extending his right hand.

The young man involuntarily rummaged through his pocket with his left hand. He laid his pole on the ground and searched with his right hand in another bag. But all he could find was a piece of candy wrapped in red wax paper twisted at both ends, with the label 'Victory' printed in white. Without saying a word, he handed it to Xintai, who gaped greedily at the candy.

After Xintai took over the piece of sweet, he opened the wrapper quietly as if it might fall apart and put it carefully in his mouth with his shaky hand. As he savored that piece of mellifluous confection, he felt life instantly open to a rare aura of the long-lost sweetness of his childhood. He treasured the moment so much that he held the wrapper dearly in his right hand, unwilling to let it part.

All the while, the young man kept looking at Xintai in tattered gray clothes, his loose, unkempt brown hair tinted with white, his cheeks hollow with bulged eyes.

"Are you from China?" After a while, Xintai asked.

"Yes." came a crisp reply.

After a brief pause, the young man continued, unable to resist his curiosity. "Are you local? How come you know Mandarin?"

"The army deployed my father here during the war," Xintai explained.

"And is your father still around?" The young man inquired.

"No, he passed away two years ago." Xintai shook his head and broke down, sobbing.

Despite nudging fifty, Xintai was always tearful, bearing a lachrymose mourner in the face of adversity. He could not remember having ever smiled before. If a smile were a natural expression people inherited, Xintai, as a human being, would never have gained that feature.

Life on this part was an antipoetic reality even before the famine struck. Men and women toiled the land with their own hands and bodies. Women wearing harnesses attached to a plow pulled while the one at the other end pushed. They plowed up a row and back, then up and down, from dawn till dusk. Exhausted, they slumped against a chair, their breathing wheezing, their back stooping, and their eyes fixating in a vacant stare. They said in monosyllables if they spoke at all and nothing more, for there was nothing else to cherish.

"But I don't understand. What's your father's name?" The young man asked.

"Dongan Chen."

At that moment, Xintai felt weak and dizzy. He moved closer to the side of the house, leaned against the wall, and then sat down on a stool. In the bright light, the man looked spent, his face ashen and haggard. There, he gradually recollected, and his memories slowly carried him back to his childhood.

* * * * *

Xintai's memories of his mother were vague. He could not recall what she looked like, for she passed away during childbirth before Xintai reached the age of five. All he remembered was her being busy all day, if not in the field tilling the land, then in the kitchen cooking meals for the family. She talked a little. When she did, she conversed mostly with Xintai and his sister. Rain or shine, she never took a break all year round.

His father, hardened by socialist causes that a man should never show personal grief over private matters, seemed not to mourn his wife's death. But he became silent and withdrawn like someone so lost in thought that he forgot to eat. More precisely, he refused to eat as if food might assuage the effect of his grief, which helped him sustain himself in times of sorrow.

One night in early spring, after his father sowed the field, he told Xintai about his hometown in China and his uncles and aunts. Xintai asked where China was, to which his father pointed his finger in the northwest direction and said, "close to here."

Xintai then asked if they would one day go to see them. His question, though expected, betrayed his father's deep sense of sorrow. A bitter answer leaped to his tongue, and his father mumbled 'maybe,' but not in so many words.

His father told him he was drafted into the volunteer army, wearing a gifted uniform designed by his beloved second-in-command, and sent to resist America and aid Korea.

His father then replicated a passage from a long-lost script and repeated, "Since defending the fatherland is a sacred duty of a citizen and the greatest duty is defending the fatherland, which is the source of all my happiness, I put on the military uniform of the revolution for the sake of protecting the Supreme Commander."

He continued, "Led by one brave general who fought alongside us, we fought bravely and fearlessly. The enemy was afraid of us. Launching wave after wave, we charged at them until they got scared and fled. That was how we won the battle. That was how we served the state, for the state."

Fascinated by the story, the boy responded, "For the state." To which his father affirmed. "To the state."

That was the most vivid account Xintai had of his father. After his mother died, his father became quieter and withdrawn, but never complained. Even when things did not work out as intended, he did not express his anger; he remained secluded.

Once, a neighbor told him about some men who had fled to China. Upon being sent back, they were beaten and forced to eat a clump of grass, along with the roots and the soil, as punishment. One of them became severely ill with diarrhea and died two days later.

With a somber expression, his neighbor said, "The poor fellow died a miserable death. He died with his eyes open."

Upon hearing that story, his father slumped into a deep silence, eyes gazing off into space.

Stoic resignation had long been part of Chen's fortitude. Confronted by many past misfortunes and injustices that he was powerless to change, he slowly learned to give in to stoic submission. From this impassive submission came fatalism, which let him accept destiny and would help him face adversity with calm.

Yet, indoctrination in his early years also compounded his fatalism. Because of this, he came to accept his indoctrination as part of the predetermined and, therefore, inevitable whole.

Tragically, this outlook on life had a lifelong lasting effect on Chen and gave him a consistent view of one icy, colorless world. In times of adversity that preceded him, he always tried to mitigate his misfortune with the age-old refrain, 'To endure is human, to prevail divine.'

This attitude lurked around the edge of his subconscious and carried him along on many uneven journeys in life without him questioning.

Yet, many decades later, that bond between him and the state faded as he lay on his deathbed. In those last moments, he felt a sense of lightness and ease. He was relieved that he would soon be free from all burdens. Gradually, his memory of past events became more precise and vivid.

On two occasions, when Xintai was old enough to ask his father why he stayed behind, his father never vouchsafed a full explanation. Each time he raised that question, his father would become quieter and bitter. His father would vaguely state that he was to carry out some extra assignments. The tasks aimed at helping bury the deaths scattered in a desolate, scorched landscape, rebuilding the nation now laid to waste, and fostering a population almost decimated.

Shortly later, Chen became affianced to a local woman with whom he followed the Party's line to build a family. They heeded the line in silence, for men and women in this postwar scenario benumbed by widespread destruction to forsake, too hungry to defy. In silence, the two procreated for the sake of procreation.

As days turned into months and months into years, Chen cast doubt on the meaning of his existence. No sooner than after the unworldly bond of marriage, the harsh realities of sustaining Chen's family set in. Chen tilled the ground for years to maintain a living, leading a hand-to-mouth existence. By then, they had their two offspring. But as always, they went to bed every night hungry, for there were too many mouths to feed and too few to spare.

But if constant worries of sustaining self-sufficiency troubled Chen, his illusion of going back home soon vaporized. He soon learned that, contrary to any heroic fantasies, soldiers faced cruel punishments for exposure to foreign influences after returning home.

At this stage, while lying in bed, Chen's memories, hoarded in his heart all these years, drifted in and out of the past and the present, of his childhood, of his parents and relatives, of his siblings and friends. But eventually, his mind would settle on some fuzzy scenes of fighting in the dead of winter.

* * * * *

For most of his life, Chen often used florid bits of speech, describing battles he ultimately lost track of their true meaning or how and what took place. Yet, only in his last hours was he able to present the events in a different, albeit unsentimental, unpoetic narrative.

Chen's vision of this heroic battle rooted in heroism. However, as Chen later reflected on it, heroism was not the familiar iconography of the revolution depicted. Instead, he came to see the whole outcome from a different perspective.

Not long after Chen arrived, he came in contact with a black and white border collie, later earning the nickname Ning the Plucky. When Chen found him, Ning was in terrible shape. Chen took the starved, sick dog to his tent and nursed him out of sympathy. From that day on, the dog always stayed by Chen's side and cemented a bond of friendship that would last a lifetime.

Then, as days wore on, an impending military offensive finally came.

That night, near to where Chen deployed, a unit of an entire volunteer army, wearing canvas shoes and thin cotton uniforms with hands ungloved, some crouching on the icy ground, others in an upright posture, all solidified by cold, like ice sculptures.

Dozens of soldiers rushed to the windswept front line in sub-zero, bitterly cold temperatures, only to be mown down instantly by machine gun fire. Many would only be in that momentous second to notice their fingers and limbs falling apart.

Not far away, hundreds crossed a frozen lake, whose trousers got drenched and quickly frozen up while their guns jammed. Scores moved like unpliable chunks of wood and fell halfway through. Impelled by 'Nothing we Chinese communists cannot do,' more followed in a tactical gambit, more human trunks fell.

By the time of the assault, frigid weather, nonfunctional weapons, and bombardments had debilitated a massive, irreplaceable number of soldiers, not to mention the complete shattering of an entire division at the outset. But that did not deter Chen, for he, like any others, gambled on the fact that they still had enough soldiers to make up a significant number of the volunteer army needed to form swarm or wave tactics.

Fallen bodies soon littered the icy landscape, hither and thither, rendering a white frosty panorama splashed with brownish, stiff remains. Soldiers trampled above these corpses, mounting successive attacks. Layer upon layer of bodies piled high. But they kept coming, moving and falling.

Amid chaotic fighting, bullets whizzed past thick and fast with a menacing hissing sound, while ear-splitting explosions shattered the air, lighting up the desolate sweep. In this momentous second, as Chen was ready to charge, he noticed something was amiss.

All the time, Ning was always three steps ahead, leading the way. But amid the confusion, when brave souls rushed in where angels feared to tread, Chen did not see Ning in front of him.

At first, Chen wondered whether Ning could have raced ahead without waiting for him. He glanced back briefly, and to his surprise, Ning was three steps behind him, sitting upright on his hips.

Chen waved to him to come forward, but it failed to prompt a response from Ning. Instead, Ning's eyes flicked over to Chen in silence, then toward the front line, then back to Chen, and the front line again, as if he was suggesting Chen go first.

Caught in a split second of this historical moment while seeing Ning not budged, Chen had no time to haggle over who should go first or lead the way. He moved without Ning.

But then, right at that critical juncture, Ning gave a sudden loud, sharp bark. He ran up to Chen, darted left and right, and herded Chen across the plain to the right. Ning kept driving at Chen, intercepting and controlling his every movement as if preventing Chen from breaking the fold until they reached the side of a hill.

Much later, Chen conceded to the intelligence gap between him and Ning. Even though both processed the capacity for intelligence, zealotry colorized Chen's. Conversely, Ning was free from radicalization and allowed himself to dwell more on practical intelligence and resolve.

Following that experience, Chen remained closer to Ning than ever. Years later, the day Ning's shadow passed, Chen broke down and wept. Never had he felt as connected to anyone as to Ning, who stood by him through thick and thin and accompanied him on many roads and journeys together and in trying times.

Yet, the outcome of Chen's interaction with Ning threw not only light about intelligence; it also served as a channel through which patriotism could bring about breakneck heroism.

Lying on his deathbed as the bond between him and the State slowly faded, an admission of silent consent evolved. Lured by the notion of collectivism and the masses as an inexhaustible and expendable resource, the State cashed it indiscriminately through the masses' unexpressed assent. By taking advantage of their silence, the State leveraged the unsaid acquiescence of the masses into wanton aggression.

Chen now saw hundreds advance toward the defensive line, but machine guns from their adversary mowed them down. Hundreds more followed.

Soldiers from the Allies clutched the triggers with their alternate fingers while gun barrels turned red. They would not let their fingers go until they became sore and numb, that they could no longer hold. But it was not about physical numbness that distressed them. What disturbed them was the mass of corpses scattering all over the landscape in plain view.

As the Chinese troops indiscriminately flung themselves upon the enemy's line, wave after wave, the enemy finally ran out of ammunition. They abandoned their posts and ran.

Chen eventually reached the enemy's line with Ning. Standing atop a hill, he planted the red flag and relieved his anxiety by relaying the message of victory.

At the sight of the victory, Chen betrayed a faint sign of a rare smile while lying on his deathbed. He then slipped into a subconscious state, murmuring in his final breath, "I'm going home. I'm going home."

He passed away in the dead of night one December at 67.

*** * * * ***

The day his father ceased to cast his shadow cast Xintai's darkest moments. Overcome with immense grief and distress, he felt completely numb. He was alone, burdened with the care of two children. Without his father, he became helpless and hopeless. Caught in a maelstrom of grief, he wept day and night.

When Xintai had narrated it up to this point, he turned to the young man and ended the story by telling him, "Our path ends where no bridge to overtake, no crossing to revival to be seen."

With that, what time witnessed the stoic endurance in his father was the dolorous resignation in him.

Xintai's account, at odds with the young man's prior knowledge, troubled him. He floundered for a few moments before assuring Xintai that nothing was like what he had said.

He then assuaged Xintai, "You might just be too tired. When you're extremely hungry, it's easy for your mind to become hazy and confused. I will let our people know your concerns right away. After that, we will take care of you and your children. Everything will be fine. We care about everyone."

The young man then took his leave, with many assurances that he would return soon. As he took another step away, he turned and said, "Stay here. I will ask for help now and get you some food, too."

At that stage, Xintai became very emotional and thanked the young man repeatedly, feeling his wishes finally heeded.

Xintai then waited and waited. But when the light faded away, the young man was still in no sight.

Shortly after the darkness enfolded him and the young man still failed to return, Xintai became uneasy.

At that moment, he recalled the pole the young man had laid down that afternoon. But with a sweep of his eyes around the area, he saw no sign of it, and he did not see the young man take leave of it.

In his semi-delirious state, Xintai was now uncertain whether the chance meeting was actual or simply a culmination of self-imagination.

To attest to the occurrence, he looked down and slowly opened his right hand, followed by his left hand.

Both of his hands turned up empty.

ASHES OF AGGRAVATION

Like any other time, his wife badgered him again about work one evening. Kai Wu jumped to his feet and hit back in a huff. "I will find it!" Then he stormed out of the cramped kitchen, still hearing his wife whining from behind.

Had he stayed for another minute, more issues would have sprouted from her mouth. Kai knew it all by heart. As always, there was no lack of topics for initiating a dialog, albeit all would eventually lead to a subject about his passivity. He always suspected it was his in-laws who egged her on.

Once, she goaded him by telling him the neighbor thought her man was a sponger. It hit upon him as the nastiest putdown. But just as he was upset about the neighbor who brandished that derisive remark, he was hopping mad at his wife, who knowingly picked up the galling term and deliberately hurled it back at him. As much as he was boiling mad, he directed his anger at his wife than at his neighbor for not helping bury the insult. Indiscriminately, he flew into such an uncontrollable rage that he swung his arm at her. Had she not stepped back and dodged in time, his swing could have smacked her face like a hammer.

Aloof and laconic, Kai was medium build and muscular. He carried a streak of stubbornness and meanness that one could not miss in his manner. He had a swagger pose with a sideways glance, seeing things but not seeing them. But if those apparent traits were not enough to show his brute demeanor, his lips permanently curved, his looks cold and distant, and his reactions abrupt and forceful.

Yet, as tough as he was, he had difficulty to live off his hump. He still needed his wife's help to extract himself if he ever floundered about in an unpropitious time. But as mulish as he was, he clung fast to his pride and stubbornness. Every so often, he solaced himself with the assertion that 'You don't know who I am?'

However, if he sought comfort in that contention, it lasted only a fleeting moment. For a man in a slew of despair, troubles dogged every step. Nothing could heal.

In the past many years, Kai pounded the pavement of Zuozhou in central China, looking for work on and off. However, the thought of those menial and degrading works grated on him more than the prospect of finding one. As the summer drew near, Kai smirked at the thought of his son's exam, thinking that was the silliest thing. For a family whose history of long-standing petty crimes, he dwelled on his maxim that 'he who takes up street codes of survival skills is better off than any educated man.'

Still feeling discontent after a brief squabble with his wife, Kai stormed out of the house, slamming the door behind him.

It was late evening, and he was strolling aimlessly nearby. He seemed abstracted, his eyes musing on the surroundings. Yet, he thought of nothing; he felt dejected.

As Kai wandered casually in his sulky mood, he passed through a narrow pedestrian street. Food vendors and restaurants on both sides and those in the middle lane had laid tables and chairs for local night visitors and vacationers. Some were still busy setting out many small dishes in front of their stalls - meatballs, meats on skewers, tofu and vegetables, fried noodles, dumplings, and whatnot.

Amid this setting, clouds of hot steam emitted in mad rushes from food steamers. Meanwhile, the smoky flavors of roasted meat and the elusive aromas from frying woks on top of the burners' bluish flames wafted through the air.

Above the street, lights were strung across the outdoor venue, casting an amber glow with a relaxed ambiance. They rendered the whole place a semblance of a nighttime oasis while the darkness enfolded all over in that warm night.

But this oasis offered Kai no sense of easement. Behind his vacant eyes, with a touch of detachment, he was deeply melancholy.

People all over this culture knew how to secure their livelihoods. It was a silent acquisition gained from the early years that foretold who would do well in life. But some preferred to keep it unspoken lest it might invite ill luck, while others treated the subject as a divine privilege.

To Kai, born and raised amid this culture, he knew it all too well, like the back of his hand.

Life in many parts of this culture had always been very rancorous, contentious, and unkind behind the veil of a harmonious culture where activities bustled around the power of a backdoor connection, a network of secret, furtive, or illicit dealing.

Since immemorial, people had sustained their livelihoods and relationships based on bias and favoritism, not by laws or the concept of equality or fairness. All these concepts had never been as practical as the backdoor connection, which had always appeared more appealing, accessible, and manageable.

As a reciprocal exchange, a rear hatch connection was a straightforward affair - a suppliant as a seeker demanded a favor, and a wingman as a provider to return that favor. The risks were modest for the suppliant because the reward might be greater than the humility embraced. As for the wingman, the hard cash and gifts they received could only help bolster their status and self-worth.

Those who believed in what most were deemed the interconnectedness of lives through this illicit core were an answer to justice, equality, and fairness. But when those could not get their fair share, the system would be unjust, unequal, and unfair. Much like distorted reflections of an object that created twisted, deceptive images of the surroundings, it was a system of equality of inequality depending on how one viewed it.

Thus, not all outcomes were alike, for it all depended on the benefit angle. To those who saw their demands unfruitful or unheeded, however, they would slip into the night and simmer with resentment.

At the outset, people in this relationship were no thicker than thieves. Conversely, it could deteriorate into unwanted consequences. When parties involved did not get what they wanted, their relationships could become sour and contentious. Bitterness, resentment and malice ensued, followed by plots geared toward destroying others. The atmosphere could be belligerent, toxic, and hostile as a result.

Kai remembered a fellow named Nian Lan, whose relatives somehow established connections with an official, and implored him to find Nian a job. Long after, the official secured a position for Nian as a vice director of a corporation through his well-connected network. This unexpected offer came as a bombshell for everyone.

However, Nian soon became overwhelmed by his newfound status and challenged his boss to run the corporation. Squabble ensured.

When news of Nian's turbulence reached the official, he called, presumably out of his mortification, by telling the director by insinuation that he 'would support whatever decision the director would like to take.'

Nian was dismissed from his job soon after.

This incident, undoubtedly stranger than fiction, illustrated how connections could stretch to such an impossible reach, especially how a nobody went on to become a vice director. But it highlighted the sudden meteoric flare in this part of the world, made possible only by crooked practices.

Still, in a society marked by dependency, where individuals lacked help, many must rely on others for material, financial, and psychological support to sustain themselves. This reliance only deepened their dependence. Individuals could only find their sustenance and achieve a sense of wholeness through this dependency.

With connections, one could effortlessly and satisfactorily solve problems, whether they related to finding a better job, getting a permit, dodging a charge, getting better marks in school, exculpating an offense, falsifying a record or document, buying quality medicines or powerful painkillers, conducting illicit trades, or secret dealing within or beyond the country's borders.

However, the outcome could be adverse if one lacks contact. One might go through endless hassles and end up nowhere, much like having to cover a distance of several hundred kilometers to one's destination with no mode of transportation.

Therefore, the hope for justice, equality, and fairness relied on contacts. Any other way was purely fanciful. As everyone else sped away, those left behind would take months or years to catch up or might wither away along the way.

That was the situation Kai was in. But what made his situation the more ironic was the notion of harmony itself. Despite boasting of its long and civilized culture with a homespun philosophy about harmony, mainlanders inherited a society that was so indifferent and ignorant towards others while disfavoring or bullying anyone over 35. The aftermath of treating aggravation and grievance with a notion of harmony thus ended up pouring salt into the wound.

Kai grew bitter and resented those around him, including his in-laws. He saw them as the roots of his miseries. He became vindictive, thinking justified violence might be the only resort to placate his vindictiveness.

Irreversibly, he became a loose cannon who could break loose in any choppy incident any time now and could smash into anyone, anything, on his way.

* * * * *

One night, Kai was hanging out with a circle of his pals. They gathered around a table at an eatery by the side of a quiet street, drinking their beers. At first, their conversation kick-started with a spurt of random, unconnected topics. But after a few drinks, they soon lost their inhibitions and voiced their frustrations: wives badgered them to get a better job; sons and daughters needed money for school, or in-laws ordered them to do this or that. At one point, a fellow became sentimental, verging on mawkishness, and sobbed for leading a dog's life, scornful and unease.

As they carried on with their conversation, their irritation soon turned to resentment when they vented their vexation at the locals: stuck-up rich kids showcased their sleek cars; snobs cast a side glance and treated them like the unwashed; street vendors refused to sell them things on credit; or haughty divas who brushed them off with all ten delicate fingers.

Afterward, their outpourings of bitterness seemed to bring them calm and consolation. Amid their griping and bellyaches, their unhappiness gradually amended with one delirium of satisfaction.

But like any party, their gathering would eventually end. At their parting near the small hours, their moments of graphic diversion from reality slowly opened up to the harsh existences of life in plain black and white again.

Afterward, they hesitantly bid so long for each other before heading separately into a lonely night.

Kai was reeling when he left, swaying left and right in unsteady steps. As he turned a corner, he walked plumb into a lamppost. Dazed from the smart, he heard a stern voice bawling, 'Watch where you're going!'

From his drunken stupor, he first realized two men were standing about three feet from him. At the sight of these men wearing black uniforms and donning peaked caps sporting a white emblem in the middle, his ills suddenly recurred, and hatred rose to his head.

He shouted back in a slurred speech, "Screw you! I know where I am going." One of these men yelled back, "What did you say?"

Suddenly, Kai lunged forward and swung his fist at one man uninvited. Both men dodged, and each swiftly grasped Kai's arm and shoulder. The man on the right brought his foot backward and swung it forward at Kai's feet in one forceful sweeping motion, resulting in Kai's feet off the ground. Kai fell flat onto the concrete pavement with a heavy thud.

Moments later, an unmarked black van pulled over, and swiftly, they threw him into the back of the vehicle. It then sped off and disappeared into the night.

The encounter was over fast, but those who witnessed that fracas were of the same mind that riffraff like Kai should be locked away.

Yet, often, prejudice might prejudice itself against man's fate.

What followed was unclear. The following day, Kai was freed from custody with no charges. Surprisingly calm and swaggering, he looked unharmed and more collected than those around him had ever seen.

When asked about the circumstances of his detainment, Kai was chary of disclosing details or what took place, aside from coming across a very nice guy who let him go on compassionate grounds.

However, he eventually told his wife he had found a job in the capital. Not soon after, the man disappeared for weeks, and people thought he got held up again. But when he came back, he looked confident and arrogant.

For the first time in many years, Kai filled empty jars with tea leaves, packed the fridge with fresh legumes and fruits, and appeased his wife with cash.

Details were slowly emerging only when he confided to his buddies that he met an official, Mr. Su Zon, who also came from the same hometown in Hubei, that the townsman sympathized with his plight and that Kai would repay Su's kindness.

However, when his pals pressed him about the exact nature of his work, Kai seemed more uncertain than anyone else. He could only say that he collaborated with the judicial system to maintain social order.

But why would someone like Kai gain his worth and attention?

He explained by likening himself to a club. He stated that what made a club function depended not entirely on its thick end, but on the shaft that formed the handle. This nation's tasks or ideology was the key element that formed the thick end, but it would need the handle to wield that power effectively. It required bruteness, loudness, and grip to make the club applicable. He concluded by boasting that was why he was hired, for whatever reason, for whatever purpose.

Despite his thoughtful analogy, Kai had attended a gathering a year earlier that unknowingly provided him with a version of the situation he currently found himself in.

There was a park that stood kitty-corner across the street where Kai lived. Some older people would stroll around in the evening and hang out after dinner. They sat on wonky wooden step stools, which they took with them wherever they went. There, they would spin their yarns in a now tranquil and peaceful surrounding at night while a group of negligible listeners gathered around listening. Occasionally, Kai would stroll into the gathering and listen to their idle chatter as he dawdled around.

Some people often went there from their nearby residences to eliminate their boredom and prattle on about nothing but everything, especially things in the past. They collected and recounted anything and everything connected with them, often droning on and on about many selfsame old stories in different ways occasionally. For younger people, it was a harmless distraction. For older ones, it became their means of subsistence to maintain their presence by harking back to the halcyon days, and it made them happy.

At his last visit, Kai heard elder Ahxin share a story about the history of thugs.

Ahxin began his story by stating that in the past, when laws were weak or nonexistent, powerful regions saw themselves as above the law and often operated under

gangster-like rules.

Ahxin explained that gangsterism in China has existed since time out of mind. Long before the rise of Chinese communism, wealthy people often supported those of misfortune, inviting them to live in their houses as guests. They put them up in different quarters, vouchsafed them with meals to ease their hunger, and sheltered them from the elements. While some wealthy families housed fewer than ten guests, others took in many more, with some even capable of forming sizable militias.

In times of conflict, these wealthy patrons would send their now guests-turned-thugs out to resolve disputes or conflicts with the locals. They would terrorize towns and villages and even commit acts of violence, all under the guise of seeking justice.

As Ahxin continued his story, he adopted a sanctimonious demeanor that was hard to miss as his voice grew increasingly louder.

A classical novel later celebrated this tradition, he continued. It depicted the exploits of a group of men and women who were, in fact, a mishmash of robbers, kidnappers, murderers, brigands, cannibals, freebooters, and petty criminals. These fictional characters, just like other fictional works written by romantic writers, were flattered by the Republic's founder, who demanded that every member read it.

Endorsed and propelled further by socialist conflict theory, thuggery is often driven first by opportunity and then by authoritarian impulses. Inexorably, the notion of thuggery emerged amid the struggle to dominate the masses, infiltrated the communist network in the early days, and settled at its lowest levels.

As a crucial instrument of control, these thugs-turned-warriors have been brutal, engaging in a wide range of activities. These activities include addressing minor issues, monitoring behaviors, conducting ruthless crackdowns, implementing land reforms, executing land grabs, seizing property, issuing death threats, and committing other gruesome acts of violence while claiming to act in the name of justice.

Yet, against this backdrop developed much in the later days, the crack between two opposing societal groups would eventually appear and collide paradoxically. On one side, the authoritarian relies on brute forces to exact order. On the other, acts of violence would emerge for the masses to demand fairness.

Ironically, amid this metaphorical ocean between the two groups, Kai fulfilled both functions back-to-back.

Indeed, that was one story that Kai indulged in during his days of latency and long before any events were to follow.

One afternoon in late autumn, Kai and other helping hands convened a meeting with their boss. The lead man told them that a small group of troublemakers was causing chaos on the east side and disturbing the locals. They were tasked with making those people 'show some respect.'

The men had endured monotonous work in recent days. Their routine became dull, their food bland, and their drinks insipid. Upon receiving this new assignment, these men suddenly felt energetic and eager to seek something beyond their boredom. At once, they all piled into the van and hit the road.

Situated two blocks south of a main road, the troubled area was on a four-lane, two-way street. Small, closely attached single-story shops lined one side of the street, while the other was housing complexes.

Closer to the intersection, a small group of people barred in front of an office next to an unfinished complex where construction work had halted. They were mostly men in their 30s or 40s.

Kai rounded the van into the street and pulled it onto the pavement. He and his men got out of the vehicle and walked toward the protesters in a macho manner.

As the protesters saw these men in civilian clothing approach, they could not be sure who they were. But before they could react, Kai shouted, "What are you people doing here?"

The protesters looked nervous. They gave these men a long stare but didn't answer back.

Having not squeezed any response from the protestors, Kai shouted, "Why are you blocking the way? Move!"

One protester objected. "We want our money back."

Kai hit back. "Your amount contributes to the foundation on which it belongs to communist China. Be it."

"No."

Infuriated, Kai snarled back, "How dare you differ from our communism?"

By this time, tensions among Kai's men had reached a boiling point. Just as Kai let out a stream of expletives, he noticed one protester was recording their encounter. Infuriated, he suddenly lunged forward and punched the man in the head without warning, causing him to stumble backward while knocking out his phone.

Kai's pals joined the fray. The peaceful scene instantly erupted into chaos, filled with bursts of yelling, screaming, and shouting, mixed with pleas for calm.

The confrontation ended swiftly, leaving many protesters with bloody noses and some lying on the pavement.

One of Kai's men yelled, "We're going to break your legs next time!" They then returned to the van.

None of the protesters fought back, and none of the onlookers intervened. Because of the potential consequences, any confrontation could cause a mass attack, riot, or widespread bystander effect.

After the ordeal, three protesters left feeling injustice and went to a police station to register a complaint.

Fearing a further reprisal, the other two decided not to join them.

Once at the station, a stout officer with a broad face and puffy eyes did not promptly address their complaint. Instead of gathering information about the incident, the officer asked perfunctory questions about what they were doing there. Why did you protest?

Did you have a permit to stage a protest? Did you cause any disturbance? And others alike.

After a lengthy and random questioning session, the officer asked, as if out of concern, in a friendly tone, "When they beat you, did you run?"

The unlikely question dumbfounded the two men standing near the counter. The shorter man at the back craned his neck between them and replied, "It happened suddenly and with no provocation."

But the man's comment seemed to fall on deaf ears as the officer chattered in an irritating tone, "I just don't understand. You folk just stood there, let them beat you up, and now you want to file a complaint? The next time you see them, run!"

He looked askance at the complaining folk before continuing. "If you have not done something wrong, why did they beat you? There must be a good reason for it."

From there, he went on unleashing his nuggets of wisdom. "As you know, people here have always adhered to non-interference in other people's internal affairs. Speculating or accusing others of trying to provoke confrontation is completely groundless and malicious speculation."

He finished telling his savvy with a satisfactory nod, as if he had just hit upon a revelation to himself.

Finally, he concluded his prosaic advice by saying, "Both parties should come together and talk things out, trying to resolve things peacefully."

By now, the two complainants at the front looked frustrated at the officer's wise counsel and became completely speechless. The third fellow at the back, visibly riled by the officer handling their complaint, got excited and rejoined, "We come here hoping to seek justice. We are not here to seek your fanciful tea leaf reading."

The speaker, who tried to vent his frustration, set the fur flying instead by hurling a saucy remark. Yet, he had some vague ideas of what it might have rendered.

The retaliation visibly offended the officer. Having a hair-trigger temper, he wanted to lambast the fellow for his impertinence. But the fellow stood at the back and was now visible, now obscure from view.

His face darkened. Seeing his advice not heeded, he was getting testy with the complainants' incessant gripes. Feeling he had lost hope of restoring peacefulness in the office, he petulantly hurled himself up from this chair and quietly went over and talked with another officer in the far-right corner.

Afterward, both officers returned and charged the complainants with "picking quarrels, provoking trouble, and disturbing peace."

Amid the confusion between parties shoving and pushing, a clamor rang out—what did we do? What is the meaning of this? What kind of law is this? Don't push! I warn you.

Despite their overwhelming protests, all three complainants were subsequently detained.

Back at the melee scene, the onlookers had long dispersed after the protesters left. The street was once again returning to its tranquility—for now.

That late evening, a couple was crossing a deserted street at the same spot where the melee took place that afternoon. Halfway through the crossing, a black sedan traveling at least twice the speed of the street limit approached them from nowhere. Gripped by fear, the couple clung to each other, unable to move as the car barreled down on them.

At approximately ten meters away, the car veered right into the next lane but hit the curb and became airborne. It landed in a pedestrian area, bizarrely missing the contentious unfinished complex. The force sent the car sideswiping a newly built complex half a block down instead, five meters from the road.

After the collision, the vehicle stopped momentarily. However, the driver remained in the car, seemingly uninterested in assessing the damage. Some bystanders approached the vehicle to check on the people inside. But before they could reach the car, its taillights flashed, and the vehicle suddenly shifted back into motion. After slowly returning to the street, it revved up the engine and drove off.

After the incident, many residents of the damaged building came out to assess the extent of the damage. The impact left a long rift running along the siding, and bits and pieces of debris - glass, rubber, fiberglass, concrete - scattered everywhere. The scene also attracted a large crowd across the street.

The couple who crossed the street said the two men in the car wore black. But the commotion among the crowd drowned out their comments. Amid confused words bartered back and forth while tittle-tattle took flight, accusations flew around.

Heightened by pre-existing negative sentiment that might have contributed to the outcome, it roused the crowd's mood to anger.

As the seething resentment over the beating that had preceded that evening had reached a boiling point, many were awaiting a foolproof excuse to seek justice. Unbeknownst to others, a small faction shifted the blame to a foreigner who drove a black sedan and lived several blocks further north. In an instant, people overheard someone in the crowd shouting obscenities about a foreigner in a Wu dialect, "A Luobodou!"

Strange enough, as soon as the group heard the epithet, they seemed to go off the deep end without good reason while their blood was instantaneously boiling. Came high water, a time to settle for overdue retribution. And that was what they said afterward.

No sooner had it developed into a full-blown hue and cry than the crowd trickled north.

At an intersection several blocks further north, some police officers, at one point, sensed something imminent. As the group moved, they drew even dawdlers and deadbeats fell behind along the way.

When the mob reached their presumed destination, the police slowly trickled in and asked the group to disperse. As more people swelled up at the rear, the number mushroomed to at least a hundred, blocking traffic from all directions. By then, the police had formed a line in front of the building where the crowd thought the Luobodou was staying.

When Kai and his men learned about the disturbance in the area, they felt an ominous presence. Realizing that the location was near where the protesters had gathered that afternoon, they sensed it was more than a coincidence. Together, they headed to the troubled area to find out what it was all about.

Upon arriving at the scene, they witnessed a disordering multitude. Kai instinctively felt a surge of hostility and mistrust rising within. Seeing the disorderly masses reminded him of his past miseries for unknown reasons. The more he saw his wretchedness in those days reflected through the crowd, the palpable threats he perceived, and the greater hatred he felt toward them.

A distance away, some people pestered the police to let them through, while others attracted them to talk to the driver responsible for the property's damage. But the police responded to their requests with deadpan expressions.

Not long after, their anger roused to fever pitch by the drama as the mob themselves fed off of one another's behavior.

Amid the turmoil, someone among the crowd started singing "The Internationale." Instantly, the multitude all broke out in unison.

Arise, slaves afflicted by hunger and cold, Arise,

suffering people all over the world!

The blood which fills my chest has boiled over,

We must struggle for truth!

The old world shall be destroyed Arise, slaves, arise!

The song seemed to comfort the crowd, even though they were unsure what it had to do with this protest. They appeared to sing for the sake of singing.

However, as if spurred by the group's collective mind, they sang only the first part of the anthem. They repeated the same one afterward, stopping short at the second part, which began with,

This is the final struggle.

At that point, the crowd's chanting visibly irritated Kai. The authorities had recently banned the anthem, citing that it contained radical current politics or ideology.

As Kai and his men were mulling over whether they should intervene, the crowd surged from behind, causing some at the front to push against the police line. The police shoved them back, but the mob at the back kept on pressing forward.

Seeing the crowd surge from the back, Kai and his men jumped at the group on the outer ring and dragged them away.

But unlike that afternoon when the protestors got caught unprepared, the mob this evening was on the offensive. Fueled by their immense hatred for the 'Luobodou' that was egged on by the state, scores of protesters lunged at Kai's men and swung punches in fury.

When the police at the front noticed fighting broke out to their left, they started swinging their batons at the front line. In an instant, pandemonium broke out; punches wielded, batons charged, expletives hurled, bottles thrown while cries rubbed the air.

Amid the chaos, officers clashed with the mob, the rabble beat the thugs, and riffraff pounded the crooks. All convinced they were fighting for the right cause, whatever that cause was.

But, for many, it felt as though they had been waiting half a century too long to express their resentment and heroism, risen from the ashes of aggravation - crooked officers, corrupt mandarins, forced evictions, arbitrary detention, the battle of

Chosin, the Olympics, Russian comrades, American hegemony, eastern devils - all swelled into one humongous, chaotic mess of grievous and heroic themes.

Unbeknownst to either party, every act of hostile aggression the state generated culminated in an equal feat of reactive hostility. Simultaneously, the intensity of the state's repression was proportional to the obsession of people's outbursts at other outlets.

As the fighting continued, more police arrived, and the mob took the beatings. Those smarter ones receptive to the fact that those who fought and ran away might live to fight began to disperse and flee as the wind changed. Those honor-bound ended up in custody or bashed mercilessly.

As the police dragged one protester to the waiting van, the man's shirt appeared worn or torn, somewhat anarchically fashioned, and his long, unkempt hair was all revolutionarily awry. The fellow pleaded earnestly, "Please let me go. My impulsive reaction stems from climate change."

Ignoring the man's attempt at humor, a slender officer with a stone face dragged him to the van.

The protester persisted, "Look, I am only here to protest the Luobodou. The government should hold me in high esteem for fulfilling my greatest patriotic duty, don't you think?"

This time, the officer retorted, "What Luobodou! There is no Japanese here!"

The fellow was wide-eyed with disbelief. "No Japanese?"

Kai finally returned home and could not be happier. The routine habit of his wife nagging now came to pass. His icy stare would be enough to silence her now. Unlike before, when he had to endure the snubs from his wife and in-laws almost daily, he now had a say in the family's running and felt contented. After all, making a house a home took a heap of living, he reckoned.

Yet, unlike the many occasions he strolled around with his exaggerated swagger, he seemed to carry the weight of a recent beating. The man had a bruise on his left temple and one on his right chin.

Almost immediately upon his return, one of his in-laws, who got a streak of permanent smugness in his look that seemed to find just about everything, everybody disagreeable, asked Kai with feigned concerns about the purple marks on his face. "How did you get that, bro? Are you OK? I've got some ointment for that. You want it?"

Kai explained he had slipped on a wet floor, striking his head against the side of a table before falling to the floor. A freak accident, he said.

After hearing that, his in-law silently cut eyes at his brother and parroted back with a slight bob of his head, "A freak accident!" He then rolled his eyes while his little brother, with his buck teeth, had yet to hold back his snicker.

Kai saw it all with his eyes closed and took it in as a personal affront. Afterward, he chewed over how best to get even with them.

Moments later, he told them his boss would visit him in the next two days and suggested they rearrange furniture in the living room.

After that, the house bustled with activities and sounds - chairs scraping against the floor, echoes of dragging and grinding objects, footsteps stomping, floorboard creaking, furniture thumping, interspersed with occasion hollers.

For the duration, the two in-laws were busy moving an unyielding wooden cabinet to the right, a bulky sofa to the left, ungainly house plants big and small to the sides of a window, and a clumsy TV set to the far end, followed by dusting, cleaning, and sweeping.

All along, his in-laws sullenly complied with Kai's request without a sound, for they feared that the man might turn his future assignment against them. After all, they knew he was a man not to mess with.

The sun began to set when they started rearranging the furniture. By the time they finished, it was late evening. Both in-laws were dripping with sweat and completely exhausted from their efforts. Finally, they excused themselves and took leave with their fatigued steps and sulky mood without saying a word.

Kai silently followed them with his glare until they were out of sight. With a sneer, he spent some peaceful moments alone while sitting on the balcony facing a deserted street bathed in a warm amber glow, a semblance of an oasis.

Both in-laws later learned that the expected visitation never took place.

LISTEN TO ME

"National Health Link, my name is Caroline Tang. May I help you?"

"Hello, I have some problems. I need help." A male voice came over at the receiving end.

"I will be happy to assist you, mister. But first, where are you calling from?" "Zh... zh...ong... gu." The caller was stuttering a little.

"OK, let me check where Zhong Gu is." Then Caroline was heard trailing the name in a singsong voice, "Zhong Gu, Zhong Gu, Zhong Gu..."

Suddenly, she stopped. What followed was an incredulous silence.

Caroline, at this moment, thought the caller might have slurred the sound 'Guo' as 'Gu.' She then asked in a curious tone, "Wait a minute, you just said... China... if I get that right?"

"Yes, China," came a brief reply.

Caroline still did not trust what she had heard. To validate that it really meant what it meant, she asked again, "China? Mainland China, you mean?"

"Yes." came another terse reply. There was another long pause.

Caroline finally broke the silence and said, "Mister, are you aware that you are calling Taiwan's national health line?"

"Taiwan? Oh! I didn't know that... A friend of mine gave it to me."

There was complete silence from the other end, but not before long, Caroline continued,

"Sorry. I can't take your call."

"I seek answers regarding my psychological well-being, but no one takes those calls here. They might simply refer me to a political session." As if the caller feared being cut off, he rushed at the receiver without stopping.

"What is that?" Caroline asked.

"It is a self-criticism session."

After a brief silence, she said in a sympathetic tone, "I am sorry, but I really can't help you. Sorry."

"Please! I have a question, that's all." The caller seemed anxious enough to seek help.

Caroline did not respond, so the caller continued pleading, "Like doctors, medical advisors can answer anyone regardless of race, status, or nationality. I just have a question."

After a long pause, Caroline resumed, "OK. Tell you what. I will talk to you as an acquaintance, not an advisor. Are we good?"

"I am fine with that." The caller sounded happy enough.

"First, what is your name?"

"Xinming Tu." the caller replied.

"How old are you?" "I am in middle age."

"As you stated earlier, you seek psychological well-being advice." "Yes."

"Since that is your wish, I want to clarify one thing. I am aware there is a school of psychology in China. But understand this. China's psychology, or dictatorial psychology, is exploiting people's fear and anxiety while deliberately altering facts and admissions to force them to remold or reorientate their perspectives, feelings, or behavior. However, I am not here to give a political discourse. Let's talk about your problems."

After a brief pause, Caroline resumed, "I will tell you how this works. But first, I am going to gather some facts from you. After that, I will offer my insights and recommendations. Alright?"

"Yes."

"What do you do for a living, Xinming?" "I am a cadet."

"A cadet?" Caroline sounded a bit surprised.

"Yes."

"You mentioned at the beginning that you have some problems. Can you tell me a bit about that?"

"I always feel I have anger bottled up inside me. All the time, I feel anxiety and palpitations. I don't know why."

"How long have you had this pent-up anger, Xinming?"

"I don't know. When I think of it, it must have been for many years, if not a decade. But lately, it gets so bad that I have chest pain."

"How do you normally react when you get angry? Did you express your anger openly?" "I never do that."

"You never do that. Can you tell me why?" "I think anger and sadness are bad."

"Do you ever cry or yell?"

"No. I equal crying or yelling as weakness."

"So, you always hold back your anger and sadness to show a strong character." "You can say that, yes."

"You mentioned you have chest pain. Do you have difficulty breathing?"

"It looks normal to me, even though my heart constantly races. Every time I breathe, I feel like heaving a stone in my chest."

"Do you have a headache?"

"Yes."

"How about constipation?" "Ah... Yes."

"How often do you have a headache?"

"On and off, I would say. It is more obvious when I have some pressure." "Have you ever discussed or talked to someone about your anger?"

"No. I have no one to talk to, not even my wife. She doesn't understand it, and I don't believe anyone else does. There was one time I overheard someone talk about his anger and sadness. His superior just laughed at him for being silly and impractical."

"You mentioned before that you often hold back your anger and sadness. But at any point, have you ever overreacted and your temper just exploded?"

"Yes, I did. That is why I want to talk to you. But, unfortunately, something awful happened last week."

"What happened?"

"I still had some pressure from work when I got home. My wife wanted to watch a movie together even though I felt I wanted to be alone. I reluctantly gave in. But when I saw it was an old black-and-white film, I suddenly felt anxious, agitated, and upset without reason. For no apparent reason, I felt someone compelled me to do something I did not want to. When my wife asked me why I acted like that, I suddenly lost my temper and exploded. In the ensuing outburst, I shouted and screamed. I openly denounced her for acting in cahoots with others to find me guilty and accused her of being so base and so low as to betray me and my relatives. My wife cried, my children got scared, and my parents intervened on behalf of my wife. Only afterward, when I was alone, I found my reactions bizarre and unintelligible. It was just like I got possessed and acted out of character. I could not explain why I acted or said things like that."

After a brief pause, Xinming continued, "There is something else I want to mention, but I don't know if it is relevant."

"Tell me."

"I had a terrible dream another night. It still scares me."
"What did you dream?"

"Well, Mr. Xian, my superior, I seldom talk to him. There are no apparent issues between us. But, in that dream, I met him in a dark room. It looked like he was discussing my performance, my conduct, or something. The moment I left, I heard him shout from behind that I deserved a slap in the face. Suddenly, I became so enraged that I intended to beat him up. But the moment I turned to confront him, the corner where he stood was so dark and blurry that I had to squint my eyes to get a good look. When I saw what was in that corner, he vanished. I then woke up, feeling my heart racing."

"How did you feel when you discovered he was no longer there?" "I felt relieved."

"You felt relieved?"

"Because I have trouble understanding why I became hostile to someone I have no difficulty with. I don't know why I had such a dream. What would happen if I attacked him? I know it was only a dream, but extracting such a violent act without justification is unthinkable. I was fearful that it could influence my behavior in real life. It bothers me because my behavior evoked what happened to Professor Guo."

"Now, what about Professor Guo? Who is he?"

"That is a long story. I knew him personally. He got educated overseas. After he finished his master's, he returned to China."

"What happened to him?"

"Word got around that he got killed." "Why?"

"It resulted from a falling-out that caused a loss of life... Professor Guo had a tenure with the university, where he carried out his research and teaching for many years upon his return. But it was not accessible from the beginning. He constantly complained bitterly about the Party secretary, who used highly coercive tactics and demands. For context, a party secretary is appointed to universities to ensure teachers' and students' loyalty to the Party. He is a significant apparatus installed in every institute to drive people's mindsets. Anyway, you would hear Professor Guo rail at being framed and abused over the years. A practice that has been so rampant that he referred to it as elicitation before being outmoded. That must have caused a significant mental toll on him. I say he was being pushed to extremes."

"You've just mentioned something about elicitation? Can you tell me more?" "That's all that I was told."

"What happened then?"

"One day, suddenly, Professor Guo was fired for poor performance. That must be a terrible blow to him, for I know he devoted himself to his work and family. People said they heard them arguing and the party official shouting. Ensuingly, things went rough and violent, and the party official ended up dead."

There was a brief pause before Xinming resumed. "When we tried to find out what would happen to Professor Guo, news got round that he was no longer with us... a few weeks shy of his thirty-third birthday."

"How did you react to this?"

"I was shocked, angry, and confused... I remembered thinking a lot that day. Who are we? What are we and our worth? What would happen if that were me, etc.? That is senseless... I gather he rued the day he returned in his last moments."

"But you mentioned earlier that you are scared, too?"

"Yes, I am scared because our circumstances mirror each other's predicament differently. I don't want to end up like him."

"Did the dream you told me happen before or after Professor Guo's death?" "After."

"Let's go back to the problem of anger. Have you ever suppressed any unwanted thoughts or memories?"

"I don't know."

"But have you ever had any slightest unpleasant feeling about certain objects, thoughts, or memories directly and indirectly related to you?"

"Yes, I think I did, especially some negative thoughts." "Are you living with your wife, children, and parents?"

"Yes, in a high-rise building, on the 20th floor. Our unit gets sandwiched in between others, shaped like a long rectangular box, with a window in each of the two bedrooms at the far end."

"So, there are no other windows?"

"Why? Those windows are useless. The two windows that we have are thick with grime and dirt from outside. Surrounding buildings also block sunlight. Besides, the further up we live, the more disconnected and isolated we feel."

"Do you feel better when you get out?"

"Look. The needful always wants to be brought closer to earth than high heaven. The greater the gravity one feels, the greater the chance of feeling lost and forgotten."

"I see."

After a brief pause, Caroline continued, "I will ask you this question. I don't want you to think. You tell me the first thing that comes to your mind."

"OK."

"I am leading you through a dark corridor. In the end, I opened the door. In front of you, you see a surrounding in black and white. Tell me what comes to mind first when you see this."

As if collecting from a hazy memory, Xinming replied almost word by word, "I see... mobsters... paranoid... with foam at the mouth..."

He briefly paused before continuing, "I am worried... children ... might get bitten."

There was a long silence after that. Caroline finally said, "Xinming, I need time to assess. Please call me back tomorrow and ask for me, and we will talk more. Can you do that?"

"Yes, I will. Thank you for listening to me."

"You're welcome. We will talk again. You have a nice day."

* * * * *

Caroline didn't hear from Xinming until Monday morning when she picked up the phone and addressed it in her accustomed greeting, "National Health Link, my name is Caroline Tang. May I help you?"

"Hello, Caroline. How are you?" Came a familiar tone.

"Hello, Xinming. Nice to hear from you again. I'm fine, thank you. And how about you?" "I'm OK. Thank you."

"It has been a week since I last heard from you. Is everything going OK?"

"Yes. We have been busy preparing for the coming lunar new year, the year of Rat. People say this is going to be another good year. Hah! I want to say..."

"Yes?"

"After the last call, I felt eased up a bit."

"That happens when you talk openly about something. I will talk more about that later." "So, have you made an assessment?"

"No, there will be no assessment. As I mentioned at the beginning, I could not act as an advisor, let alone with the limited information I have. I can offer you a suggestion. You take that suggestion as a piece of information."

"OK."

"Good! Based on my information, it could be a combination of repression from the past and suppression in the present."

"I don't understand."

"Try to imagine this. You are standing next to a vertical liquefied wall. On your side of the wall is your consciousness in the present time. On the other side of the wall is the liquefied state of your subconsciousness in the past. When you encounter something highly unpleasant in the current time, you inevitably take a step backward and end up submerging on the other side of that liquefied wall. Once you immerse yourself in the subconscious side, you pick up the behaviors and any defense mechanisms or hostility in the past to help you cope with the unwanted experiences in the present. That is repression. With suppression, you stay clear of that liquefied wall and remain in a conscious state, knowingly and deliberately blotting out any painful or unwanted thoughts in the present."

Caroline stopped, then continued, "By combining them, many things happening concurrently in the past and the present could bring them about. Things like concepts or ideas compel you to accept against your will; orders pressurize you into obeying without your consent; intimidation browbeats you to admit without judgment; or experiences you encountered earlier that make you feel ashamed, humiliated, agitated, upsetting, etc."

Caroline paused, anticipating Xinming's reaction to her comments. But it was silent at the receiving end.

Caroline resumed, "When you suppress something inside you, it creates pressure. Your constipation results from holding in negative feelings or trauma. Your headache or other body pains, such as neck aches or chest pain, result from the weight of this trauma or experience."

At this time, Xinming seemed perturbed and asked, "Is... Is this uncommon?" Before Caroline could answer, Xinming fired another question. "Am I mentally ill?"

"Understand that definitions and categories can vary from one culture to another, from one region to another, and from one reason to another. In China, physicians may assume that it is normal. For us, it is not. However, it is more critical for you to understand what they are. In the long run, they can harm your health."

Caroline stopped for a moment, then continued. "Your dream betrays you in a precarious stage where the threats against you become so unbearable that they manifest themselves in your dream. But the thing is that we rarely have power over our dreams. However, your last one was instead influenced by what you did not want to see. First, it turns into a dark, amorphous shadow, and then it vanishes; this occurs when you try to avoid any unpleasant experience. While being beset, you instinctively learn to cope."

Caroline halted and expected Xinming to raise some questions, but the quietness at the other end was disconcerting. Her curiosity grew.

"So, how can I... Is there any medication for my problem?"

"Medication is beyond our discussion. However, I want you to know that we live in a different world. In some parts of the world, people can resolve these types of problems effectively, but on your part, it is a tricky situation."

"Why?"

Caroline explained, "Try to understand this. It is impossible to heal another with persistent denials of facts, and nobody can make progress while surrounded by widespread misbelief. I liken this to you being trapped on the lower deck of a sinking ship and told that your fear and anxiety are merely a result of your imagination.

"There is a way, however. Your problems can be assuaged by expressing and releasing your feelings, discussing and deconstructing your past and present repressed experiences, or experiencing catharsis. Cathartic cleansing has many ways. One of the best ways to release your repressed experiences is through writing, such as journaling your daily exposure.

"However, despite my suggestion, beware. In a system where everything is surveilled and censored, your writing, even though it can act as a cathartic discharge, can also at the same time serve as a harbinger of ruination. You could be in a very dicey situation where a universally recognized remedy can instead become a dose of treason or a spoonful of poison. When that happens, a much-needed universal antidote exacerbates your symptoms further."

"What else can I resolve this, then?"

There was silence on the line. Finally, Caroline resumed, "There are general guidelines on how to deal with this, but I don't think they apply in the world you belong to."

"Why... but what if they might work?" "Alright, regardless."

Afterward, Caroline gave him complete guidelines and other advice. At the end of the instruction, she said, "I hope these guidelines might work for you. Do you have questions?"

"No."

Caroline continued, "Keep in mind - for every coercion exerted, there is an equal and opposite reaction. The outcome, predictable rather than unpredictable, leads to actions that lack valid will. That might be food for thought."

After a brief pause, Caroline resumed, "Is there anything else you wish to ask?" Xinming broke the silence and replied, "No. I appreciate all the help."

"You are welcome."

After pausing for a moment while feeling Xinming still reluctant to hang up, Caroline continued, "It has been my pleasure and privilege to talk to you, help you, and assist you. May you live a healthier, freer life and a happier, more meaningful existence with those you share with. Goodbye, and take care."

"Bye, Ms. Caroline."

After that last call, Caroline never heard from him again.

THE TEST OF TIME

Nawdida village was in West Africa. Beset with high hills to the north, it was bound by a main dirt road that led to a meadow in the east, where an ancient river flowed.

The villagers sustained their livelihoods by raising cattle and sheep, while farmers cultivated grains, vegetables, and fruits. In times of need, they would come together and offer each other help and support. They had kept their lives simple, just as their ancestors did when they settled in this village over two centuries ago. Like their ancestors, peasants tilled their fields in peace and contentment from dawn till dusk and maintained a self-sufficient life.

Most people lived with their extended family in small huts and bonded with traditional social values. They respected elders and honored their ancestors for their efforts and contributions.

A chief, Elder Abdalla, a wealthy man chosen by the community's consensus, guided the village. He oversaw all village activities, planning for ceremonies and festivals, and providing direction and guidance to the people. When disputes arose among villagers, he would try to mediate a peaceful resolution. Together, they enforced rules, norms, and values that reflected their unique worldview.

Amid this simple life, Adio Chidike lived happily in the early part of his life.

Adio, the youngest of the two children and the only boy in the house, relished his playtime all day. Unlike him, his sister, Adebola, allocated much of her time to helping her mother, shouldering most household tasks such as washing clothes, cooking, and looking after the young sibling.

Adio was free from all the chores. He had much time playing with toys, drawing, or diddling with anything he could set his hands on. Occasionally, when he grew bored and threw tantrums, his mother would relent and allow him to play outside. There, he would chase chickens with a stick, dig up worms, or torment rabbits with a carrot.

But if Adio was apt to disturb everything in his path, he had an affinity with a wood warbler that made him quiet. Some mornings, when he spotted the songbird perching on a tree, he would sneak out quietly and listen to its melodious song. Under the soft rays of the sun amid gentle breezes, he found peace and bliss within.

Under the care of his mother and sister, Adio spent many carefree years studying, playing, and, later, hanging out with friends in the heady days of his youth.

As Adio reached his thirteenth birthday, there was talk of a new school opening in the city, the Great Sage Center. Long after, a representative from the Center visited his village to highlight the benefits of learning the Chinese language. The delegate asserted that knowing the language could enhance their livelihood. He arranged a single class for the village and urged the locals to take this opportunity.

Adio's mother, hoping to keep Adio out of trouble, enrolled him, making him busier by taking up his regular schooling in the morning and then the Chinese class in the afternoon.

Lively, exuberant, and adventurous, Adio was initially very excited about the new language, just as he expressed his interest in almost anything he could dabble with. However, he soon discovered that this tonal language posed a significant challenge. Not only did the characters look alien, but they also sounded strange. Every attempt to recognize a character or detect a unique tone strained him.

Yet, given an even chance, it might cast doubt on whether someone with a skittish nature could manage. To gain a new language, one might need patience and perseverance, which Adio might lack.

* * * * *

Months after the announcement, the school opened its doors to the public. The school tasked Ms. Xiu Wen, a middle-aged old-school teacher from Xiaojing in southern China, and her assistant with teaching in the village.

Ms. Wen had a slim figure and shoulder-length black hair. She wore no makeup and had a stern mien that contrasted with her assistant's friendly nature.

On the first day, sporting a pearl necklace over her red shirt, Ms. Wen looked proper and solemn. She was mindful not to muss her clothes whenever she took her seat and seemed conscious of everything around her.

When she addressed the class, Ms. Wen's attention took in everything around her, moving or stationary. One time, Adio noticed her looking at the window intensely, as if trying to stare out danger. Curious, Adio quietly glanced over his shoulder but saw nothing except some green leaves on the tree's branches fluttering in the breeze outside.

One day, near the end of class, Adio saw Ms. Wen place some files and documents in a locker. After she closed and locked it, she pulled at the compartment handle to see if it locked. For some unexplainable reason, Ms. Wen unlocked, opened, closed, and locked it again. Like before, she tugged

71

on the handle with her left hand to see if it locked while her right hand held the key aimed at the lock. After that, she seemed to waver from her next move, but eventually decided against it on the third try.

The more Adio drew to her eccentricities, the more he became curious about her. There was one time when Adio joked about her being a spy. She responded with a frosty look to show the joke was inappropriate. She ended the exchange by saying, "We don't joke with each other."

One day, a student asked her how she enjoyed teaching there. She relayed her reply through a translator: "It is nice to be here, to bridge the differences between East and West, and to provide and adopt each other's values and education system."

As she spoke, she seemed to recite her words from a script. While maintaining a cold, blank stare, she showed no emotion and little or no head movement.

As her reply sounded so mechanical, Adio found it comical and parroted it back. Little did he know it caught Ms. Wen's attention. As a result, she marked Adio down for being disruptive for the second time in only a few weeks.

Once, the village invited her to a seasonal festival, where the locals gathered with their families to celebrate their roots and culture. The highlight of the event was a festival dance. Wearing close-fitting costumes and headpieces of embroidered cloth, the dancers followed the musical rhythm of the drums with their light, repetitive foot patterns.

From the beginning, Adio noticed Ms. Wen was not enthusiastic about it. She kept glancing left or right during the dance, visibly not at ease. The local hop vastly contrasted with the ones Ms. Wen saw in her native land, where performers typically presented a large-scale systematic arrangement to attain a special effect. Yet, once acculturated to symbols of control, order, and grandeur, she failed to appreciate the occasion as a social and cultural event.

His teacher's atypical personality thus partly motivated Adio's attendance. The more he paid attention to her, the more he became curious about her.

Between and after school, Adio enjoyed hanging out with his friends at different places, cracking jokes all day. Their jokes always cracked up with the rest of the group. But for Adebola, she felt their talks often teetered on the edge of absurdity, leaving her feeling foolish and speechless. As usual, she would shake her head and continue with her chores. But as silly as his sister presumed, sometimes their jokes went too far and raised someone's eyebrows for more than a laugh.

One afternoon, Adio, in his usual bubbly mood, told his friends, "You know how Elder Abdalla's daughters are being cared for?"

Their friends demanded, "How?"

Adio said, "His two daughters always indulge in juicy chicken breasts while their father has drumsticks and chicken feet."

Upon hearing this, his friends rocked back and forth with raucous laughter.

When this joke reached Elder Abdalla one evening, it flipped his lid. Pacing back and forth, he was so indignant at being held up as a butt of mockery. In the next moment, to seek retaliatory action, he ensured Adio would not get away with his impertinence.

The next day, he summoned Adio and his mother to his side and chastised the boy for his reckless remark. He said he and his members always upheld traditional values and beliefs and would never let his daughters do such a thing. He also blamed Adio's mother for failing to give the child a good upbringing and concluded, "His failure as a son is your failure as a mother."

Only after he let loose with his indignant outburst and stern admonition did Elder Abdalla feel satisfied. Afterward, he waved them away with a show of arrogance.

On the way home, Adio's mother got really upset and forbade Adio from eating meat for a month, for Elder Abdalla also punished them each with a chicken.

As months passed, Adio learned more Chinese words. However, the gap between him and his teacher seemed apparent as he grasped more. Their differences had been simmering unobtrusively for quite a while until they grew into a full-blown disagreement.

The fundamental clash between Adio and his teacher came when the students began learning to write Chinese characters. His teacher quickly noticed Adio was using his left hand to write. She objected to that and insisted on Adio writing with his right hand.

Her demand seemed unreasonable to Adio, who had used his left hand as a dominant hand since childhood. By insisting on him using his right hand, Adio would have to use his right hand to write Chinese while using his left hand to write his language. That would not work, Adio asserted. For that reason, he continued using his left hand.

The next time the issue arose, Ms. Wen confronted him again. Again, Adio disagreed with her, saying other people were also using their left hand. At that point, Ms. Wen fixed him with a cold-eyed stare and responded with an emphatic denial, "No!"

She then declared, "No one in China uses the left hand. Not one!"

Her response frustrated Adio even more, but he argued, "Just like walking, either you take a first step with your left or right foot first, you're still walking. And whether I use my left or right hand, I am still writing."

At this moment, Ms. Wen looked at him blankly, and without another word, she walked away. She never brought up the subject again.

One day, one student asked Ms. Wen what the term 'fu' meant. She explained it meant 'subservience.' Without solicitation, she pontificated until she submerged herself in her pontifical delight.

At an inopportune moment, Adio interrupted her while she was elaborating on the topic. Her reaction was one of a mixture of indignation and confusion. In China, no one dared to question a teacher lest he dared to brace a cracking skull, and Adio dared to challenge her.

Yet, she was hesitating about why she said what she said. She then clarified that she intended to define the word's meaning and nothing more. Ultimately, she reiterated her role was to teach the language.

Like many new learners, Adio needed help to understand the overall meaning of words when combined. Owing to that fact, he could only pick out the singular significance of each symbol while leaving the general sense of the series of words to guess. That might leave him understanding one thing while missing a broader picture.

Decades before Ms. Wen set foot in this far-flung place, another unnatural seismic activity engulfed her hometown nine thousand kilometers away. Even though no one here at the time had heard of it, it did not mean that this manmade seism was out of sight, out of mind. Only many decades later, when the repercussions eventually reached them, the demise it left behind was some two million souls biting the dust.

At the height of another brutal campaign, their ruler carried out in China, radical fringes, brandishing red notebooks, roamed the land indiscriminately. What they aimed for was to manifest their maniacal obsession with eradication and extermination. In the ensuing decade, their acts of violence went on without cessation. They smashed, thrashed, and hammered old cultural artifacts, relics, and monuments and even targeted people, trees, sparrows, or anything they could lay their hands on.

One day, amid the campaign, a radical named Amo stumbled upon an old handbook written by scholars centuries ago. Fascinated by the beautiful lettering and calligraphy, Amo hesitated momentarily, but ultimately took it home to look at it.

Once at home, Amo pored over the handbook page by page. The author recounted an event two centuries earlier when someone discovered three hefty volumes left by a Confucius disciple at an archaeological site. Because of their unwieldy masses, a scholar had to study them on-site. But because of the gigantic volumes, it took the scholar his whole life to finish just the first book. After that, he wrote the summary and passed it on to his son, who continued to the second volume. Like his father, the second scholar could only finish one book, so he wrote the summary for his son. The final author of the handbook was the third generation of the original scholar who, at long last, finished the last volume.

At that point, Amo was excited as he waited for the great wisdom given away by the third and final author. But he was deeply shocked upon learning the author's last revelation was "nothing!"

The author continued, "It is just a set of values devoted mainly to filial piety that hint at physical care, love, service, respect, and obedience. How one should be dutiful to his parents, wife to husband, etc."

The author then implied that this belief system, mainly composed of ethics and morality, lacks logical thinking or analytical reasoning. Inevitably, it circumvents skepticism while fortifying obedience.

But almost immediately, Amo hit on the epiphany that would change the outlook. Unlike the author, who saw the structure from the bottom up, he saw it from the top down.

Because of the chain of duties, the population could be tied collectively to debts, obligations, punishment, responsibilities, jobs, advancement, compliance, etc. All subjects must be responsible for anyone they related to or associated with what they did. When someone infringed or breached the law or rules, all others, including their immediate family, siblings, relatives, friends, and associates, were all incriminated.

Any criticism could only aim at those at the same level or below; anything above would be punishable and worthy of retribution. Therefore, if anyone handled wrongdoing, all three generations of the related subject were accountable.

This structural subservience gave way to the nuclear concept that everybody deemed interrelated to someone else and that no one was free. Because this notion saw people as interdependent, people must be responsible for anyone they knew. To make people accept this collective obedience and submission, the ruling class molded this system into customs and laws to impose on them.

Established as a set of values, this collective obedience, or structural submission, eventually gave rise to collective punishment for any infractions around which all crimes or offenses, regardless of their size or severity, revolve. From this dynamic, it also spawned other forms of sadistic, animalistic nature that took pleasure in seeing other subjects' self-abasement as a punishment, such as kneeling, self-criticism, obsequiousness, self-induced crying, etc.

Even though this collective system might not initially be deliberated as a restraint system for the masses, it would eventually become one and evolve as a stepping stone for dictatorship.

Under this system, those wholly absorbed in submission and acquiescence rendered their independence and originality obsolete. Because of people's strict compliance and passivity, innovations and political beliefs could only emerge through imitations, transfers, or exact replication.

Amid this revelation, Amo realized that once Confucius was idolized and venerated among deities, he became absolute and unchallengeable. But if Confucius's system was unchallengeable, what would or could the campaign he followed accomplish?

The Great Culture Destabilization campaign was supposed to spearhead a new idea to bring about a complete change. In reality, it was destined as a pretext to drive people to greater fear. It elevated old structural obedience to a new level of fear, securing a new, unbreakable submission inherited from the old one. Thus, what Amo and others were following should transfer that cruel old yoke to new control and secure the foundation of a present and future dictatorship.

Drawing from this revelation, Amo now believed that the only remaining action was to inflict fear substantial enough to drive a mass psychology of fear, making that fear permanent.

Developing along this line, Confucianism would be present as a harmonious system with ulterior motives in the distant future. Serving as a conciliatory bridge linking socialism to democracy, it would facilitate subsequent propaganda, surveillance, censorship, control, and other transfers. Amo surmised this scheme could someday expand eastward and westward under the disguise of language outreach and friendship, exploiting the vulnerabilities associated with democratic openness and transparency among other third nations.

One day, as usual, Adio was loitering around with his friends. He briefly went into a shop owned by Elder Abdalla and brought some snacks before joining his friends outside.

Together, they strolled to the other part of the village, bantering with each other until they gathered by the side of the river. As they sat there cracking jokes, their laughter and shrieks continued to rise and fall, reverberating beyond the meandering.

In a good mood, Adio shared a joke with his friends.

Adio revealed that sheep a long time ago differed significantly from sheep nowadays. Sheep roamed and frolicked about in rolling fields and grasslands, living a relatively free, untethered life. Because of that, they wandered off occasionally and constantly challenged nomadic pastoral people elsewhere.

One day came the Great Sage. Upon hearing a shepherd's problem with his sheep, the Great Sage assured him he would handle the situation. He promised the shepherd would sleep like a log once he resolved the issue.

The next day, the sage led the flock of sheep deep into the mountain. There, he instilled and indoctrinated the sheep into one unbreakable fold.

When he re-emerged from the mountain, the sheep followed him submissively. As if bound by a contract, they became attentive, always heeding to the lead sheep, and followed him.

The sage then led the flock back. The shepherd, at first, was not convinced, for "animal nature, just like human nature, can take time to evolve but cannot be forced or trespassed by extemporaneous means."

The sage then gave him a look of unconcealed contempt and riposted, "Of course you can't. I can!"

Feeling partly convinced yet still skeptical, the shepherd led the sheep on nearby slopes. By the time he came back, he was genuinely impressed. As the sage had said, the flock was orderly, heedful of the group's movements, and none of the sheep strayed.

After that, praises were plenty, and gifts were never barren.

One day, like any other day in late autumn, the shepherd herded the sheep up the mountain. As they ascended, lightning quietly flashed among the distant dark clouds on the horizon. By the time the shepherd and his herd reached the top of the cliff, the black clouds had gathered ominously in the sky above them.

As the sheep were grazing blithely on top of the mountain, there was a sudden clap of thunder. The bellwether of the flock was startled, dashed to the right in a panic, slipped, and fell off the cliff. The sheep closer to the lead sheep caught sight of their lead jumping off the cliff; they instinctively followed. Sheep in the inner second ring saw the first group jump; they, too, jumped.

In an instant, the shepherd, witnessing the horror swiftly unfolding before his eyes, felt a wave of sheer panic wash over him. In a race against time, he made a mad dash to the edge of the cliff, stretched out his arms, and yelled, "Stop! Stop!"

However, the sheep, driven by their instinct to follow the animals before them, were not heedful of the shepherd's desperate pleas in that split nanosecond. Instead, they dashed either left or right, made a bolt over the cliff, and plunged to the bottom below. In a matter of seconds, the top of the ridge was completely deserted; all the sheep lay in heaps at the bottom of the cliff. The shepherd was left standing alone in a state of shock and grief.

The panic and grief-stricken shepherd hurried back to his farm to impart the tragic news and hoped the sage could somehow backpedal what he had done to the sheep. Yet, they knew it was futile, for the sage had taken leave of time long past, and the outcome of the discipline instilled in the new sheep race could no longer be undone or reversed.

As Adio recounted this part of the story, his friends listened with rapt attention. Their mouths hung open, and their eyes popped in disbelief. Then suddenly, the silence was broken by Adio's burst of laughter, as if he was expecting his story to send all his friends into hysterics. However, his friends remained motionless, like waxwork dummies, looking severe and solemn. None were laughing.

One of them then finally broke his silence and scolded him. "That is not funny, Adio." "Don't you see how funny it is?" Adio burst out laughing again in his playful mood. "No, I don't see it, just heaps of dead sheep at the bottom." Remarked one friend.

"How many? There must be... What? at least hundreds of them?" Commented a conscientious listener.

"Well, that is what the sage made them become. That is how sheep behave nowadays." Adio replied.

"Really?" One seemed to come across the matter seriously.

In the end, Adio's friends were still not amused by the story. Instead, they found Adio's story annoying, if not upsetting. Then, predictably, they decided they had had enough fun for the day and headed home.

* * * * *

Rumors of Adio making fun of the Great Sage reached Ms. Wen one late evening, perturbing her deeply. She could not concentrate on anything upon learning that. Instead, she felt deeply insecure, volatile, and helpless.

From the beginning, Adio had cast a negative image in Ms. Wen's mind. Long trained in stringent conditions herself, she inherited and used that same rigid attitude to teach others. In due course, she developed an implacable hatred for those with happy-go-lucky attitudes. Because of that, and being mentally incapable of understanding anything else, she was always preoccupied with orderliness, perfection, and obedience, bordering on obsession. But when her attempts failed to regulate her environment, she felt like she was being held captive by others. When students did not follow her demands, she would become angry. And when her anger gave way to vindictiveness, she was hell-bent on seeking punishment.

As her mind drifted in and out of this furor, she sat, apparently making mountains out of molehills. The more she thought about it, the more she became overwrought. The more she became overwrought, the more she started seeing images in her mind. Amid her immovable frame that appeared to lose track of time, her eyes gaped at an invisible presence that seemed perceptible out of thin air. As she continued sitting there nursing her anger and letting her emotions toss and roil inside her, she became angry and angrier to the point she could no longer hold it back. Then, suddenly, her body made one involuntary, forceful lurch at an imaginary object or person in front of her desk, much like suddenly finding oneself on the edge of a cliff resulted in an uncontrolled movement of leg cramps at night, almost knocking out her cup of tea. The tempestuous mishap abruptly brought her back to reality. At once, she gave a surreptitious glance across the room and was relieved to find no one around.

As she sat upright and regained her poise, Elder Abdalla came by to say hello.

After a brief exchange of pleasantries, Elder Abdalla asked about her teaching. She insisted everything was fine before continuing in a dragging voice, "But..."

Elder Abdalla became concerned and followed up.

She started by saying it was only a minor problem. But she would uninhibitedly let on the full details of Adio's behavior. Upon hearing this, Elder Abdalla slumped into a profound thought.

Without waiting for Elder Abdalla's comment, she continued, "I have advised him not to use his left hand to write. But he won't listen to me."

The unanticipated subject came up as a complete surprise, as much as it perplexed Elder Abdalla. He asked with a frown, "What's wrong with using your left hand?"

"Well, you see... We have statistics to back up that those using the left hand are prone to committing crimes."

This allegation deeply stirred Elder Abdalla. For a man who led a seemingly reclusive community, he seemed paralyzed by the term, which implied something unimpeachable. Subsequently, it aroused his reasonable fears as he remembered his daughters complaining that Adio was teasing them. Elder Abdalla suddenly became so disquiet and worried. He briefly tried to get hold of himself.

Afterward, both continued to converse quietly with each other for quite a while.

Elder Abdalla largely stayed silent during the conversation. He appeared unable to think clearly for a time, but he eventually said, "Good night."

Saying nothing further, he left.

For many years, Adio's mother warned her boy that he might get into trouble someday if he continued to cause mischief. Problems did finally come, however serious ones.

The next day, the tribe's guards detained Adio. They accused him of stealing merchandise from a shop and causing disturbances. Adio maintained his innocence, saying he went to the shop only to buy snacks. Elder Abdalla refused to budge, even when his mother and sister pleaded for release. Without giving definite answers, he sent them home and asked them to wait.

The matter, however, proceeded swiftly. Adio was forwarded to the next town on the first day of light to face a hearing. The accusations against him were many: stirring up trouble, picking quarrels, shoplifting, and causing a public disturbance.

Charges that local people had never heard of and accusations they could never comprehend.

Briefly detained in one town, he was transferred to yet another. This time, more accusations were added to the list: not cooperating, encouraging disunity, threatening unity, defiling the symbolism of sheep, a presumed act of inhumanity to animals, disrespecting a foreign subject, and disrespecting an alien figure.

Ink was cheap, and it bore no weight. Human lives were treated like flakes, like fish flesh, wilfully pecked at mindlessly.

The final destination was the city, and Adio's fate boarded up.

Many seasons came and went. In an unexpected turn of events, the Chinese school closed down. Nobody knew why, and it closed down without an announcement. As a result, Ms. Wen was no longer there. She went back to her hometown.

Spring came when Adio was released. Villagers said he was a changed man. They said life in a camp must have done a number on him, life in the re-education camp. He was no longer energetic like before; he was so quiet. Every evening, people would see him walking silently toward the river, where he would sit by himself for hours on end.

Years later, after Elder Abdalla passed away, the villagers found a logbook he had left behind. It contained a chronicle of the events and activities in the village through the years. It also listed other prosaic details of life, such as what activity was, who attended it, how much was spent, etc.

There was one conspicuous segment near the end of the log where he made no bones about the seriousness of Adio's offenses. It said, "Over the years, our village has withstood the test of time and continued to prove that our unity will always prevail. Yet, despite our village not changing much, it is no longer the same. Since Adio returned, we have seen the first recorded offender living among us."

UNFORGIVEN

As fall drew to a close, a helicopter hovered above the northern part of Xishuang in southern China and slowly circled toward the western skirt of the forest. Onboard, a crew member conducted a visual survey of the areas below.

As the helicopter approached the southern fringe near the outer pocket of the forest, one crew member spotted something unusual. He nudged the crew member beside him.

Pointing below an endless vista of towering trees near the horizon, they saw a puff of white smoke rise from the forest floor beneath. Without delay, the pilot circled to that spot for a better look.

Once hovering above the location, they saw a makeshift structure resembling a hut with a man standing beside it. At first, the crew found it hard to believe what they saw, for the area was deep inside the forest, far away from human habitation. They circled again, and amid the blasting chopping sound from the furious whirring blades of the rotor, they waved to the man below. However, he did not wave back. He just stood there and gawked at them. Although the crew was eager to talk to the man, they realized it was impossible, as below them was a vast, dense forest with no clearing in sight.

The helicopter made one final pass overhead while one crew noted their bearings. It then headed north and was gone.

It had been a week since the crew returned to their base in Ainon county outside Xishuang. Afterward, they told others and the county chief what they had found and discussed ways to get to the man or maybe a group living there.

At first, the county chief needed clarification, for the location was far from a human settlement. Even though it begged for belief, he reluctantly agreed to let them meet the man.

Figuring out how to get there proved challenging. With no roads or access points available, the county chief appointed a team to devise a plan. After mulling over the geographic areas, they formed an expedition.

At the end of the week, they finally assembled a team of two men and a woman. Before they set off that morning in a nearby town inside Xishuang, they wondered whether they should get some firearms.

One man said, "I heard tell there are tigers and leopards deep inside the jungle."

The other fellow added, "I am less concerned about wild animals. We don't know what people we might run into. I get wind that many gangsters and thugs operate all kinds of illegal activities southwest of the border. It is a dangerous area. If you were captive, you would be extremely fortunate to cut and run with only one kidney missing. You know what I mean?"

For their protection, the two brought firearms to guard against the vagaries of the jungle.

The trip proved to be an arduous and taxing journey. Equipped with a compass to determine the location, the crew trekked through a canopy of trees and dense vegetation, scrambled up mountains, and waded through creeks.

In the daylight, they walked through the jungle without a letup, hoping to shorten their distance to their destination as much as possible. When the light of day faded and before darkness enfolded them, they stopped and pitched their camps. There, they rested and waited for another crack of dawn to lead their journey again.

By the fourth day, they finally arrived at the presumed point but found no sign of the man. Neither the hut they had previously encountered was nowhere to be seen. At that point, one crew member suggested they split up and search in different directions to locate the man.

Mr. Ren Lang, the team leader, objected, "Forget that. If one of you gets lost, we must organize another expedition to find you."

Instead, they resolved to call out to the man. Suddenly, their yelling and screaming broke the tranquility of nature, scaring away animals and birds alike. They continued to shout until their shouts made them hoarse.

Once the silence returned, Ms. Tan Xing, exhausted by her yelling, shuffled around and squatted down on a broken tree trunk. Only at that point did she spot someone hiding in a bush at eye level. She involuntarily shouted a greeting, "Hello!"

After hauling herself up, she called out again, "Hello!"

By then, she had drawn the attention of the other two. They now cautiously approached the individual in the bush.

Standing at a safe distance, Ren Lang greeted him. "Hello! Are you living here?" The man in the bush stirred slightly but did not respond.

Tan Xing asked, "Are you alone or with someone else here?"

At that point, the man attempted to communicate, "Ah... I... my... self."

Eagerly, another member of the team, Mr. Jin Ping, got closer and courted him in a gentle voice, "Can you come out? We won't hurt you."

The man made a stir and was slowly hauling himself up. As he emerged from the bush, the crew saw a tall, slender figure who looked haggard. He had bony cheeks and long, white, unkempt hair. Wearing worn-out clothes and shoeless, he looked advanced in age, pushing for seventy.

"What is your name?" Ren Lang asked.

"Vin... cen... t." His speech seemed impaired a little.

"Vin Cen, how long have you been living here?" Tan Xing asked.

"Most... my life."

"Most of your life? How did you get here? From where?" Tan Xing exclaimed in astonishment.

"A long... long story."

Seeing Vin Cen in a muddled state of mind, the crew tried not to ask him many questions. Instead, they offered him some food and snacks they had brought along. Vin Cen looked at the snacks greedily and savored every bite.

Afterward, he led them to his makeshift shed, about the size of a small bedroom, with a thatched roof and walls made of twigs and mud. He then shared how he and other family members ended up there, how they survived in the jungle, and why they stayed away from civilization. Their conversation continued late into the night before the crew set up their tents and hit the sack from their exhaustion.

The crew had been discussing the situation since they woke up the next day. Initially, they tried to persuade Vin Cen to leave with them. But little did they know, Vin Cen was more obstinate than they had first thought. He refused to leave and told them in no unexplicit terms that he wanted to stay.

Yet, after lengthy persuasion, Ren Lang got frustrated and asked, "Who will take care of you here?"

"Myself! No one I need."

"But..." Ren Lang intended to push him a little, but his voice died out.

"Us, they persecute." Vin Cen explained.

The crew understood what Vin Cen was referring to. It was a time when demented agitators-turned-thugs with red armbands terrorized and brutalized the entire nation. Under duress, the inhabitants had to kneel, beg, and double-cross each other while those firebrands sneered, mocked, and spat.

That was during the bleak period when Vin Cen and his family fled to the forest.

"That was a long time ago. Everything has changed since then. Nobody persecutes you anymore," Jin Ping assured him.

Vin Cen remained unconvinced. "Everything? Really?" "Of course, we are in a new era now."

Still, Vin Cen remained recalcitrant and would not budge.

Ren Lang initially felt it was wrong to leave the man behind. But on second thoughts, he had to accept that Vin Cen had been here most of his life. He might have been homeless, but he had the survival skills they might lack.

But there was another issue. Ren Lang reminded his team that they would not fancy making the journey from the nearby town whenever they wanted. It would be absurd if the county chief expected them to make another trip.

Tan Xing, at that point, suggested, "There is a creek nearby that has a small clearing. Maybe we can make the clearing slightly bigger for landing."

After a lengthy evaluation, Ren Lang finally relented. "That might be our only choice. We will head there first before we leave."

The crew gave Vin Cen whatever they could - snacks, canned food, and drinks. Before they bid him farewell, Ren Lang told him, "We might meet again."

Vin Cen at once requested, "Salt! I need salt."

The crew nodded, realizing that all they could think of were items like snacks or instant noodles, the essentials of city life.

Vin Cen stood on a hill waving to them until they disappeared.

*** * * * ***

The county chief, Mr. Wan Xang, was upset when the team reported about the man they found in the jungle.

"Why didn't you take him with you? You think this is a leisure tour?" he snapped.

"What could we do? He refused to leave." Ren Lang tried to defend himself.

"We have to get him out. We care for everyone. My word is my bond." Wan Xang said, while pacing back and forth about the room.

Little did the crew know, he had a very different agenda. He theorized some criminals who started and handled the violent episode of the past event. Their relentless crimes have since faced justice, and the nation has moved into a different era. Vin Cen would be an eyewitness to this new progress firsthand.

Wan Xang paused and said, "That's all for now."

Wan Xang was a stout middle-aged man, standing barely five feet tall. He had a round face and a crew cut, which gave him a look younger than his age. A pragmatic man, he liked to handle things swiftly and effectively. He hated procrastination, and he strongly appreciated speed.

Yet, he was also headstrong and enjoyed getting his way. Once he committed to a specific plan, as unyielding as a tree stump amid a garden, nothing could sway his mental obduracy.

As had happened many times before, he habitually interrupted further suggestions by bawling, "That is enough!" That was typically how a discussion usually ended.

After the team left, Wan Xang summoned his assistant, Mr. Youwen Dang, to his office and said, "You need to go with Ren Lang to get that man out of the jungle. He can't remain there. He needs help. Talk to Ren Lang. Get ready for the journey."

Wan Xang made it clear just as Youwen was about to take leave. "If he refuses, tie him up and bring him back here. I am serious. I don't want to see you come back empty-handed. You hear?"

After a day of preparation, Ren Lang and Youwen took off the following day in a helicopter and headed south.

After the crew left Vin Cen behind last time, they located the creek that Tan Xing had suggested. Following some hard work, they secured a small clearing by the stream.

The challenging task ahead was to find that specific landing spot. However, as they closed on the presumed landing area, they needed help to locate the site. Much to their relief, they spotted it on the second attempt when the aircraft flew further east.

As they were about to land, Ren Lang was busy gathering provisions like salt, rice, and other supplies for Vin Cen. Youwen considered telling him to leave the supplies behind, but ultimately decided against it. Initially, he had reservations about the trip, uncertain he could fulfill his boss's expectations. Conspicuously, the implication of his occasional distraction revealed his unease.

After a short trek from the landing spot, they saw Vin Cen standing atop the hill, watching them. Once they reached him, Vin Cen was grateful for the provisions. He went through the items individually and thanked them now and then.

Long after they arrived, Ren Lang and Youwen brought up the topic of the decampment. They began telling Vin Cen about television, movies he could watch in a theater, a waterbed, friendly people, etc. Finally, at the end of the lengthy persuasion, they asked Vin Cen to leave the jungle. To their disappointment, Vin Cen remained as obstinate as a mule.

At this stage, Youwen was not just disappointed; he was desperate. If push came to shove, extracting Vin Cen would be tantamount to kidnapping, Youwen thought. Even though the idea did not sit well with him, he knew the practice was not uncommon.

He became jittery and took a stroll around to ease his anxiety. When he returned, he found Vin Cen sitting alone.

"Too hot," Youwen grunted as he squatted down on a tree trunk, fanning himself with his hand.

Together, they sat idly in that sultry afternoon under the dense canopy of the jungle, where birds trilled and chirped now and then.

This time, Youwen started babbling with Vin Cen, talking about his childhood, school years, or kith and kin back home. At one point, when he mentioned rainy days, Vin Cen interrupted him.

"Have you to the sea?" he asked.

"Yes, a couple of years ago," Youwen, distracted from decampment, replied absentmindedly while staring at the ground.

"The adults told me... when small," Vin Cen continued.

Upon hearing that, Youwen replied in a desultory manner, "Well, two hours by airplane, maybe."

"They too. They wanted to. But..." Vin Cen pointed to where his family members lay under a nearby tree.

Youwen continued to reply halfheartedly, "I'm sorry to hear that."

Youwen had been a straightforward man. Unlike some people who preferred a roundabout, devious approach to resolving matters, he inclined to take issues mano a mano. But at this instant, when he offered his condolences, a curious sensation struck him that something was amiss.

Youwen now became attentive and heeled. He asked, "You want to see the sea?" "I don't know... What like?"

"Look at the blue sky above you." Youwen looked up and animatedly swept his arm across the blue above the towering trees. "You see how big it is? But the sky is where you can never reach. However, the ocean is much like that vast sky stretching before you, and you can float on it. It makes you feel pleasant and peaceful."

Vin Cen was staring off into space, completely lost in thought.

Youwen paused briefly before continuing, "Vin Cen, come with us, and I will arrange a trip for you to the sea. It is something you've wanted all your life, isn't it? If you'd like, you could even live by the sea."

At his moment, Youwen held his breath, anxious over how Vin Cen would react. Yet, he was slightly assuring when he saw Vin Cen remain silent while immersing himself in a trance.

Youwen continued to coax, "Come with us, Vin Cen. Come with us to the sea."

The minute when he returned to the county with Vin Cen, Youwen felt elated. His boss praised him enthusiastically and flattered him. "I always have confidence in you. That's why I sent you. Good job!"

No sooner than Vin Cen arrived, news and gossip spread fast to towns nearby. People with eager faces all wanted to sneak a peek at 'the jungle man.' But for Wan Xang, he had carefully hammered out the details long before Vin Cen's decampment.

Amid the ballyhoo, not soon after Vin Cen's arrival, the county chief announced the date for a press conference and forwarded invitations. After Wan Xang informed Youwen of the day and time of the interview, he told him, "There are things we have to prepare for."

Unaware of his boss's intentions, Youwen expressed doubts about this whole thing.

"Don't you think the local press is enough?"

"This is significant. What you have to do now is tell Vin Cen what to say and what not to say. Tell him to cooperate with us if he wants to see the ocean. You understand?"

"What am I going to tell him?"

"Tell him to describe the past event as a cruel act committed by a group of gangsters. They had no empathy for anybody and disregarded the nation's progress. This incident had nothing to do with our great socialist beliefs or causes. What happened before, let the past be the past. When he returned, he expressed great gratitude that the government had saved only one man. He praises progress and adheres to our core socialist values: prosperity, democracy, civility, harmony, freedom, equality, and justice."

Wan Xang continued, "You must train him by asking and telling. Prepare a note and ask him to read it and sign it."

After Youwen took leave, he felt the interview might not go well. Long habituated to a reclusive life, Vin Cen often appeared unspeaking and uncommunicative. His speech was fractional, disconnected, and incomplete. How to get him to talk intelligently was not something he could gain within a couple of days. Vin Cen was experiencing both mental and physical decline. How well could he handle this situation?

That evening, Youwen informed Vin Cen about the interview and what they expected of him. The request appalled Vin Cen, and he snapped back, "Why me to do that? I say not a word!"

Youwen immediately defended himself. "Not me. It's my boss. Not me."

Both descended into complete silence before Youwen continued, "I know it sounds silly, but listen, you just brave it for a while, and the interview will be over quickly."

A long silence of hesitation washed over Vin Cen. Submitting himself to the contradiction of the murderous event in the distant past only deepened his anguish and aggravated his profound sense of inferiority.

Realizing that the longer Vin Cen took to think it over, the more likely he was to refuse. Youwen pressed on relentlessly. "After the press, we will arrange a trip for you to the seaside. Just think of it. There are plenty of exotic fruits already there waiting for you. Anything you name it - mango, guava, coconut, papaya, pineapple, etc. You can stroll around, pick whatever you like, and eat until your heart's content. You don't want to miss that, do you? Besides, you can live there too. We will arrange it for you."

Mentioning the sea, Vin Cen envisioned the vast expanse of water before him and felt buoyancy.

Noticing Vin Cen lost in a trance, Youwen quietly prodded, "Life is short, and time is swift."

Upon hearing that, a light flickered in Vin Cen's eyes. He seemed stirred by the adage, and after a fractional hesitation, he eventually agreed by silently nodding his head.

Elated at Vin Cen's consent, Youwen exclaimed, "Good! Now, let's go over the material together, shall we?"

Youwen then went over the speech in great detail with Vin Cen. Throughout their discussion, he also slipped in anecdotes about how their beloved leaders' hair turned white overnight because they stayed up all night thinking and worrying about the welfare of the ordinary; how they declared, in a time of crisis, all for one and one for all; and how their hair miraculously turned black again when they fought and saved the lesser mortals from danger in defiance of an angry sea.

After a long rehearsal with Vin Cen, Youwen felt satisfied and left with a sense of relief.

As he was in a lighthearted mood walking down the entrance stairs, Youwen accidentally stepped on a feline's tail resting at the bottom of the dimly lit porch. The cat gave off an ear-splitting caterwauling that made him jump. That harsh, piercing cry frightened him silly. For a moment, he presaged it as a harbinger of something terrible.

Standing there, reeling from the inquietude, he tried to cast off the spell by cursing it back. "Stupid cat. Watch where you're going. Maybe you find living such a nuisance. Silly cat."

But for all his grumbles, his exclamation seemed too wordy.

A moment after pulling himself from the ordeal, he slowly returned to his quarters.

Meanwhile, Vin Cen was grinding away at the preparation speech in his room. But then things took an unexpected turn.

The night before the press conference, Vin Cen had a fitful night's sleep. He woke up several times to take a sip of water. After midnight, he, at last, fell sound asleep.

That night, he had a dream. Vin Cen floated in an ocean full of corpses. There were so many that they seemed tightly packed together, making Vin Cen's body movements immovable. The water was like thick brownish mud while fetid smells filled the air. Amid this horror scene, Vin Cen knew he was in a dream. He tried to open his eyes to free himself. But despite how hard he tried, his eyes remained glued shut.

Overwhelmed by terror while writhing, twisting, and thrashing in utter panic, he then saw the water's surface ripple in the heat mirages from a distance ahead. Through his half-closed eyelids, a misty figure now and then shimmered and flickered in the heat of illusion. The blurry figure slowly approached him until it revealed itself as a middle-aged woman.

Suspended in mid-air above him, the woman calmly bent over and plunged her hands into the water. With one hand behind the back of Vin Cen's knees and one behind his back, she gently hoisted him out of the water. At this moment, Vin Cen felt his body slowly uplifted into a supine position. A profound sense of peacefulness and serenity washed over him.

In a fleeting moment, he found himself in the forest, seeking shade under a tree on a scorching afternoon, feeling enervated and debilitated from semi-starvation.

Standing before him, the lady said, "Do not take the low road of subjugation. Honor yourself and honor your forebears. Take this nurture for your ailing body and mind. And honor me."

Afterward, she fed him with a piece of fruit.

Vin Cen eventually opened his eyes. Amid the darkness enfolded, his eyes swept, hoping to catch sight of the divine being. But, as this spiritual nurture betokened sustenance for his body and wisdom for his mind, her caring also held a place so precious in his heart that he cried. If her caring was so sacred, she also gave a dying man the dignity a human should have.

In silence, he vowed he would honor her.

The preparations were underway for the event. The press conference took place outdoors. Set against the backdrop of a nature reserve, a makeshift raised platform was put up in front of an entrance to a public garden flanked by two rows of red Jacaranda trees.

Two rows of folding chairs lined up in front of the platform. Above the platform, a table and two chairs were placed in the middle—one for Vin Cen and another for Youwen.

By nine o'clock, the reporters had taken their seats while a crowd of townspeople gathered near the entrance. Shortly after, Vin Cen approached the table gingerly, followed by Youwen.

The meeting began with fifteen minutes of brief questions and answers: What did Vin Cen eat? Did he cook? Did he encounter any animals? How did he pass his time?

Afterward, a reporter asked how Vin Cen felt upon his return.

Youwen, at that point, discreetly stepped out of the spotlight, hoping that Vin Cen's upcoming comments on patriotism would not arouse suspicions about his involvement in orchestrating the entire situation.

Vin Cen, however, should have mentioned any progress or slogans as expected. Instead, he broke into an impromptu speech,

"How I feel now depends on what you know about how we ended up in the jungle from the beginning. At the outset of the campaign, sensing the danger that might ensue, my parents took me, my grandpa, and grandma, along with our dogs and cats, and fled to the forest's edge. We only planned for a temporary stay, but little did we know the campaign had yet taken its worst turn. Those radicals beat up and humiliated townspeople. People died by execution, hanging, throwing off cliffs, or drowning themselves. Our beliefs put us at further risk. Soon, we realized we were going to stay in the forest for a long, long time. That was when we moved deeper and deeper into the jungle until we ended up where the team found me."

A reporter asked, "Are you happy with what you see now?"

Vin Cen picked up where he left off and continued, "At the beginning, seeing what happened in those towns, the thought of death might make us entire. The sheer impulse of brutality tore asunder cultural fabric, woven since time immemorial. Lives, fostered by a long past, scattered over barren landscapes. White bones exposed, wild grasses grew, windswept plains waited in silence, but cold, lonely nights."

At that moment, the reporters below fired a barrage of questions. But Vin Cen did not bother with any of their questions. Instead, he kept going. "But we lived and endured all kinds of hardships. All the time, we were not afraid of wild animals, but we instead smelled fear of humans. At one point, we thought we had lost our humanity, but in the years to come, it was in the wilderness that we restored our faith in the gospel. Through nature, we learned to understand self-preservation to preserve ourselves and, subsequently, to uphold the principle that all persons should be endowed with natural rights to life, liberty, and property. Men are, by nature, all free, equal, and independent. Had our natural rights been safeguarded, just like our great-great grandparents of Celtic descent had, none of these events would have occurred. Lives would have been free.

Living would have been more meaningful."

At almost the exact moment when a reporter interrupted Vin Cen, Youwen, standing at the back of the reporters, felt deeply disturbed. It defied logic when he reflected on why Vin Cen suddenly became so talkative or about things not going accordingly. It was Vin Cen's untimely disclosure that truly unsettled him. Earlier, despite Youwen being aware of Vin Cen's height, he also noticed his straight nose, slightly pale complexion, and receding chin, which differed from the genetic inheritance in the country's southern regions.

Yet, nothing could have prepared him for the shocking revelation about Vin Cen's ancestry and beliefs. Why did he not bring it up before? A flurry of questions raced through his mind, throwing him into confusion. He wanted to stop the now

interview-turned-lecture but feared his boss might hurl accusations at him for making excuses, having contradicted him early on. Caught in this mental chaos, all he could think of was to look for Wan Xang. He looked around and dashed into a nearby building in one mad rush.

In the meantime, Vin Cen continued, "More importantly, how an event could descend into such a vicious cycle? For all I know, just like in the past, as in the present, it happens because lookers-on would always pacify their conscience by the delusion that they can do no harm if they take no part and form no opinion. Bad men need nothing more to compass their ends than that good men should look on and do nothing. But why are men so futile? The only explanation is that power tends to corrupt, and absolute power corrupts absolutely. Therefore, great men are almost always bad men."

At that moment, someone behind the scenes willfully turned up the power amplifier. The loudspeakers above jammed with electromagnetic interference, making some hissing and buzzing noise. Suddenly, a loud, booming sound erupted. Spooked by the blast, Vin Cen quickly ducked his head while his forearms anchored to the table's edge, as if to avoid a blow. In doing so, he almost bumped his nose against the table's surface.

First, there was complete silence as the crowd below tried to regain their sense of the booming sound. Then hoots of uncontrollable, raucous laughter followed as they witnessed Vin Cen's abrupt, comical reaction. Bewilderingly, this instantaneous response was unanimous feedback to what Vin Cen had said earlier.

A male voice then mocked, "You got your comeuppance, my friend!" That drew even more boisterous laughter from the audience while some rocked back and forth with their heehaw.

Inflamed by the remark, Vin Cen straightened his back and lashed out, swinging his hand across the stage. "Silence! Silence! A friend to all is a friend to none. I am not your friend!"

While Vin Cen attempted to settle accounts with the rowdy reporters below, an old fellow with a long white beard among the audience kept shaking his head in silence now and then.

Meanwhile, Vin Cen gave the audience a blank look before rambling on, "Yet, despite seven decades, Chinese political orientation, after certain transformations, remains unchanged. Our faith has never been safe, but the Darien Gap, though perilous, is now a distant past. I heard everything has changed. That is because it is in a deceptive cycle.

The invisible oppression will swing back. When it does, the end justifies humans as inferior by nature. They will live, survive, or die according to the arbitrary wishes of the state. You can not hold back the pendulum effect. Have you not seen the country long locked in a cog of a socialist mentality? It twitches back and forth, subsequently reactivates itself, and astonishingly takes tens of millions of lives on its direful historical joy rides now and then. And so, as great men are almost always bad men, those who take no part and form no opinion will also bear the crimes no less severe than those who committed them. Those who never desire to atone for their bad deeds will only embolden themselves further for whatever reasons they choose not to redeem."

By this time, Youwen and his boss were rushing back. Immediately, Wan Xang darted to the platform with four men at his heels.

Wan Xang and the men demanded Vin Cen to come with them. But he was so obstinate that he would not budge. Even though much had met his satisdiction, he still intended to carry on to his next topic to reach his satisfaction. He just sat there, looking at the sky obliquely in silence, oblivious to their presence. The men then pulled him out of his chair.

In an ensuing scuffle, two men grabbed his arms and shoulders while the others held his legs. They then hauled him up and sent him on all fours up against the sky, flailing and wailing. But his struggle only made him feel swimmy with each heaving motion as they carried him away, confounding the audience below with mouths wide open.

In the ensuing moment, the unfolding scene above drew a howl from the audience below at another sight of Vin Cen's comical reaction. Some brought attention to others by pointing a finger at Vin Cen and rocking back and forth with their shrieks of laughter.

Vin Cen did not have time to reciprocate with the boisterous crowd below this time as the men carried him away. Still, people could hear him yelling, "Put me down! I have not finished yet! I have much more to say. I haven't talked about the bad things about democracy yet!"

$$* \ * \ * \ * \ *$$

As Youwen mentioned before, the interview would be over in no time. Yet, he would never expect things to go so awry.

Wan Xang took the rap for 'digging up this guy out of nowhere and letting him lecture us? Unforgiven!' For that reason, he got removed for failing to secure permission. It later became known that he was sent to a farm some 200 kilometers away where he attended hogs and underwent the hands-on experience of how hogs lived to comprehend the concept of dependency and reliance as core interests in the state.

Youwen was demoted too and retired to who-know-where.

The guests were neither exempt from the castigation nor exempt from it. They paid the price for accepting the invitation in the first place and subsequently witnessing things unfold. "You have a good time there, don't you think?" So they were told.

They got a fix. They were all eventually referred to re-education programs, underwent self-criticism, admitted guilt, and cleansed their thoughts. Afterward, they went to another location to learn and reaffirm their patriotism.

Yet nobody knew what fate had befallen Vin Cen.

There was an elderly in town with a long white beard. Nicknamed Ahwai, locals revered him as a wise old soul. People turned to him for advice whenever they faced unresolved problems or encountered strange phenomena.

On this day, curious people came to discover Vin Cen's whereabouts. The wise man told them, "After that day, they threw him back into the forest, told him to stay there, and never ever come out. They said they have had enough of him."

The old man wagged his head and lamented. "He talked too much!"

Slouching over in his chair while gazing off into space, he shook his head again.

Life went on as usual after that. Occasionally, against the backdrop of the forest, ambient sounds of children playing nearby in a park resonated with merriment, and people heard them sing,

Over yonder lives an old man in the jungle, Carefree and untroubled, he likes to be called uncle. He loves to ramble and mumble,

But people want him to be humble, not grumble. His name is Crusoe, and he likes to mingle.

EVENT HORIZON

Part I - The Specter of Deprivation

It is a long story about how a man named Lao Mao came to people's attention. It all began when the rebels spread some intriguing tidbits about him. These tidbits mainly contained anecdotes containing amusing activities or other incidental details about him.

Some of these depicted how peasants risked their lives to bring the rebels food, how the comrades cared for each other and never left the wounded behind, how his

second-in-command, AhEn, preferred to go hungry to give away food to the hungry peasants, how the comrades joined and helped the peasants in harvest time, how Lao Mao exalted the peasants as gods, and how the comrades sewed and mended worn clothes for the needy.

These anecdotes, from which no one could verify, little by little, offered much bigger images and many meaningful messages that helped the population relate to Lao Mao and his comrades' ways of life.

Later, the faction added additional artworks to bolster Lao Mao and the rebels' images, such as one giant painting that depicted Lao Mao marching bravely alongside his comrades in battle, providing an alluring, awe-inspiring portrait.

These anecdotes and artworks evoked feelings of compassion and humanity. They ultimately captivated the public's imagination and won their support.

However, as much of the stories lazed in histrionics rather than grounded in actual historical accounts, they did little to strengthen the reality beyond these fairy-tale-like portraits of Lao Mao or his comrades until a man showed up.

One day in early spring, a strange-looking man appeared in a land northwest of China out of nowhere. The locals inquired about his name but learned of something uncertain. In a moment of creativity, the stranger pointed to a patch of snow on the ground and patted his chest. The locals simultaneously burst into an uproar, "Oh, Bai! Bai is your name! Fancy that! We could have guessed."

'Bai' is the local language for 'White' in his mother tongue.

To make it easy to call or remember, they added a repetitive sound to his name, dubbing him "Bai Bai."

Bai Bai later revealed that he came from the New World and was a reporter. Longing for a break from the humdrum of his life in his hometown, he always wanted to seek excitement and adventure abroad.

Once arriving, the man contacted the rebels in their dugouts. However, as he attempted to gain Lao Mao's trust, he first had to show his loyalty to the faction, hoping to become their confidant.

As Bai Bai attempted to endear himself to the group, he slowly gained the Bai malady: he was well received and well-treated to the degree that he was being cosseted and pampered. Then, they demanded him to return a little favor, which he was happy to compile.

As time went on, more insidious requests silently seeped through. At every turn, Bai Bai appeased and conceded. He even allowed his works to be censored, edited, and manipulated afterward. Eventually, acting as a shill, he presented his works as

second-hand propaganda relayed to the New World and beyond.

Being new to the environment, Bai Bai likely adjusted his behavior to meet his basic needs and function in a unique setting. In doing so, he opened his way to assimilation and accommodation. However, this disposition affected more of those seeking better returns, recognition, or advantages. For those eager to be thrust into the spotlight through appeasement, Bai Bai would not be the last.

Shortly after, Bai Bai carried out the message for Lao Mao, presenting him as a man who awakened millions to an issue of human rights and encouraged people to fight for a life of justice, equality, freedom, and human dignity.

It was unclear whether Bai Bai's statements, filled with grand rhetoric, were sincere or merely empty talk. The authorities quickly reeled off all the fanciful, eloquent ideas in the first part. However, the second part that required their efforts to uphold their assertions might take time.

In reality, that second part had yet to materialize, as they likely needed to remember what they originally asked Bai Bai to express in the first place. As for Bai Bai, had he not hung on to his self-adulation to sustain himself through times, he might have come to terms with his statements, albeit inflated, during his later years.

* * * * *

For some time, rumors circulated that officials occasionally organized feasts in the compound where Lao Mao lived. Entertainment would follow.

During the festivities, the officials would arrange for female cadets to attend. Lao Mao would dance with the female cadets. Later, one of the female cadets would be escorted to his bedroom, the Red Chamber, next to the dance hall.

Despite being just rumors, no one could dismiss or deny them. The locals always held on to the belief that "stillness can not engender waves." Many details were too titillating to ignore: the legs at the end of the bed elevated a couple of inches higher to enhance Lao Mao's carnal desire, romantic interludes between him and his former teacher, or

advice-seeking on how a phallus could flip a stone, among many others.

Instead of dispelling doubts, these accounts only captivated the imagination regarding what had transpired. The question was how the commoners would offer what they were offering. The answer might have laid in lockstep with the structure of centralized power.

In an era when a centralized power ruled over its citizens, questioning or defying the authorities was treasonous. Everyone must remain silent and obedient to preserve a harmonious society.

Seeing that no one could question or defy the authorities, those who represented that same power below do the same: they all copied the central control as their own. The branching and emulation of supreme power kept branching down, far and wide, in one uncontrollable sprawling fashion until it reached down to lowly neighborhood watchers, measly paid teachers, money-spinning monks, or others in positions of power. They all wanted something, anything, that gave them a sense of importance, a sense of worthiness, or a sense of superiority. And they, too. They all wanted a piece of that power or an equal representation of authority.

From there, it spread across different levels of law enforcers who all shepherded a law unto themselves. As a result, this structure of imitation power formed one gigantic entanglement of corridors, with the intricacy of twists and turns that the ordinary had to navigate in mincing steps through communist deception and manipulation.

Under this structure of imitation power, unlawful activities flourished. Yet, the central control could never oversee the massive branching of the underpass, both genuine or bogus, legal or pretentious, below. Hence, fraudulent or illicit activities proliferated uncontrollably, like weeds growing wildly.

As a result, cracks lay in wait. When the total number of unlawful issues exceeded the number tolerated, it eventually posed a severe threat to the notion of stability and a direct threat to the power itself. By keeping the number down, the authority might resort to discouraging, denying, rejecting, and dismissing any claims, complaints, or disputes to preserve a state of equilibrium, a semblance of harmony and stability.

Emboldened, all these imitation powers deemed themselves secured and encouraged even further. As a result, the country saw the overrun of local powers, riffraff, thugs, power-backed corporations and organizations, or crime syndicates acting in cahoots with local law enforcers who all mirrored absolute powers.

Yet, lawless, rampant, and unchecked as they were, these widespread powers helped fortify central authorities who could risk losing control of the masses without them. For that reason, these powers, either genuine or counterfeit, might thus be left partly condoned. In contrast, others slipped past the borders, carry on with their presumed abilities, and formed secret organizations or other pursuits with or without the central authority's knowledge.

This structure of carbon powers thus formed one massive, messy network of twists, knots, and turns, spawning millions upon millions.

From imitation power came power and influence, and from power and influence came cash and wealth. These power imitators all demanded something, or anything, sometimes purely to make themselves feel good, important, or worthy. With that, for the ordinary, daily routines became burdens, movements circumscribed, and lives suffocated.

Under this circumstance, underdogs and ordinary people who wanted to become the sole survivor of the fittest must adapt to the bullying pattern, intimidation routine, absurd demands, and other hurdles pervasive throughout while waiting in line for an opportunity to reverse the trend.

Inevitably, lives always teemed with favor seekers eager to exploit every chance to improve their fortunes, elevate their low social status, or improve their livelihoods. Indeed, men and women of crooked timber, skewed and contorted in this environment, were ripe for trading off, willingly and readily, for something better, anything better.

Behind the veneer of law and order, this was how China being run, in and out, since the early days.

Yet, not all those who set out to curry favor by stooping low or relinquishing their dignity would emerge content and triumphant. Instead, those who were to be left abandoned by structural bias and favoritism, from which they dwelled their hopes, transformed themselves into a unique identity. They all ended up as negatively charged entities that repelled each other. Contrary to the implication of the proverb 'birds of a feather,' they pecked at each other, constantly and eagerly pushing and shoving each other out of the way to regain their mental balance.

Under these circumstances, those who survived abusive conditions perverted themselves by shouldering abuse and requiting the abuse to others. And those who had endured authoritarian abuse tried to regain a sense of power by exerting tyrannical control over other beings. In human terms, all lotuses that grew out of mud, all soiled in dirt. In humanistic ramifications, all souls in this environment warped and contorted. From all walks of life, no one was immune to this cycle of abuse. And from all four corners of life came the terminus of the abused and the abuser.

For those whose wishes were left wanting, bitterness and hostility would become parts of their lives. Some quietly faded into obscurity afterward. The majority would simmer with resentment and slowly gain a dour, bitter look. Their indescribable, hateful, and accusing eyes reminded one of past abuses or empty promises. In silence and lurking shadows in their minds, they slowly gained sadistic personalities, took malicious pleasure in seeing people's misfortunes or failures, and harbored deep-seated ill will against commoners, strangers, or anyone they hardly knew.

Yet, among those companions who went to the Red Chamber, one was an unlikely guest.

To begin with, Mrs. Lo could have been a better pick. She was uncultivated, loud, and bold. The lady saw the affair as an opportunistic liaison worthy of sacrilege devoted to patriotism, only if there was a catch. She expected a returned favor, something like a post among party members. But nothing, as she vouchsafed in her own words, "Not even a watermelon!"

Armed with her mighty indignation, she shot her mouth off, "You don't want to fancy what that man did to me."

Despite her allegations, no one was certain she was telling it like it was; neither was anyone denying her claims. Being a rumormonger herself, no one was sure what her actual intentions were.

However, just as everyone knows that in a nation steered by wayward arbitrary rules and standards, denying facts was always concluded as the government's basic measure; in contrast, rejecting government explanations was considered a person's common presumption. On that basis, any wrong reason could be a good reason; any wrong cause could be a good cause, and vice versa.

Amid the frenzy of name-calling and slander peddling, a small circle picked up the smearing and spread it like wildfire.

Months had elapsed, but rumors and gossip refused to budge. Throughout this time, AhEn, second in command, maintained a discreet distance from the unfolding drama.

Once the gossip began, the tittle-tattle ran amok. Just as loose talk laid it on thick, ill news spread apace. When Lao Mao eventually caught wind, he could hardly contain his fury. From being a self-proclaimed drop-dead charming prince to being cast off as a dirty man, it completely shattered his notion of romanticism.

Suffering with indignity, he lashed out, "How dare you bite the hands that feed you?" But when his fulmination failed to calm him, he vowed revenge with more profanities and hyperboles at those who spread malicious gossip

Yet, his intentional act of vengeance was only to herald ridicule. "Don't be as cruel as the first emperor," some said. Yet, unbeknown to others, when the man whose egomania defiled with cruelty, this mockery only egged him on.

When this tidbit of the slur passed on to him, instead of enraging him, it pleased him. He crowed in a highly spoiled and pompous manner, "Only if I am many times crueler and more brutal than him. You shall see."

When that incident occurred, Lao Mao's second-in-command, AhEn, remained cautious. Being second only to one man but commanding millions, AhEn knew well how to react. If he could please only one man, there was no need to jeopardize the privilege of overseeing millions. Yet, far from being a man of timidity in spirit nor nobleness in color, there was something deeper to his character.

When AhEn became the first premier, the fate of Li Ssu must have weighed on his mind early on. Like AhEn, Li Ssu became the first chancellor under the first emperor some two thousand years earlier. He was so powerful that he would later be charged with treason and cut in half by the brutal retribution he created, along with his three clans and people he related to or associated with. His alleged crimes tightly crammed one after another, jamming into at least several pages long.

When AhEn became the first premier of a newly formed regime, he understood the importance of avoiding the fate that befell Li Ssu. He must have taken the actions to stay in power and prevent a long list of charges, especially during internal turmoil.

He likely recognized that being a successful revolutionary was not about showcasing one's talent in this turbulent era. It was about evading a brutal demise.

Besides, AhEn must know men and women under this system were depraved enough and inferior enough to be served as instruments; they could also be anybody's instruments used against him.

Revolution was not a theatrical production that everyone could appreciate. Instead, it represented a moment human nature reached its lowest point—a time when people lost their humanity and descended into animalistic, barbaric cruelty. It was a time when individuals might experience immense pleasure in inflicting harm on each other, witnessing the pains others endured, and jeering at others in their hours of agony.

It was an age of iniquity where no one would stand up for anybody, not even their parents, children, or spouses. It was an age of wickedness when everyone would betray anyone they could - their friends, relatives, or forebears. It was an age of degradation where people all over this nation refused to stand by anything rational, righteous, or moral.

On account of that experience, be it in the past or the future, be it called Democratic Dictatorship, Chinese Marxism, Maoism, Communist China, Socialism with Chinese characteristics, Autocracy, or authoritarianism, this was a political system that would bring out not the best but the worst in people, against people, any people.

Thus, if AhEn made one false move, they would surely be pleased to see him expire, just like the way he had made sure his expansive network of subordinate collaborators would never see the light of their day again.

If Li Ssu was a historical hotshot, AhEn knew he was better off being a live dog than a dead lion. He thus embraced the role of servitude - to become humble and subservient. AhEn, viewed as a socialist survivor of the fittest, would trespass any human acceptance or common decencies. He was a man of great sacrifice, both body and mind, in supine subservience. He pampered. He cosseted. He mollycoddled Lao Mao on every whim. He stooped low, he obeyed, and he complied with every order.

But if a haphazard collection of men and women with conflicting personalities ran the course of history, Lao Mao and AhEn complemented each other well. While Lao Mao represented a mash-up of a malignant narcissist and a dreadful battleaxe, AhEn was a perfect classic fusion of overt benevolent and covert malevolent personality. Their pairing resulted in a kind of self-adulation sustained by both kindness and underlying malice, which ultimately fed off their nature. Thus, they needed each other. They craved each other. They spoon-fed each other.

And so when hell hath no fury like Lao Mao scorned, AhEn kept his guard and lay low.

In the week that followed Lao Mao's outburst, rumors reached towns that the ruling party had reconsidered. They granted clemencies and forgave those who had made malicious gossip earlier. Many viewed this significant shift as a gesture of kindness and leniency.

However, when people were spreading these rumors, farmers were contacted by mysterious sources to replace their grain seeds with ones that were said to be scientifically engineered and changed. The planters took the promise that these seeds would produce higher yields while helping to keep costs down. The complacent folks were thrilled and eager to compile, pinning their hopes on these seed hybrids to make life easier.

After the planting, the farmers waited days in and days out. As weeks passed, nothing came except for some clumps of weeds or grass from the soil below. As the farmers could recall, agreeable weather and plenty of rainfall marked that year. But nothing came.

In the meantime, a bolshie man, Kim Bo, was full of non-stop arguments. As the town's smart aleck, he often shared his opinions on productivity and how to live life. However, the locals had grown weary of his endless rambling and homespun philosophies about achieving harmony or other nonsense. Dismissing him as an empty vessel that made the most sound, they never warmly received him.

One day, Kim Bo showed up at an impromptu gathering. As the locals expected, he mouthed off about planting and seeding. That was how one local described it later. This know-all claimed that the mysterious seeds in bulk were instead boiled seeds.

Upon hearing that, the people looked confused by his unexpected assertion. "What?"

they exclaimed, taken aback.

Kim Bo stated, "Because they want to show that our communism can go to extreme lengths to bring them back to life to triple production."

Already in a state of agitation and nearing panic, the farmers became furious, not only because of Kim Bo's accusations but also because of the additional distress he caused. The farmers would have none of it, despite Kim Bo's pledge to hear him out. They just threw him out, all the same.

Details about what happened to those towns afterward were scanty, for communications among cities came in dribs and drabs and ceased altogether. Soon, the event reached its nadir when people who fled those towns were arrested and sent back. Many told of the lingering specter of deprivation. Others spoke of tales of threats, intimidation, and incarceration for spreading 'malicious gossip' and 'false news.' Aside from that, only a little came out.

Time dawdled on. Came autumn eddies of fallen leaves glided high and rolled in the field. In came spring. Flowers budded and then bloomed under the warm sun and gentle breeze. Time and time again, decades went by.

One day, a stranger appeared in a town. He claimed he came from the Old World to study the local culture. When the locals learned his name, the locals, speaking in tones, tried to replicate the pronunciation that did not exist in Chinese. They mimicked the first part of the name's pronunciation, 'fœ... fœ... frr...' but struggled to pronounce the second part correctly. Despite many attempts and variations, they needed to be more straightforward. As a result, they referred to him as 'Lao Wai,' a term that denoted someone from afar.

When it was his turn to inquire about the town's name, Lao Wai learned it was uncertain. No matter how hard he tried, he couldn't roll his tongue in to pronounce it correctly. Ultimately, he decided on the complicated articulation by naming it Eastern Never, as it was not his desired destination.

Long after Lao Wai settled down in Eastern Never, he studied and recorded the local customs, their codes of manners, the food they ate, and the clothes they dressed. But just as much as he learned from the locals, the locals also unexpectedly picked up some peculiar habits from him.

The visitor got one of his quirks of placing his chopsticks backward, leaving the tapered ends sticking out on the table. Later, people with whom he came into contact also discovered that he had one of his eccentricities of counting how many grains of rice were in his bowl before finishing his meal.

Other times, he caught some local folks gawking at him in silence when he laughed at his jokes or talked to himself in eerily sounds that reminded one of a feline's plaintive mating calls.

One day, after having a few drinks with the locals at an evening meal, Lao Wai went alone for a walk. He rambled down the street and went to the outskirts of town. From there, he continued west to an open field, waded through a small creek, and dawdled to a nearby hill. The sun set, throwing its last light to the red roofs of the houses beyond into relief.

Lao Wai planned to stay a little longer in the shadows beneath the hill before returning. He sat on a rock by the hillside in the gloaming, taking in the atmosphere. From his vantage point, he could see the town's lights slowly coming on.

As he enjoyed the atmosphere while watching the shadows of the surroundings deepen, he saw some hazy figures yonder by the creek now and then, drifting in the wind. Uncertain about what it was, he squinched his face into the surroundings, now getting darker. Soon, the shadowy figures appeared to be moving in his direction. At that point, Lao Wai could not fully entrust his perception, as he worried his blurred vision might result from the alcohol he had consumed earlier.

Just as the shadowy figures drew closer, only then was Lao Wai able to make out an alarmingly pale-looking man leading a little girl by the hand. Their eyes were fixated on the ground, oblivious to Lao Wai's presence.

Lao Wai then hailed the strangers. "Hello! Are you from the town?"

But it did not evoke a reply from the man or the young girl, who seemed disoriented and confused, as if not knowing where they were.

Lao Wai gently asked them again, "Where are you from?"

At that moment, the man, who had a vacant, mournful look, slowly raised his right arm and pointed to the ground in silence where Lao Wai was sitting. Confused by a strange, unexpected gesture, Lao Wai reciprocated an instinctive reaction to the man's motion by lowering his head to where he was pointing. Yet, it was too dark to make out anything.

When he raised his head to look at the strangers again, both were no longer there. Only then, a dart of sudden fear seized him. He stood up, looked around in the semi-darkness, and saw no trace of them.

Without a second thought, he was slowly retreating from where he came from.

The moment he woke up the following day, Lao Wai tried to recollect the encounter the evening before, as it was still so vivid in his mind. He asked whenever an opportunity arose for any missing man and a little girl. The locals needed to learn what he tried to inquire about. But as people were busy with their tasks, they downplayed his concerns by replying, "It's all peace here."

Toward the afternoon, unable to gather any clue, Lao Wai returned to the site to get a look at daylight. Once he set off after a short walking distance, he turned back and borrowed a spade from a neighbor. Taking with it, Lao Wai went to the outskirts, through the field, past the creek, and then to the hillside.

Once there, he went to the same spot where he sat last night. Lao Wai dug the spade into the earth beside the stone, the size of a sandbag, and heaved it out of the way. Then he started digging. About a foot down, his spade turned up some small pouches made of hemp.

Not knowing what they were, he kept digging until he unearthed more and more.

The next day, Lao Wai went to gather some tidbits about the pouches. To his disappointment, the locals could provide him with little insight. Towards the evening, feeling disheartened, he gave up and started heading home.

On his way, he unexpectedly ran into a familiar face, a man named Liao, whom Lao Wai had known for some time. Upon getting word of what Lao Wai was inquiring about, Liao suggested he speak with an elder named Siku. He was a repository of knowledge about their history. He might help, Liao said.

The houses along the main road to the northern edge of Eastern Never became less and less densely packed. The further the road moved north, the more it opened to a natural setting until it bore a faint resemblance to a semi-outback. At the end of the road stood a small house where Siku lived. Siku was tall and slim, with a long white beard and an avuncular mien. Despite being nudging seventy of a robust constitution, he was.

Lao Wai visited Siku the following afternoon. At the sight of a visitor, the host became enthusiastic and received Lao Wai with a warm welcome.

At once, he invited Lao Wai into his house and treated him to an elaborate tea ceremony. While enjoying their tea, Siku also fondly showed Lao Wai two of his recent scenery brush paintings mounted on scrolls. Seeing these paintings that used effortless brush strokes to depict a landscape, Lao Wai shared that he, back home, was also an artist.

In his early childhood, Lao Wai showed an interest in art. Using his innate talent and imagination, he made many artworks in the past, including paintings and decorative and installation art.

Upon hearing that and being an artist, Siku was excited to find a kindred spirit. He said, "Artworks that allow us to convey our thoughts and feelings should be universal across all cultures. So continue to make use of your talent while you are here."

Amid their light-hearted conversation about artworks and nothing and everything, Lao Wai, at length, raised the main reason for his visit. He reached into his pockets, removed those pouches, and asked, "Have you ever seen these?"

The moment Siku laid eyes on the pouches, his complexion turned grim. His good-natured amiability earlier seemed to fade away instantly, replaced only by a somber expression.

Siku promptly demanded, "Where did you get those?"

"I found them buried below the earth outside the town." Siku grimaced and asked, "You dug them up?"

Siku seemed slightly annoyed by his new acquaintance's behavior and objected, "Why?"

Lao Wai contemplated bringing up the encounter with the ghostly visitants, but Siku took over those pouches. While he was weighing them upon his hand, his mind seemed to drift somewhere.

After much delay, Siku said, with his voice dragging, "These are... They are..."

Unlike being highly articulate and expressive by the time they met, Siku had now descended into a stammer. "They are... amulets... for the..."

"For what?" Lao Wai was impatient.

At this moment, Siku appeared to grapple with whether to carry on with the topic. Then, unwittingly, he let words slip out aimlessly, "For those sacrificed for..."

Lao Wai asked with a scowl. "I don't understand. Sacrificed for what?"

Siku seemed to lose concentration and continued mumbling, "Patriots who died doing... works for humanity."

As Lao Wai continued to stare at Siku silently, waiting for a response, Siku fidgeted in his chair, clearly uncomfortable. In a moment of spontaneity, he suddenly stood up and blurted out, "I will tell you tomorrow."

That concluded the visit. As Lao Wai stood on the porch before leaving, he expressed his gratitude again for Siku's hospitality and promised to call again.

To Siku's awareness, Lao Wai was a practical man. Once he committed to something, nothing could deter him. He took Siku's word fairly and squarely as a person grounded in reality. When Siku told him 'tomorrow,' he meant it had to be tomorrow—not the day after or several days later.

Yet, the minute he arrived the next day, he was unprepared for the unexpected. As he raised his hand to knock, he noticed a note pinned to the door. The message said, "Out traveling the world. Not expected to be back soon."

At that point, his acquaintance's whim on an unannounced global gallivanting utterly bewildered Lao Wai. Little did he know as soon as he left the day before, Siku gathered his belongings and some supplies and fled to the forest bordering the town for unknown reasons.

After much ado about nothing, Lao Wai was left disappointed and slowly making his way back.

Back at his abode, Lao Wai was still in his befuddled state. However, based on what he had gathered from Siku the day before, these amulets were considered the marks of humanity and should be venerated.

Brimmed with optimism, Lao Wai came up with a plan. He would first gather all the amulets and start counting. The man thought that if it took him one second to count one, the total number of a day's count he could tally would be 60 seconds, 60 minutes, and 8 hours. He thought the counting would be over in a few days.

To monitor the counting, Lao Wai thought of affixing amulets to the bricks. By continuing to do it this way, he expected, his work would run into a few feet long by the time it was over.

Yet, Lao Wai had never prepared himself for what he had uncovered. As more and more amulets he found, the prospect of getting over it in a few days had now turned into weeks. He was determined to figure it out.

By the 29th day of the first year, when the estimated number of deaths from the Huaxian earthquake centuries earlier reached, the counting was still far from over.

At that stage, Lao Wai was highly pleased. While the figures elsewhere highlighted brutalities, here they represented achievements for humanity. Nowhere else could one find such an awe-inspiring number of sacrifices for humanity as in China.

As Lao Wai remained preoccupied with counting, the clock ticked by. But the tally increased dramatically as weeks turned into months and months into years.

By the 138th day of the third year, which marked an estimated number of bubonic plagues that swept over the Old World in the early centuries, the counting was still far from over.

Inspired by the record of selfless acts for humankind, fostered by the most outstanding government the world had ever seen, Lao Wai continued his work relentlessly into the fourth year.

Part II - The Moral Rust Belt

Siku had been living on the edge of the forest, bordering the northern part of Eastern Never, for over three years. Yet, for all these years, not a single day did he find it lonely. Long habitual to a life of simplicity, Siku instead was pleased with his newfound reclusive life surrounded by nature.

He spent most of his time painting, journaling daily activities, catching fish, watching birds, or chasing after wild chickens. As no human beings bothered him, as an essential requisite for a peaceful life, he felt content.

One day in the early spring of the fourth year, as Siku was fishing in a pond, a sudden thought dawned on him that living in the woods might no longer suit him. As he got older, he thought he would not be fit and healthy for this lifestyle forever.

But returning to his humble abode inevitably reminded him of Lao Wai. He must have left a long time ago, he thought. As time passed, men could not linger in one place forever. He convinced himself that Lao Wai must have returned to his hometown. The following day, Siku packed up his belongings and returned home.

The minute he stepped into his house, he felt his home enveloped by its immense comfort and sweetness. He then spent about an hour cleaning and tidying the space. Afterward, he made himself a cup of tea while sitting by the windows overlooking the forest beyond; he was overcome with nostalgia for the carefree life in the woods again.

Towards the afternoon, on the spur of the moment, Siku wanted to check out some quaint streets in town. Once he stepped outside, he leisurely strolled south, occasionally exchanging greetings and pleasantries with passersby.

As Siku reached the town center, he got a whiff of the sweet aroma of freshly baked bread emanating from the bakery he often frequented before he left. As the thought of those delicious delicacies got him, he turned left, thinking of dropping by the bakeshop to get some pastries before returning home.

Yet, little did he know he was heading straight into the section Lao Wai chose to be the onset of his work three years earlier.

As Siku was blithely strolling down the road, he noticed someone approaching from the corner of his eye, waving and cheering in great excitement. Siku squinched his eyes, trying to make out who that was. Only to his great astonishment did he recognize the man as Lao Wai.

Even though Lao Wai hailed him at that point, Siku failed to respond. Instead, he was taken aback by the scope and magnitude of the work he saw behind Lao Wai. Then, as he continued to gawk at the immense work, words slipped through his mouth, "What have you done?"

Lao Wai turned and gestured at his work and replied enthusiastically, "That? It is my contribution to human achievement."

Siku looked confused and reacted with alarm. "What? What human achievement?" "Those amulets, remember?" Lao Wai tried to remind him.

Once Siku realized what had happened, he covered his face and said, "No, no. You've got it all wrong. All wrong."

Lao Wai was now baffled. "How?"

Initially, Siku believed paying less attention to detail was better than saying anything fussy would make things copacetic. But instead of making things all right, it only caused Lao Wai to snafu everything. The outcome was chaotic. Siku was now left bewildered about how to get out of this mess.

Siku patiently explained to Lao Wai. "The way we talk here differs from how you talk. This difference stems from the policies that shape our lives. When people twist every fact out of shape, you conform to those distortions to make you whole. It might confuse you, but it never confuses us. In a world of illusion, you might accept these false impressions and learn to live with them; for example, 'yes' means 'no,' and 'no' means 'yes.'"

For a moment, Siku seemed confused by what he had just said, but carried on anyway. "To 'hold it' means 'loosen it.' You might get yourself used to it while being here. But once you are back in your own country, you will re-adjust; 'yes' means 'yes,' and 'no' means 'no.' You understand?"

As Lao Wai tried to process what Siku had just said, Siku was mulling over while shifting his weight from one foot to another.

Eventually, he let out the first few words, "You have to stop this. You put yourself and others in danger."

Siku, glancing around, still struggled to find the right words. He seemed nervous and fidgety. After a moment, he uttered a few reluctant words, "Before I went into the woods... No. No. I meant before I traveled the world... I offered advice to a fellow countryman and was apprehended."

After a brief pause, Siku continued, "As you know, my friend, time never idles by while aging never lets up. I can ill afford their special treatment."

Concerned that he might not have communicated his thoughts clearly, Siku tilted his head slightly, inched closer to Lao Wai, and asked with his intrusive eyes again, "You understand? Huh?"

With a sheepish look, Lao Wai bobbed his head in response. For the first time, Lao Wai seemed to realize the seriousness of the situation he had gotten into. As he pondered how to exonerate himself from the troubles he got Siku into, Siku continued, "Those were charms of disburdening."

Wary of passersby who might eavesdrop on their conversation, Siku grabbed Lao Wai by the elbow and led him to a quiet corner.

Once they were alone, Siku explained, "Decades before you came, a great calamity resulted in many deaths. Only a little was known, for communications between towns got disconnected. We later learned from the locals who mentioned only 'the specter of deprivation' amid crop failures."

Lao Wai felt things were becoming more clear than ever before. He interrupted and asked, "But how does that relate to the amulets?"

Siku just continued, "The local archive mentioned that the famine did not occur immediately as first thought. Against all odds, the farmers held out despite the crop failures. Therefore, it asserted that the famine did not occur immediately afterward."

Siku looked disquiet as he continued. "The famine occurred only when these amulets broached." He continued.

Lao Wai, at this moment, looked more puzzled than ever. "I don't understand."

"All I know is food became scarce, resulting from acts of pure malice. However, instead of adhering to the communist ideology that we ideally share everything, Lao Mao and the Party did not want to share anything with the multitudes. They wanted more than just being half-filled. So those with the amulets had to forgo themselves and made ways for the others so that Lao Mao and the rest could eat to their fill."

At that point, Lao Wai remarked, "I have always thought that socialists were supposed to be humanistic."

Siku seemed agitated by the remark and snapped back. "For the uninitiated, they have always competed for resources with the masses. That is what it is all about. That is the essence of collectivism: who will get more and who will not? Stupid!"

No sooner than Siku said that, his own words took him aback. He could not believe he had let such a word slip out of his mouth. Sensing a word once spoken was now past recalling, he momentarily covered his mouth with his hand and issued a mea culpa: "Pardon me!"

"But don't they have any sense of decency?" Lao Wai asked out of curiosity.

No sooner than Siku offered his apology, Lao Wai's other odd remark rattled him again. He at once retorted, "Decency? For socialists, decency is a curse nobody wants because it prevents them from expropriating things they want. Unlike The West, which has built its standards upon liberalism, political tolerance, and public opinion in the last seven decades, Chinese socialists, on the contrary, reject these positions. Do you know why?

That is because liberalism, political tolerance, and public opinion, in the eye of the socialist beholder, are the weakest visible sections of a rampart for attacks and, concurrently, for expropriation. That is what they see.

"By rejecting liberalism, political tolerance, and public opinion, they allow themselves to expropriate things they want. In doing so, they transform themselves into a different, opposing body - a dark entity, a system of anti-human nature, anti-rational, antipathy nature. That is why this system willingly let the notion of appropriateness be indeterminate to make way for appropriation. Do you understand?"

Still perturbed by the remark, Siku parroted back, "Decency? Pff." He then gave Lao Wai a blank look and shook his head, leaving Lao Wai standing there, rolling his eyes.

After a while, Siku got on with the subject and said, "But Lao Mao was not a fool. Surrounded by many faithful servants of his, he expected someone would come to him than he would to them to get his full fill. Don't you think?"

"Who then?" No sooner than asked, Lao Wai seemed already to know the answer.

Siku carried on. "AhEn ordered grain taken from farmers by any means necessary over three years. This action was beyond the pale in disturbing contrast to the dramatic airlift 1948. One was helping people, while the other snuffed out their kind within a border, wiping out people of all three generations.

"But what happened here simply because it adhered to the core of a socialist mentality and AhEn's utmost courtesy to only one man. AhEn's actions starkly contrasted with the image of an honest man with refined and composed manners. Deep inside, the man was, in fact, a double-cross, double-dealing twister."

At this time, two burly men passing by gave Siku and Lao Wai a stare. Not sure they had overheard their conversation, Siku became stiff and remained quiet.

Siku patiently waited until those men vanished from view before continuing in an almost whispering tone, "Throughout it all, our wise man was so obsessed and preoccupied with being the most devoted servant to feed one man above him while willingly bypassing the needs and interests of tens of millions below, manifesting conduct morally repugnant and contradictory to all human values. What the man did draws no parallel in history, while the conduct itself met the characteristics of gangsterism: the strongest get the most, the weakest die."

Lao Wai suddenly exclaimed, "Just like nonentities!"

Siku let out a sigh and continued, "You might say there were good Nazis and evil Nazis, but there are not such good communists. AhEn, hailed as the most righteous and decent man in the world, is a portrayal of an accessory. At the same time, Lao Mao could not have become so wicked without another half of the vileness that stemmed from this man."

Lao Wai interrupted again, "But the man himself rose from a status of commoner, just like millions of others."

Siku continued, "This echoes patterns from the past. Groups of revolutionaries have historically relied on the people for support, only to turn against those who sustained them. Contrary to traditional belief, those who sow courtesy reap demise, and those who emanate kindness garner greed."

After a brief moment, Siku said, "Thus, the masses must sacrifice themselves to settle whatever the ruling class needs and be willing to cut themselves out whenever necessary or called upon. Tragically, this massive gamble on the masses for an aim is not unprecedented and would not be the last. Look at the wholesale starvation of Changchun before the founding of the Republic. Pay attention to a series of patterns from there, and you will understand.

Lao Wai then quizzed, "You mean the whole thing is expected? But could this happen under an elected system?"

Siku clarified. "Collectivism is a fancy term for legitimacy making way for illegitimate appropriation, and communism is nothing more than a collection of high-flown theories and elaborated excuses to conceal gangsterism aimed to exploit goods, resources, technologies, and human capital and to grind human nature into inferior races. The debris and destruction communism has left behind are extreme. It ushers a revolution-induced capricious nature and brings about an amoral society. Now we see where everyone expropriates whatever people can lay their hands on. And for only a few decades, it completely wiped out the long-standing tradition of sharing and caring.

Subsequently, it chokes out compassion and relinquishes all sense of decency; acts of kindness and the perception of morality vanish. What is left is the moral rust belt all over."

After a brief pause, Siku continued, "Under this system, nothing is deemed rational or irrational, human or inhuman; whatever they want, they will get it by fair means or foul. That is the ruling class's attitude toward its people, and so is the people's attitude toward other people for things they want, come what may. The aftermath leads to an implosion, drawing everything and everyone inwards, ultimately culminating in an event horizon effect."

At this moment, Siku was dropping his tension into a relaxed pose. His gesture showed he had reached the end of his talk. "This system could not have endured this past century had it not resorted to deception and tall tales. If you don't see the brutality and cruelty that belies communist vulpine charms, you are delusional, my friend."

Near the end of their conversation, Lao Wai descended into total silence. He stood with his head hung low and his back bent while gazing at the ground, utterly oblivious to passaging time. Gradually, Lao Wai raised his head and stared at his work.

He met Siku's eyes in silence while bobbing his head as if to acknowledge the reality of the situation. Without a word or ceremony, he turned and left.

Siku watched Lao Wai's silhouette against the bright sun, moving with a shuffling, weary gait down the road flanked by rows of tulip trees that early spring until it disappeared over a corner.

That was the last time Siku set eyes on Lao Wai.

* * * * *

Back at his dwelling, Lao Wai cried. He now came to accept that what he had built upon for all these years was not a record of humanity, but a symbol of death.

The night before he left, while lying in bed contemplating the fateful vicissitudes of history, he suddenly remembered the shadowy apparitions he had encountered some three years earlier. Before bidding everyone farewell at daybreak, he went to the site.

Once there, he set up a makeshift memorial marker. In silence, he quietly urged, "Life on Eastern Never has been one of turmoil. What injustices have unfolded shall be unfurled in remembrance. But dwell not, this earthly plane. Endure not the realm of eternal darkness. Go gentle to the light. And may your souls be free."

As he walked to the edge of the land, he looked back, still lingering in doubt.

The inherent traits of mainland Chinese temperament remained constant throughout, especially in the early days, marked by ingenuous, considerate, and sincere characteristics that made them exploitable. Even in the present day, when subjected to an authoritarian order known for its lack of compassion, the complacent masses of an indoctrinated nation became easily abused and manhandled, not solely by outsiders but by internal conspiracy and manipulation. Amid this, the outcome of an ideology-driven or manmade disaster was a surefire increment that was more catastrophic than a natural-caused disaster.

Amid this, the greater landmass would warrant the greater number of deaths. With a profound sense of sadness, Lao Wai began his long journey home.

Yet, Lao Wai did not go away quietly.

Years later, a group of central authorities inadvertently wandered into Eastern Never and were shocked to discover that Lao Wai had left behind an unfinished spiral brick wall.

The wall was the height of 20 stacking bricks, each bearing an amulet that protected people against misfortune and adversity. It spiraled away clockwise from the original point and kept revolving around the axis until it reached an equal distance of some 450 kilometers.

Upon their discovery, they went completely berserk. They bumped around and questioned whether this unhinged Lao Wai had better things to do. They hurled oaths and imprecations at him for doing something stupid out of ignorance and not respecting the government and its people. In response, they vowed to dismantle the wall.

Yet, the true extent of the aftermath remained unknown.

BARREL OF A GUN

Zhang Bo was disappointed by his friend's last-minute change of plans. They expected to depart for Krong Kep the next day, where they had booked a resort villa for a few days. His friend informed him he had just received a new assignment and could not join him. Through an interpreter, Zhang learned it was too late to cancel the reservation. Left with no other option, he went alone.

Before heading out the next day, Zhang needed to pick up some antacids and pain relief medication from a pharmacy in the town center. He occasionally struggled with stomach problems, which his doctor warned resulted from taking irregular meals or bolting down instead of savoring his food.

It was a sultry afternoon when Zhang set out. The roads were congested and echoed with the revving sounds of motorbikes, tuk-tuks, and scooters pulling carts heavily laden with cargo. Along the sidewalks, shoppers bustled about, chatting and bargaining with one another as they engaged in their daily activities.

As Zhang was tacking through the crowd, he reached a three-way thoroughfare and paused. At the intersection, Zhang hesitated whether to turn right to take a shortcut through an open market on a dirt road that ran diagonally connecting two major streets or to stay on the main street, which would take longer. Even though the dirt road had turned into a muddy morass because of the earlier rain, he took the shorter route.

On both sides of the road, vendors piled their stalls high with wares and colorful products ranging from cheap electronic accessories, showy clothing, hair products, exotic fruits and vegetables, grilled sausages, steamed buns, silkworm salad, crunchy fried crickets, and whatnot.

Zhang sauntered along the stalls, pausing occasionally to look at some items of curiosity.

As he turned and continued to steer through the crowd to the next booth, he noticed a man blocking his way. Zhang took a cursory glance at him while yielding to the man. But just as he was about to take the second step to the right, he did a double-take at that man. The stranger simultaneously turned and looked at Zhang. Both frowned and squinted their eyes at each other.

Then, Zhang blurted out reluctantly. "Paisan Sima?"

The man seemed equally surprised and let out, "Zhang Bo?"

Both spontaneously burst out laughing while extending their hands for a handshake. Zhang then padded at Paisan's shoulder, saying, "I would never expect to see you here. The last time we met..."

Unable to rein in his excitement, Paisan barged in. "It must have been eight years since we last met. So, what are you doing here?"

Amid the excitement of chancing on each other in this strange land, Paisan's immediate inquiry put Zhang in a very awkward position, for he seemed to hem and haw for a second too long before replying halfheartedly while his eyes rolled. "Oh, ah... some work."

Paisan frowned and inquired, "What kind of work? I thought you were..."

Being 6-foot tall, with an angular face and muscular build, Zhang still had his crewcut hairstyle.

Immediately, Zhang interrupted, "Ah, some works for a company here... ah... marketing. How about you? What are you doing here?"

Paisan could tell Zhang was evasive about his work, so he dropped the subject and replied casually, "Oh, ah... I was thinking about taking a stroll."

He illustrated his remark by pointing his two fingers downward and wiggling them.

Paisan's reply puzzled Zhang a little this time, who felt something seemingly out of context. He tried to clarify, "I mean, in Cambodia."

"Yeah, Cambodia. A peaceful country. Ha!" Paisan giggled while avoiding eye contact. Zhang became increasingly perplexed, raising his eyebrows. "By yourself..."

However, sensing their conversation was going nowhere, he changed the subject. Instead, he mentioned his reservation in Krong Kep and asked Paisan to join him.

Zhang told Paisan that this was the first time he got some days off. He wanted to spend the time lounging on the beach, watching sunrise and sunset, a moment he had ached for.

The resort, set against a mountain backdrop, comprised a ring of bungalows encircling a spacious outdoor swimming pool. Along with tropical gardens and a restaurant and bar area, Zhang bragged, giving him the feel of a tranquil sanctuary surrounded by nature.

However, to his surprise, Paisan declined, citing his unfamiliarity with the area. To Zhang, Paisan was worried about being robbed or taken advantage of.

But then, feeling alien to this part of town, Paisan had spent many lonely hours looking at the street where people came and went. He thought he desperately needed contact. So, he added, he would drop by for a chat.

Afterward, both exchanged more small talk. Before parting, Zhang reminded Paisan to come. If he had changed his mind and stayed instead, Zhang stressed he would be more than happy.

Zhang met Paisan many years ago when he went to the capital city of northeastern China for training. But the encounter with Paisan was uneven right from the very beginning.

As always, Zhang envisioned himself as a war memorial sculpture, leading a group of soldiers crouching behind him. In that vision, he wished to emanate the courage and patriotism of a warrior.

But when the man met Paisan, he found it difficult to reconcile his ideal with the reality before him. The man Zhang encountered was of medium height, with a round face and round spectacles that gave him a meek and mild appearance, almost boyish.

By the time he met Zhang, Paisan was a researcher and lecturer in history at an academic institution. Because of their diverse interests, they got into trouble initially. Their conversations could have been more comfortable if they had been more cordial toward each other.

For Paisan, his words conveyed excessive philosophy about the quality of life, frequently going on without pause, as if it were nobody's business. In contrast, Zhang's speech entangled with negative adjectives that lambasted or found fault with almost every soul he encountered or everything he ran into. When people spoke without using negative modifiers to colorize things they said, Zhang became confused about their intended meaning. His confusion thus led to a barrage of follow-up questions to confirm whether their references were "good" or "bad."

Practically every time, at the end of their conversation, no one could sum up or remember what the other had been discussing.

But as their indifference and aloofness ebbed away, their conversation would become more manageable and thus more meaningful. Over time, their acquaintance would grow from their shared interest in history, even if their perspectives differed. While Paisan mainly focused on the cause and consequence of historical events, Zhang treated the subjects like fairy tales.

In the beginning, Paisan emphasized the importance of understanding history beyond the Party's version, not only in Chinese history but also in world history. Zhang, whose head was one unabridged volume of heart-thumping slogans and mind-boggling propaganda, knew next to nothing beyond that. Instantly, he took offense at the remark, thinking Paisan intended to hint at his crass incompetence for being an 'intellectual pygmy.' In response, he hit back, saying intellectuals should recognize themselves as 'rotten' who spouted nothing but idealistic flimflam. Paisan, however, ignored his taunts and other jejune comments while patiently making his point.

Initially, Paisan began by sharing some interesting anecdotes from classic literature. From there, he explored various historical accounts, mainly focusing on the years 1203, 1683, and 1989. Zhang, having long been wearied by communist history and bored with stiff propaganda himself, found himself captivated by these stories. As time went on during his stay, the more he listened, the more engrossed he became.

However, one late evening, he learned something equally intriguing and stranger than he would have expected.

It was late one evening when they stopped for some beers from a street vendor. They settled at a table in a dimly lit alley. As they chatted, Zhang noticed that Paisan occasionally faltered. During these moments, silence reigned, and everything around Paisan seemed to cease to exist while he stared at the tabletop. He would continue immersing himself in his catatonic state for a few minutes without a single word coming from him.

Afterward, Paisan would resume their conversation. But his attention would shift to a dark corner where he would stare in complete silence with his glassy stare. Curious, Zhang quietly glanced over his shoulder but saw nothing there.

On this occasion, Zhang witnessed Paisan's bizarre behavior and ascribed it to a highbrow conceived as 'an odd man out,' a bookful moron hounded with loads of learned lumber, lumbering through life. The man, Zhang thus concluded, should be duly subject to a 'mental class struggle' to knock some sense into, especially an 'intelligentsia' like him.

However, little did Zhang know that Paisan's oddity stemmed not from "too much studying, too much reading," as he had suggested.

Memories of intense training sessions flashed through Paisan's mind intermittently. Through those flashbacks, which took place during his first year at university, he saw a kind, modest, and sincere young man sitting in a dimly lit room.

The trainer, Mr. Shao Xu, began the session with Paisan in a friendly and pleasant manner. He alleged that people all had negative thoughts. Unhealthy thoughts would stray people away from the right path and pervert them to become ill elements. He stated that by eliminating these harmful thoughts, Paisan would lead a peaceful life.

The purpose of that meeting was thus to align Paisan's thinking with the Party's beliefs. Mr. Shao Xu asserted everyone was capable of reform. Only through the process of reform would Pasan become an ideal citizen.

Halfway through the interview, Shao Xu alleged China was one peace-loving country. At that moment, Paisan was eager to show his willingness to comply with Shao Xu's suggestion, so he faithfully agreed.

Yet, little did Paisan know his response instead sent Shao Xu into a violent reaction. He slammed his fist on the desk and shouted, "That is a lie! You're not telling me the truth."

Completely stunned by Shao Xu's sudden change of attitude, Paisan got quite a jolt. Looking pale, he attempted to reply, but words stuttered on his lips, and nothing came intelligently. "I... know... true... I... don't know."

Like before, Shao Xu adjusted his voice to an appeasing tone. "What did you hear? Tell me!"

Despite the conversation having lasted only a few minutes, Paisan became exhausted and weary. He instantly transformed from a gentle, good-natured young man into someone visibly nervous and terrified. Overwhelmed by fear, he lost all his ability to answer anything coherently or correctly; he was numb with dread.

Shao Xu continued, "We always encourage citizens to express their opinions openly and take part in governmental policy-making. But, Paisan, when you major in history, you must have known what our first premier said long ago?"

Paisan still looked distraught.

Shao Xu went on, "Our first Premier once said, 'The government needs criticism from its people. Without this criticism, the government will not be able to function as the People's Democratic Dictatorship. Thus, the basis of a healthy government is lost. We must learn from old mistakes, take all forms of healthy criticism, and do what we can to answer these criticisms.' You may need some time to think, to collect your mind."

Long after he became a history lecturer, fragments of these memories came back to haunt him. As time went on, these recollections occurred more and more frequently. Often, when he spotted a figure in the distance, he could not be sure whether it was real or just a figment of his imagination.

Different episodes had taken place over time, each causing him great distress.

From the beginning, Paisan assured Shao Xu that he had reflected on many matters and had no negative thoughts.

Eyeing Paisan askance, Shao Xu said, "Why are you worried about your criticism of our party? It's OK. We listen."

In his late adolescence, Paisan was idealistic and had a great sense of duty. Despite knowing not to talk back, he took pride in expressing his belief that 'let history be known, else what we know. If we disown the gateway to the past, how do we know which road ahead to take?'

Thinking that Shao Xu could provide a different perspective this time, he reluctantly broached the subject. "The thing is that during the period you mentioned earlier, when the government was encouraging criticism from its citizens..."

"What?"

"It... It witnessed hundreds of thousands face persecution."

Upon hearing this, Shao Xu flew into an uncontrollable rage. He jumped to his feet, banging the table with his fist and lashing out. "Don't you dare challenge us! No one dared challenge our absolute authority. Our leaders are all of omnipotence, benevolence, and omniscience. We never betrayed the principle on which we invited people to take part. We are always on the right side of history."

As the meeting proceeded, Paisan fixed his gaze on the table, hesitant to make eye contact.

Shao Xu continued, "We don't need you to recount history. We want you to be more creative and resourceful. As we know, a cause will lead to certain results. But, if you propose a different source, it can yield a different outlook. Your task is to look backward and identify what ideal causes could bring about positive outcomes. Only when you can transform something abstract in your mind into something tangible, will you truly understand socialism with Chinese characteristics. It is the version you present to the people and the world."

Years later, Paisan's perceptions of his surroundings suffused with a sense of constant danger. He developed a stiff posture, harbored irrational fears, and perceived anything could spiral out of control and become violent and destructive. People's aberrant behavior, change in tone, rustling sound nearby, or anything stirring could trigger an overreaction or panic. Much like the aftermath of an encounter with a snake, the fear instilled in him, both physical and mental, in those early days became everlasting.

Paisan, now in his late thirties, was not only aware of his ailment and unwellness, but he also understood that the cause of his condition was neither accidental nor hereditary.

These cruel, mock practices gained from the early days were to dehumanize human nature through distortion, threat, and menace by men like Shao Xu.

During those tormenting hours, Paisan wished to end it all by selecting more qualified candidates. Given the opportunity, he vowed to hold those who cultivated and spread sick minds just as accountable as those who started such acts.

In recent years, those memories had haunted him more frequently. Other times, he found him sitting in a room from a different location, illuminated by a dim light bulb. A bully figure loomed over and howled. "You sully our reputation."

When it happened, Paisan's face would contort with anguish. He would raise his hand to shield his face as if he were enduring unbearable pain from the past, the pain of being inflicted by cruel practices, and the burden of grappling with twisted historical logic. In those moments of torment, he also fantasized about a new life elsewhere.

If not, he must compromise his principles, even if that meant contradicting human nature or moral judgment.

After arriving at the resort the next afternoon, Zhang thought about taking a leisure stroll to familiarize himself with the area.

As he stepped outside, he encountered a middle-aged woman sitting on a chair next door, soaking up the sun. Seeing Zhang, she greeted him in Mandarin and introduced herself as Klara Viklund.

Zhang was surprised to see a Caucasian woman who was fluent in Chinese. He enquired about how she had gained this skill so well. "Ni shuo zhong wen na mo hao!"

Klara was flattered and replied, "I studied the Chinese language at an early age. I am a professor of Asian Studies at a Baltic institute."

Zhang then asked if she had traveled much. To which she replied, "No. It is my first trip with my partner in many years."

Zhang then suggested. "Or maybe China next time."

Klara flashed a smile and returned the compliment. "I am certainly looking forward to it."

Zhang recommended a destination: "Because of your interest, I suggest you visit the Memorial Hall."

Klara became curious and asked, "What does it dedicate itself to?"

"It dedicates itself to the memory of the civilians killed by the invaders during the war. It is also a glorious chapter that recounts how our communists risked their lives to protect our fellow citizens."

Klara exclaimed and said, "Oh, so it is like The National War Memorial that I visited years before in Ottawa. I will keep that in mind."

They continued to share pleasant conversations before Zhang took leave and headed to the beach.

Before it started getting dark, Paisan arrived. Zhang, known for being chatty, piled Paisan's glass with drinks. After more toasts of each other's health, they exchanged much chitchat and indulged in more beers and spirits while sitting outside.

After watching the sunset, they continued their conversation inside, engaging in lighthearted small talk about the weather, the local beaches, their families back home, fond memories, movies, and other topics. By this time, Paisan had felt tipsy from many toasts. He got up to the washroom, swaying as he walked. When he returned, Zhang poured another drink for both, raised his glass, and said, "Cheer, my brethren."

Together, they drank some more.

All the time, because Paisan was quiet and slow-talking, their conversation proceeded at a sluggish pace. Their chats would halt, leading to complete silence. When that happened, Zhang would attempt to introduce some lively topics to dispel the awkward and stuffy atmosphere.

At that point, Zhang picked up snatches of conversation by mentioning Preah Sihanouk's inner-city nightlife. He told Paisan he could find many streetwalkers, both Cambodian and Chinese.

Paisan asked in a curious tone, "You see them a lot?" Zhang scoffed, "I don't have to go to them."

"What do you mean?" No sooner than he asked, Paisan reminded himself of what Zhang said about 'marketing' that afternoon.

But before Paisan could rephrase, Zhang continued, "These local Cambodians are very dumb. They trust you and will listen to whatever you say."

Paisan deemed Zhang's statement blunt and promptly retorted, "Surely you indulge yourself in their unsophistication."

Zhang seemed to find Paisan's reply a mixed message, teetering between a compliment and a mockery. He clarified anyhow. "They need to eat, to live. I give them just a few dollars, but I bring in more in one day than a paycheck in one month. I see that as an unexpected leverage resulting from our rising influences."

Unable to hold back his excitement, Zhang made a suggestion. "I will take you there after we head back."

Unexpectedly, Zhang got a terse reply, "Thanks, but... No!"

At first, Zhang thought his attempt to enliven Paisan's spirits might work, but to his dismay, it fell flat. He felt annoyed when Paisan rebuffed his offer. With a sense of letdown, he got up and went to the bathroom.

When Zhang returned, he was surprised to find Paisan about to leave. Finding the man's behavior whimsical and unpredictable, Zhang coaxed his friend into staying a little longer.

Zhang sat down, sipped his drink, and started afresh by asking Paisan how long he planned to stay in Cambodia.

"Maybe a week," Paisan said after re-taking his seat.

Zhang seemed not to follow. He asked again, "Don't you have a scheduled return airfare?"

Paisan replied faintly, "Yeah, yeah, I have. I have."

Zhang did not like Paisan, for he seemed to bottle up something inside.

Zhang carried on with their conversation as usual by mentioning a trip he had joined the other day. Leading a group of tourists, mainly from China, the tour took them to places like Siem Reap, Kampot, Koh Rong Sanloem, and Angkor Wat. After these stops, the tour guide led them to the Tuol Sleng Museum. Zhang owned up to knowing nothing about the museum beforehand.

He said the building looked like a run-down school, but it surprised him to see many skulls kept inside. What shocked them even more was when the male tour guide pointed to those skulls and said, 'With Chinese money and support, Pol Pot carried out the period of murder, starvation, and brutality.'

Zhang raved that the remark seemed like an open assault on tourists. To most laid-back, wide-eyed Chinese tourists, this comment caught them totally off guard. They were unaware of the context and were unhappy about it, struggling to figure out how to react.

In a manner akin to someone experiencing memory loss, they confabulated evidence and falsified imagined events to fill in the gaps they were hopelessly lost. They even became angry and accused the tour guide of telling them lies. They questioned why they had heard nothing about it and if it was true. Then, a Chinese female tourist in the group made an unexpected comment. 'We are friends now. Do not talk about the past.'

Zhang chuckled. "But the guy tried to badmouth us."

At that point, Paisan suddenly raised a question. "Have you ever adopted a dog?"

Zhang frowned at the unexpected question and exclaimed, "What does that have to do with a dog?"

As Zhang recounted his trip to the Tuol Sleng Museum, it triggered Paisan's memory of a chance meeting with a professor many years ago. The encounter occurred long before Paisan quietly disappeared one rainy night.

During their conversation about world affairs, this professor alleged civilians killed in a recent conflict were fair game and that the losses were justifiable.

This professor unwittingly drew a parallel to the familiar justification that 'power grows out of the barrel of a gun,' which hinted at something far more sinister than Paisan initially realized. This so-called fair game opens up a succession of questions in the years before and after the founding of the new China. Why did the ruling party express gratitude to Japan for invading China but keep silent about the mass killing of civilians that took place in the late 1930s?

But the more Paisan dug deeper, the more it disturbed his great profound. The experience gave him valuable insights and eventually unraveled a chain of myths he had held for all those years.

Thus, when Zhang asked him about Tuol Sleng, Paisan replied, "Our fair game mindset sees the masses as expendable, and it is justifiable even at significant losses."

At that point, Zhang struggled to understand what Paisan was saying, as the subject was seemingly outside his province. But hearing Paisan mention something being 'justifiable,' Zhang seized upon that term and lashed out. "You said before that we are one peace-loving country. But now you suggest otherwise."

Half-drunk and losing his inhibition, he pounded the table with his fist and shouted,

"That is a lie!"

The loud bang on the table seemed to send Paisan into a headlong shock. He felt a sudden flash of an electric jolt from his forehead to the back of his head. The sensation gave him a shiver, and his face scrunched up. Instinctively, he raised his hand to shield his face, bewildered by his surroundings in a dimly lit room.

As Zhang took in what was unfolding across the table, he witnessed Paisan's bizarre and alarming reaction.

Slowly, Paisan lowered his hand. His face was pale, and his expression was unemotional. He stared at the man in front of him with an icy glare. Paisan knew who this man was.

Paisan replied, "What happened here was that it willed itself to our communist fair-game mindset to justify the means. Just like vicious people who would raise vicious dogs, when a dog's parents are prone to violence, the dog you adopted from those people will also be susceptible to a similar episode. Just as you asked, backward, then forward."

Zhang missed the point of the first part but attempted to paraphrase what Paisan said at the end. "What... backward? Forward?"

But on second thought, he swung his arm in the air and said aloud, "I don't want to know! You don't look well."

The man was not uninterested in knowing. Like millions upon millions of others, he was terrified of the truth. The fear imposed by the authority far outweighed his desire to learn. Subsequently, he preferred to remain some moron than to lose his head altogether.

Though drunk, Zhang realized how dangerous his situation was. It all began when he mentioned the Tuol Sleng tour and escalated with Paisan enkindling a reprehensible past. Anyone could seize upon the contents of their discussion to menace him, potentially leading to blackmail, coercion, or extortion.

Even if he stopped here, it was already too late. Zhang suddenly was seized with fear and the thought of his safety. The hunch that 'this is dangerous' kept flashing through his mind. His heart was racing, and he became even soberer. He now regretted not letting Paisan take leave earlier. Their cordial friendliness at the time they met had now turned into a cordial mistrust of each other.

He stood up to ease his anxiety a bit. As he took a few steps toward the open window, he seemed to catch a glimpse of a shadow flicking by. Nervously, he took a peek out of the window. It got slightly windy outside, and apart from the trees swaying in the breeze, he saw nothing suspicious.

Leaning on the window ledge, he pretended to get some fresh air while silently harboring a plan to report Paisan to the authorities to have him arrested and transported back to China as he and others had before.

Thinking that once Paisan repatriated, he would most likely end up in an insane asylum. Well pleased with that envisaged outcome to cure Paisan of his obsession with all these nonsensical theories, Zhang betrayed a momentary hyenic grin. He walked back to the table and sat down again.

Affecting a tone of curiosity, he said, "OK, where were we at?"

Paisan still had that unemotional look. His impassiveness bewildered Zhang even more, as if he seemed to look at something but did not see it.

Over the years, Paisan would never forget the mental torment and anguish left behind by his trainer. All the time, he was regardful of Mr. Xu's great expectations of creating 'an ideal citizen.' At this moment, he was ready to present his findings.

He said, "What happened here is not unprecedented. Decades before, the same practice was observed on our soil. This summary is a response to your original request. Reflecting on historical accounts and practices when China was caught back-to-back in the

Sino-Japanese War and civil conflict, all the lives of men, women, and children, as long as they stood in the middle of the way that hindered our communist aim, were dispensable, even at significant losses.

"On that account, the end always justifies the means, excuses any evil, and even colludes with its enemy to lay siege to its kind. But in that conflict, our communists did not gain their upper hand directly through the barrel of the gun. Instead, they lent it or support to the enemy, who, in turn, helped them achieve an aim or power at the expense of our inhabitants. This collaboration, on an unprecedented scale, will eventually carry

far-reaching historical repercussions."

Not well informed and seemingly heedless of what Paisan was saying, Zhang snapped back without thinking. "You are playing with fire!"

Paisan reciprocated. "Just as much as you are happy with those who, you said, were dumb enough to prostitute for you, you may also do the same."

Upon hearing that, Zhang jumped to his feet and exploded, "What did you say?" Paisan leaped to his feet and said, "I'm going to report you!"

When hit with the same line of action he planned to use against Paisan, Zhang's mind seemed short-circuited. "What?"

Paisan pointed a finger and said, "I'm going to tell CNN all those stories you have just told me."

Upon hearing that, Zhang was shocked beyond description. But only then did he realize what Paisan meant 'to take a stroll' earlier. What stunned him most was that Paisan's trick would make him a two-headed snake or, worse still, an American dog. Never had he been in his lifetime thought of this mama's boy who would plot such a sleazy scheme.

His face was red with rage. In an angry rush, he burst out, "You wily old fox!"

Details of what happened next were sketchy. According to the version the villagers gave, the moment the two met, great black clouds had already gathered on the horizon, menacingly sneaking up behind them. As they bandied words over some issues, a blanket of low clouds had gathered above them, whirling in one momentous whirl.

When the heated exchanges between the two flew thick and fast, their negative energy rose. The flow of their energy was so intense that it loomed high into the sky and collided with the positive energy in the storm above. It engendered a flash of dazzling lightning, crashing through the roof, hitting the propane tank, and blowing everything sky-high.

The explosion was so powerful that it rumbled the walls and rattled nearby windows. The shockwave even reached people a mile away, where they thought it was an earthquake.

Immediately afterward, the villagers and tourists rushed hurry-scurry outside to see what had happened, only to find the house was partly on fire. The blast blew off the window and tore open sections of the wall.

Some ran over to check on the people inside. They found Zhang lying face down, still barely breathing, while a puff of smoke was still rising from his singed hair. Swiftly, two men lifted Zhang off the ground and carried him outside. They then loaded him into a three-wheel tuk-tuk and rushed him to a nearby town to seek medical care.

Yet, the other fellow was nowhere to be seen. "These good-for-nothings should never be here. They talked too much. What goes up must come down." A villager, barely five feet tall, raved.

As the fire raged on, the villagers and guests formed a long human chain to the edge of the swimming pool. There, they filled buckets with water and passed them along to the first one to douse the fire. They also formed another line, which helped pass empty buckets back to the pool.

Klara was among them, who joined the effort to contain the fire near the house. At one point, she moved back to regain her balance when she stepped on something bouncy. It gave her a real scare, and she squealed to her companion nearby in a foreign language, "Det finns en död kropp här!"

Then, amid the darkness now and then lit up by the flickering flames from the burning house, she and her companion stooped over to inspect an object they thought was a body. But, much to her relief, it turned out to be just a swim ring of an inflatable tube covered among heaps of broken walls, clumps of thatched roofs, and other debris.

The other fellow never came to light.

Some years later, Klara would remind herself of this freak accident again when she finally organized a trip to China. Standing in front of the Memorial Hall, Klara remembered she overheard every word Paisan said that evening, words to the effect that the crime that aids and abets the enemy is greater than the crime that delivers. "This corridor shall mark the admission to a collaboration between Chinese communists and the invaders. Brought about by the communist fair game doctrine and the invader's brutality, this conspiracy expedited the inland incursion while Chinese communists snubbed. This unprecedented collaboration success eventually spearheaded and perpetuated a socialist mindset that no winning is possible in the future without conspiring with its enemy, any enemy, north and west of our boundaries in the present day - lest sovereignties forget."

THE WINDING DIRT ROAD

Part I - A Seed Of Life

On the east side of Dian, west of Nanzhao in central China, stood a large courtyard house at the end of a cul-de-sac. The home featured a single-story building that formed a square enclosing an inner courtyard in the middle. Rows of elevated bedroom units flanked the courtyard on both sides. The kitchen was on the right side of the main entrance, while the bathhouse was on the left. Directly in front of the main entryway, across the courtyard, was the study room, bounded by a living room on the left and a dining room on the right. It was here in this courtyard through which the life of the members of Nin Yige's different generations ebbed and flowed.

On this day, the man of the house, Nin Yige, sat in a chair in his study room. He appeared preoccupied. His back bent forward with his forearms resting on his knees while his eyes stared into space. Time quietly slipped away without knowing how long he had remained in that posture.

The silence broke when Nin Yige's caregiver, Mr. Yang, knocked on one of the open double doors. But his master didn't hear it. Seeing it elicit no response, Yang gently tapped it again. This time, it caught Nin's attention. Nin straightened his back and waved for him to enter. Once inside, Yang began conveying some messages to Nin. Both whispered to each other for quite some time in a solemn mien.

Afterward, Nin continued to relate to Yang while pointing his finger at him, apparently appointing him to more instructions. Just as Yang was about to take leave, Nin called him back and gave more directions while Yang nodded repeatedly in affirmation.

Moments later, Yang stepped out of the study room and left.

That evening, Nin barely touched his food. After dinner, he could hardly remain seated in his study. All the while, the man appeared to be very conscious of each passing minute. Despite only being in his late forties, Nin looked gloomy and tired tonight.

On and off, he would get up and pace back and forth. His expectant face would now and then turn and glance at the clock on the wall, ticking in its rhythmic, everlasting tick. He would resume stepping around, pacing back and forth in his room at his interminable, ever pace.

At around 11 p.m., after ensuring his wife and two teen daughters were asleep, Nin quietly stepped out of his study. After taking a short flight of steps, he tiptoed through the courtyard and slipped out of the house.

Outside, the street was quiet and barely illuminated by warm, dusky street lights. Amid the quietude, the whirring spokes of a bicycle passing would occasionally punctuate the silence. Nin turned left and headed south.

Two blocks south of his courtyard stood a low-rise apartment complex whose all-white façade was surrounded by impeccable lawns, giving an impression of a rather cozy dwelling place. Nin walked right to the complex and headed straight to a unit.

Upon entering his apartment, a woman in her late twenties greeted him. Nin addressed her as 'Xiao Yong' and embraced her warmly. After a few exchanges, Nin assured her that 'everything will be fine.' All the while, Xiao Yong inclined her head and remained silent while her eyes betrayed an element of sadness.

Nin left Xiao Yong alone in her bedroom, where she stayed to hold an infant and caress him now and then. Both of them remained in that stillness and waited, waiting.

At midnight, someone gently knocked on their door. As if expecting according to a plan, Nin answered the door promptly and met with Yang, the caretaker. Nin told him they would be outside shortly.

Moments later, Nin and Xiao Yong emerged from the building. Yang was patiently waiting outside while a black sedan was seen parking along a curb with an audible susurration of the car engine softly droning on.

While holding the infant, Xiao Yong held back her tears. She gently stroked the baby's cheek before reluctantly handing the child to Yang. Yang took hold of the baby, gave the couple a silent nod, and got into the sedan.

With heavy hearts, Nin and Xiao Yong waved goodbye. Together, they remained on the doorstep, fixing their eyes on the sedan, slowly heading down the street until it descended into the night.

Taafeef Eibrahem had tilled this land all his life. He grew corn, beans, fruits, and vegetables and attended to livestock, raising sheep and goats. In a village outside the southeast corner of Abou Gheit, east of the Delta Nile region, Taafeef lived with his two young sons, Adeel and Kashif, and his wife, Yasmin.

Like his father and grandfather, he grew crops along the banks of the River Nile on the rich black soil from morning till night. Like them, he tenaciously clung to an age-old way of life to scrape a modest living to raise his family.

The sun was setting on the horizon when Taafeef, looking to be in his middle age with a swarthy complexion, prepared to go home. While gathering some equipment, he heard a faint cry in the distance. At first, he was too busy to pay attention to it, dismissing it as a sound made by an animal crying or a bird. But as he continued to pack up, the sound caught his attention again. This time, he straightened his back, stood still, and listened. He heard it anew, but could not tell where or what it was. Out of curiosity, he stopped packing and headed toward the side of the river. At the riverbank, however, he hesitated about walking north or south.

The Nile was a peculiar river; it flowed north instead of south. So, one had to go up to get down and had to go down to get up. Taafeef then trekked a little south to get upstream.

As he walked along the riverbank, the faint, subtle sound became more apparent. Feeling he was walking in the right direction, he paid closer attention to the bank where the reeds grew thick.

After taking further steps, his curiosity gave way to uneasiness. Even though he associated it with an infant's cry, he was wary that it might be a fox's mimicking sound. At one point, taking a precautious step, he trod into the river and raked through the reeds with his hands. He then saw a small plastic vessel-like container struck in the reeds. Inside that vessel, he saw an infant wrapped in a blanket cry fretfully.

Taafeef stepped back to the shoreline and hauled the vessel out of the water. He then picked up the infant and cradled it in the crook of his left arm. When the infant stopped crying, Taafeef noticed the baby was not local. He looked Asian. Not having been outside Egypt, Taafeef could not tell whether it was Japanese, Chinese, or Korean. But why such a baby ended up here was the most puzzling question entering his mind.

He looked around, then up at the sky. After returning his attention to looking at the baby, he raised his head and scanned upstream, downstream, and then to the opposite shore. Noticing nothing suspicious, he gave the baby a thoughtful glance again, trying to make sense of this.

At this moment, his instinct prompted him to rummage through the container for clues. Amid the growing darkness, he found a roll of notes stuck in a corner. He unrolled it, and it read, "Our son is your son. Take good care of him, and we shall reward you."

As he continued to roll out the note further, he saw a figure '$5.' But when he continued unfolding it, he saw a zero followed by more zeros, revealing the total amount of 500,000. At that point, Taafeef had difficulty understanding that figure. He knew how much it was $5, or $50, but 500,000 was beyond him. The question 'Is this some kind of joke?' troubled him.

As Taafeef pondered over the baby, more puzzling questions beset him. He gently laid the baby on the ground and fumbled through the container in the fading light of day. After removing an underlying blanket, he felt a hard surface beneath. When he knocked on it, it produced a hollow, metallic sound. He wedged his fingers between an inner corner of the vessel and the metal object and carefully wiggled it out. Feeling heavy, he anxiously removed it from the craft and lifted the cover. In an instant, he was stunned by what he found. Even in the semi-darkness, he could see it contained cash, stacks after stacks of $100 US dollar bills. His mind boggled at the trove as he struggled to comprehend how much it was that much.

The way he perceived money was how it was associated with a quantity, likened to a bag of rice or two bags of flour. But when he saw that display of glaring notes, he had difficulty translating it into any tangible equivalent.

For a moment, he seemed to submerge himself in a daze. Once he emerged, he hurriedly put the cover back, jiggled the metal box back to the bottom of the vessel, and laid the infant on top again. He then carried the entire setup and walked across the field. He kept walking without looking back until he reached home, leaving all his farming tools in the open land.

* * * * *

The sky cast a pink and red glow over the eastern horizon when Taafeef woke up.

The night before, there was a lot of talk with his wife, Yasmin. Taken by surprise with a staggering amount of money and an infant, Yasmin had difficulty embracing her husband's strike. As they continued their conversation, their overwhelming suspicion, caution, and warning only stressed their talk. Despite Taafeef's assurances, they continued their talk until midnight. At last, they both took pity on the baby and agreed to bring him up as their child.

The first thing on Taafeef's mind that morning was about the baby's name. After running some errands, he set out to find the village's learned man, Mr. Mostafa. Following some cordial exchanges between them, Taafeef explained he needed a name for an adopted Asian boy.

Even though Mr. Mostafa, being commended as the village's walking dictionary, had little knowledge of Asian languages. Except on some occasions when he came in touch with some Chinese or Japanese tourists, he picked up a few amusing single-syllable sounds. Yet, despite all this, being a walking dictionary also hinted at his ability to collect new terms that came along.

Remembering a Chinese product he had seen, labeled "Dongfang Hong," and another called "Kun Shan," he tried to brainstorm. Combining elements from both names, he proposed two different choices: "Dongfang Kun" or "Hong Shan." After some contemplation, he decided that "Dongfang Kun" sounded better.

In the end, Taafeef and Mr. Mostafa were pleased with the name.

Dongfang was an 'amiable child,' Yasmin gushed. He cried a little, unlike their sons. All the time, the baby was cheerful and easy to calm. His mild temperament did not cause any trouble or interference, as the couples were initially worried about. As a result, life went smoothly and uninterrupted as days turned to months and months to years.

As Dongfang's brothers were at least six years his senior, they spent little time together and rarely bothered each other. As he grew older, he was often seen playing by himself but would always stay close to his foster mother, with whom he found comfort to be with.

As early as 5, Dongfang displayed a penchant for keeping things tidy. When his brothers messed with his belongings, he would act out with a bad temper.

One day in the early spring, as he was ready for kindergarten that year, Yasmin accompanied him to a school outside their village. However, on that first day, something unexpected happened.

When Dongfang encountered the gathering of large numbers of children in the classroom, he clung fast to Yasmin and would not let go of her hand. Despite his fears, Yasmin explained he would get used to it there, learn many fun activities like drawing, and make new friends. One teacher also joined Yasmin and offered many pleasant words. But despite all the cajolery and blarney, Dongfang had none of it. He told Yasmin he did not want to stay and would not loosen his grip.

As the problem protracted and when all options were exhausted, one teacher held Dongfang back from behind while another tried to remove his hand from Yasmin's wrist. At that point, the boy started screaming, yelling, and crying.

However, detaching his grip from Yasmin's wrist proved an uneasy task, as both teachers were sweating over it. By the time they had successfully let go of his grasp, Yasmin was in shock and disbelief, as her wrist was all bruised over. She could not have imagined that Dongfang, being so small, could hold on so firmly.

Once Yasmin freed herself, she turned and left the classroom without looking back.

A decade later, that was the only memory Dongfang could recall during his kindergarten years. Later, he held no recollection of how he got along with the other children or how he did there. As his traumatic experience etched deep into his memory, his adverse exposure stretched out over a prolonged period, overshadowing any pleasant contact that might follow.

Unbeknownst to his foster parents, Dongfang seemed to gain a repressive bearing after that incident, as if his identity had collided with his surroundings and remained quiet and uncommunicative.

Cemile Kougioumtzis was reciting the prayers from a book she held with her left hand outside Meryem Ana Evi on top of Mt. Koressos. Pushing sixty with

shoulder-length white hair, she had a slim, graceful figure with blue eyes.

Nearby, several pilgrims and worshippers quietly waited their turns at the Spring Water Fountain. It was Cemile's favorite place, overlooking Ephesus beyond and nestled among trees and olive gardens where hillside slopes slowly dropped to the Aegean Sea. It rendered a naturally beautiful, serene place to be and where the closest, she thought, she could get to God.

After the prayer, Cemile slowly made her way home. Once she returned to Selçuk, she dawdled down the street, occasionally idling outside a shop and looking at some display items.

About a block from her home, two kids ran past her. One child blew a raspberry at the other while the other cut capers and giggled along the footpath. Seeing these two bubbly children, Cemile instantaneously recalled some dreams she had a month earlier.

They were dreams out of the ordinary. In the first one, Cemile saw a lonely child living on a land bounded by a river on one side and farmland on the other. What was striking were the details, which were so vivid. Not only could Cemile recall the exterior with a row of palm trees, but she also remembered the features inside that mud-brick house. And in a dark corner, she saw a melancholy and strange child languish in silence.

In an ensuring overlapped segment in the dream, people were dashing and yelling and screaming in confusion in the dark. All the while, the child remained stolid and calm amid the chaotic scene.

Cemile had only a hazy recollection of what the boy looked like afterward. But she would never forget the child's gaze - eyes that emitted intense hatred and bitterness, eyes that could cast people asunder. After Cemile woke up, she felt an air of gloom lasting for many days.

Afterward, as Cemile was busy juggling between work and prayer, the matter soon slipped out of her mind and was laid aside.

Yet, not long after, another dream came to her at the very location where she saw a grown-up man now standing next to a towering tree, lost in thought. Cemile could not recognize who that man was. But in that dream, she intuitively felt he was once the same child from the previous dream.

When she saw those children today, a series of vivid flashbacks from her dreams rushed through her mind again. A thought suddenly struck her it might be the will of Meryem Ana Evi. Only then did she construe it as a plea for help from a child who seemed in distress.

A few days later, Cemile related those dreams to her friend Damla. She confided they had such a palpable weight upon her, and she was convinced there must be a meaning to them. It could be an ethereal appeal, seeking her help.

While immersed in their conversation, Damla suddenly made an impromptu suggestion to try out her fortuity. With a clear mental image of the area and the house, Cemile could try an online satellite image to locate it, Damla suggested. However, she cautioned that this approach might not be successful and would require significant time, patience, and effort. But if God were willing, Cemile would eventually locate it, she said.

Accessing a computer was a challenge for Cemile, however. She had to either go to the library or use one at Damla's house. Once she began her searches, it became clear how difficult the task was.

When zooming out, the entire region of Anatolia and the Middle East could fit into a page. But when she zoomed in using Street View, she felt like she had to hop every step at a time.

The search could have been more fruitful most of the time. Often, Cemile skimmed through results with no specific purpose in mind. As time flew by, Cemile juggled her time between work and household chores and between reciting prayers and searching. But, on and off, she kept on looking.

As the summer passed and now revived, Cemile had been searching for many seasons. However, her enthusiasm waned after the lengthy search, and she slowly distanced herself from those dreams. Unintentionally, she shifted her focus to exploring the scenery around the region instead.

At one point, she scrolled through images of various sights, zooming in on the bazaars in Istanbul, the Hagia Sophia, and the Bosporus. Other times, she would flip through the landscapes of Athens. From that point, she moved southwest to Valletta, then to the southern Mediterranean Sea, and ended up in Alexandria, in Northern Africa.

On this day, she suddenly got an impulse to explore the various locations of the pyramids. As she pored over the region near Cairo, she noticed the distributary in the upper right corner. Just as she was about to scroll up to scout the area, Damla came in with two glasses of iced mint tea. Together, they sat there bantering about work, teaching, old times, and fried sushi.

At one point, when their conversation stalled, Damla brought up some rivers, and soon their attention shifted to southern Türkiye. After Damla left, Cemile's search fell back to where she began.

Not long after the first year ended, Cemile felt tired and lethargic with her pursuit. Just as chances no longer favored a dull mind, her dreams about the child faded into oblivion, and her search halted.

As years flew by, the cycle repeated itself when the summer ended, and the leaves of the oak trees were turning red, regenerating all over again. Then, the odds arose.

One Sunday morning, while cleaning her table after breakfast, she reached over to grasp a pen rolling off the table. She accidentally knocked her cup of coffee, causing a spill.

Letting out a sigh, she stood up to get a kitchen towel to clean up. But as she was about to clean the mess, the image of the spill caught hold of her attention.

She stood with the towel in one hand, gawking at the image. The liquid formed a long, narrow puddle. At the upper end, it split into three smaller streams, heading in different directions. Seeing that, she vaguely recalled having come across it somewhere.

Standing there gaping at the impression, she gradually brought her back years ago during a visit to Damla's house.

The sight of the spill finally stirred up her photographic memory, summoning her to the region near Cairo where the distributary formed.

As years flew by, Dongfang made steady progress in school. Nothing seemed out of the ordinary. At school, he achieved good grades, and at home, he kept to himself, causing no trouble. By age 9, however, there was a sudden change in his behavior.

As time slipped by, Dongfang became defiant and domineering. He insisted on getting his way and was rude to others. Nobody appreciated how it began. When his foster parents slowly noticed the change, Dongfang seemed to have entrenched himself further.

First, his foster parents received a notice from the school about the boy's disorderly behavior. Not long after, he was sent home on one occasion, involving in a fight. Amid the disturbance, his parents were at a complete loss why he changed so dramatically.

That all started when he befriended a dumpy, dead-end kid named Amon. Amon was notable for his pranks and antics in class and his rowdiness during recess. Dongfang, for one, was known for being quick to pick up new things.

For all that, Amon was also a great fan of kung fu movies. He claimed to know martial arts. In their idle hours, he taught Dongfang some silly, outlandish martial arts movements that reminded one of someone kangarooing around, much to the bewildering of the onlooking dilly-dalliers nearby.

Coincidentally and oddly, this learned behavior carried Dongfang out of his suppressed, bottled-up disposition over the years, only straying to a different extreme attitude.

The adults thus surmised that he learned from imitating Amon's attitude, appointing all he said or did. From there, his behavior changed.

But that explanation did little to clarify what had transpired when he beat a schoolboy.

The incident stemmed from a row between Dongfang and another child, called Nasir, during recess. Dongfang believed Nasir had taken his coin and demanded its return. Not only did Nasir refuse, but he also mocked Dongfang by saying, "Ask your real mom to get it."

Even overwhelmed by an inexplicable anger, Dongfang, without saying a word, turned around and intended to walk away.

Inauspicious as it was, the moment the boy turned, he came into visual contact with a broomstick leaning against the wall to his right. Involuntarily, he just grasped the wooden staff, turned back, and raised the broom head overhead. Without saying a word, he walloped Nasir repeatedly with the broom, much like the way he threshed wheat with a flail in the field.

Surprised by this sudden violent reaction, Nasir covered his head with both his hands while screaming for help.

After spending the entire day working in the field that evening, Taafeef sat down and talked to his wife about Dongfang. Yasmin assured her husband that Dongfang's troubles might be temporary. She explained everyone might go through different stages in life that they must navigate.

Yasmin then suggested, "Maybe we give him some money to buy things he wants."

Taafeef, an honest and kind man, did not wish to treat Dongfang too harshly. He kept his promise to bring up Dongfang when he found him. Yet, Taafeef surmised Dongfang had too many idle moments, which could lead him to trouble.

In his own words, Taafeef stated, "Time and tide wait for no man. Let him accept hardships, and the road will lead him to a promise of futurity. The readies can only corrupt the mind and weaken the body. Work relieves us from boredom, vice, and want."

He concluded they should keep the money for building a new school and more wells. A knock came from the front door as they discussed bringing up Dongfang.

When Yasmin answered the door, she encountered a tall woman in her early sixties who said she had gotten lost and asked for some water. Yasmin invited her in. Once they were in, the woman introduced herself as Cemile Kougioumtzis, a schoolteacher and a clergy member.

Upon hearing that Cemile was a teacher, Taafeef and Yasmin expressed their regret about being too busy raising one of their children. Taafeef then brought up some trouble Dongfang had caused and mentioned he would appreciate Cemile's input.

In response to Yasmin's kindness in offering water, Cemile considered the offering the best form of charity. She expressed her desire to repay Taafeef and Yasmin's generosity by serving as a tutor to help instill moral values in their child. Given Taafeef and Yasmin's struggles, this offer felt like a blessing from above.

At once, Taafeef and Yasmin accepted and asked their child, Dongfang, to meet Cemile. That was the first time Cemile met the boy.

From that day on, Cemile devoted her time to Dongfang, instilling a sense of moral values in him. She taught him to be honest and to avoid deception, cheating, or stealing. Using various methods, she explained these principles and engaged him in discussions. Cemile praised the virtues of decent people, encouraging Dongfang to have the courage to do the right thing, treat others with respect, and show tolerance for differences.

Occasionally, she taught him to recite moral codes, emphasizing the importance of compassion, caring for others, expressing gratitude, and forgiving those who wronged him.

As Cemile dedicated herself to teaching, time flew by as dusk verged into night and night into day. During that period, she inspired noble aspirations by urging Dongfang to avoid wrongdoing and dishonesty; if something was not right, he should not do it, and if it was not true, he should not say it. Cemile explained false words were evil but also infected the soul with evil. She concluded that a man's deeds, not words, shall judge a man.

Cemile vouched for Dongfang's open-mindedness, listening to others, admitting mistakes, and never asking someone to do something he wouldn't do himself.

Early, Dongfang's focus was prone to wander off to other objects around or outside the house. Under Cemile's guidance, his attention gradually stopped drifting and became more concentrated. When Cemile asked him to recite particular passages, Dongfang no longer faltered and could recall every line.

Despite the progress, Cemile noticed that the boy seemed buttoned up and remained reserved. Cemile realized that Dongfang's learning journey would likely be a long haul. She would not be there to guide the boy every step of the way.

Yet, Cemile knew also that Dongfang needed more than just a branch of knowledge; he would eventually have to gain more discipline and experience before merging with the larger world.

One early morning, Cemile took Dongfang out for a stroll. Amid the peaceful surroundings, Cemile got Dongfang's attention by pointing to a row of trees and asking, "Do you know why we come to value trees?"

Cemile then explained to Dongfang a metaphor relating trees to men and women, "It takes years and patience to see a tree grow. It is like the perseverance and determination required to nurture a person. To grow a tree thus invokes the cultivation of a generation."

To ensure Dongfang listened, she suggested he plant a tree. She explained, "Let us plant this seed of Acacia as a symbol of fostering a generation of honorable men and women. With patience and perseverance, let its roots anchor, its trunk strengthen, and its branches outstretch. For the air we breathe, the shade we seek, the fruit we eat, let us nurture this tree of life. And let us hold on to the hope that we will one day see it flourish. Just like the lives of the men and women we cherish, it will grow strong and prosper."

On this day, Cemile gave Dongfang a tiny seed of life, which the boy planted near the house.

Meanwhile, the teaching continued as days turned into nights and rejuvenated.

When the first tulips heralded the coming of spring, Cemile was about to conclude her teaching. The night before her departure, Cemile took Dongfang for a stroll in an open field. There they stood, watching falling stars streak across the sky, with a glowing train trailing behind them now and then.

Cemile stood out in silhouette against the sky, where countless stars twinkled and flickered. She pointed to an exceptionally bright star at one point and asked, "Do you see that bright star?"

Dongfang silently nodded, basking in the universe's wonder on this night.

Cemile said, "The light you see traveled across the universe for millions of years before finally arriving here tonight as if conveying a message to humankind. Your actions on Earth will be much like that light, whether they are acts of kindness or meanness, of honor or iniquity. They will carry and convey your messages millions of years from now."

After a brief pause, Cemile added, "Be told. Avoid evil, and it will avoid thee."

When dawn verged into daylight, she bid farewell to everyone, while Taafeef and Yasmin bowed and expressed their gratitude.

Standing at the entrance, Cemile told Taafeef and Yasmin, "I do all I can to bring peace. Unlike before, when that peace was a distant mirage, it is now attainable. Even when darkness enshrouds, the light of courage will find its place."

Once she stepped outside the house, she embraced on a long trek back to her hometown.

After Cemile left, Dongfang felt anything but free and relaxed. Unless Taafeef needed a helping hand on the field, he wandered around the village and far afield or spent time with his friends.

In contrast, Dongfang faced restrictions on his playtime. Besides assigning various tasks to him, Taafeef kept him occupied with other work, whether in the field or at home.

One day, Dongfang was helping Taafeef count the total number of eggs needed to deliver to a customer. During the counting, Taafeef added them up in increments of three. To Taafeef's surprise, Dongfang could not follow along. He did not understand why the counting started at 3, then moved to 6, then 9, and continued in that manner. The only method he comprehended was the rudimentary method of incrementing by 1. For him, other random increments like 3, then 7, then 11 were totally out of reach.

Only at that stage did Taafeef realize Dongfang was raw with math. He perceived Dongfang could only conduct a proper trade if he was familiar with simple math. Without this knowledge, others could take advantage of him, and he might face money risks if he guessed. In the end, he might even end up owning nothing but trouble.

Taafeef was adamant that Dongfang should improve his basic math to address this issue. Weeks after he looped around inquiring about it, he found a math tutor outside the village. His name was Baahir Al-Katib.

Baahir was short, standing just over 5 feet tall. He was overweight and had a round body shape that reminded Dongfang of a wooden barrel. Because of this resemblance, Dongfang struggled to connect with his new tutor, mixing the local term "Barmil," which means barrel, with Baahir's name.

Baahir was outgoing and enjoyed chatting, often bringing up random topics and making jokes. For that reason, Dongfang had difficulty following up on the conversation. Being habitually uncommunicative and lacking intent, he either responded with a persistent sheepish smile or remained quiet as a choice.

From the beginning, Baahir explained to Dongfang that even if he were wealthy and had someone to count eggs for him, he would still need to understand math to ensure his aid wasn't cheating on him.

The next day, Baahir dinged into Dongfang's head through the timetable by memorizing techniques.

At first, the boy's reaction to the method was much like that of a mule responding to an instruction. It was slow, faulty, and awkward. Only after a month of persistence and patience did Dongfang pull off the timetable, even with considerable effort.

After the timetable, Baahir taught Dongfang math operations. To his tutor's surprise, Dongfang understood and followed along very well. One day, out of curiosity, his tutor let his pupil solve a problem mentally, jotting nothing down. That was when Dongfang fumbled. Only then did Baahir realize his pupil had difficulties with math problems.

One day, Baahir came up with a game. He told Dongfang that if he could answer a problem correctly, he would reward him with a 25-piaster coin. Dongfang became very enthusiastic.

The tutor then asked Dongfang, "You were counting sheep. There were ten sheep in front of you. How many did you count?"

"10." Without wasting time, Dongfang promptly replied.

"No, 11." His tutor replied.

"What do you mean 11? You said 10." Dongfang frowned.

"You were sitting on one," Baahir explained with a wry smile.

Dongfang was caught in a complete surprise. "What? That is not fair. You did not tell me I was riding one."

Baahir told him, "One thing you need to know when I convince you to count an additional imagined sheep. Whenever you do that, you will get a reward. Subsequently, you always include an additional item when you count because of an expected reward. In the long term, you automatically include that additional item whenever and whatever you count. That is called conditioning. Later, I will tell you more about it."

Still, Dongfang remained in a sullen resentment, all thinking about that 25-piaster coin.

Then, one day, his tutor asked another question, "The brown rabbit was born in the spring, and the white rabbit was born in the summer. Which one is older?"

Like before, without wasting time, Dongfang promptly replied, "The brown rabbit." "Wrong!" To his surprise, his tutor replied.

Dongfang was not happy and contended. "How could it be wrong? Spring comes before summer?"

"You know the season they were born, but you don't know the year. Therefore, the answer is 'I don't know.'"

Dongfang felt defeated and was unhappy with his tutor, thinking he was not very serious about teaching him math.

His tutor then told him. "Be advised that there will never be a shortage of people who want to play tricks on others."

However, Dongfang became sulky and remained silent. Rather than recognizing that he had missed an opportunity to earn prizes, he focused on losing two coins.

In the months that followed, Baahir taught the boy more mathematics. But it was only when his tutor introduced him to some algebra and rudimentary calculus that the boy became more focused. At that stage, even though the boy still had a vague understanding of how algebra and calculus could apply, he was fascinated by how a set of different numbers could bring about different outcomes.

One day, Dongfang became increasingly fascinated by a formula that challenged him to find a number that could bring a calculated result close to zero. This formula captivated him when he came to see how numbers could influence the outcome of his calculations. He randomly assigned a number to the formula to get closer to zero. But to his dismay, his attempt was fruitless. He ended up either getting a positive or negative result, but never coming close to zero. So, he just sat there tinkering with it until it got dark.

His tutor also taught his pupil a simple form of reasoning called syllogism, in which two assumed propositions would lead to a conclusion. Dongfang found it quite amusing that the boy secretly worked on one: all dogs bark; my tutor often barks at me; therefore, my tutor is a dog.

But despite his great amusement, the boy got stuck with the reverse logic: if his tutor was a dog and the tutor had a pupil, would that make him a dog too?

Meanwhile, the math lessons would continue for another two months. Before ending the tutorship, Baahir gave Dongfang a Rubik's Block as a gift. At first, the boy became very absorbed in the new toy, working on it day and night, hoping to solve it. But his enthusiasm slowly faded, and despite his persistent efforts, he could never solve it.

Part II - Finale Of Mentorship

After the math tutoring session, Dongfang felt less restricted and happier. As if he had been trapped indoors for too long, he felt the sky bluer, the air fresher, and his movement freer.

Yet, unbeknownst to him, he would be placed under the third and last tutor months later. This upcoming experience was going to differ from any previous ones.

A Chinese national in his early thirties occasionally sneaked around over the years. He came in contact with Taafeef to purchase a variety of crops. He was of slim build and medium height and distinguished by his rather salient features. He had a protruding forehead with a heavy brow ridge over his dark, sunken eyes, which gave him the appearance of a reserved and shrewd character. His name was Gusha Dao.

That day, while Taafeef and Gusha were chatting about the weather, the harvest, or the river, Gusha's attention soon fell on Dongfang, who was idling at the doorstep. Curious about him, Gusha asked to see Dongfang's right palm. After studying it for quite some time, Gusha told Taafeef that his child had an aptitude for languages.

Gusha claimed the child would profit from learning another language. Knowing other languages would significantly improve his problem-solving and communication skills, he said.

However, he cautioned that such talent would become dull and useless if left untrained.

Intrigued by these comments, Taafeef inquired about Gusha's experiences. Gusha shared he had been a Chinese language lecturer at a university in China and was now working for an export firm.

Having spent most of his life tilling the land, Taafeef, as a man of few words and practicality, always maintained that indolence would only lay waste to the harvest even when nature had done its part in fructifying the soil. When he heard what Gusha said about talent, he thought that thinking aligned with his belief that a man must learn and work hard to bear fruit. Besides, he gathered through interaction with people that language could change one's perception and character.

Ever since being shepherded under Cemile and Baahir's guidance, Dongfang had become more dependable. However, Taafeef remained cautious about him potentially falling back into his old self. Taafeef agreed he deserved further education. Recognizing that Dongfang could benefit from additional learning, Taafeef brought it up the next time he met with Gusha.

Gusha accepted Dongfang's tutor position and promised to do all he could to help him reach his potential.

At first, Taafeef and his wife were worried about how Dongfang might take to a new language. But Dongfang surprised them by staying more focused and becoming calmer than before. By the end of the first month, he became fixated on the Chinese language, likely because of pattern recognition skills and memorization techniques, which he had gained from Cemile and Baahir the years before.

As Dongfang continued to learn under Gusha's guidance, time flew by. By the end of the first year, the boy had secured his basic understanding of the language.

Soon after Dongfang became more efficient with the language, Gusha also brought up some seemingly unrelated, disconnected subjects on and off.

At first, their conversation was stilted and punctuated by intermittent silences. But as Gusha introduced more and more topics, their talks would have become more natural and spontaneous.

One day, the tutor told Dongfang, "Don't be too honest when you speak. The art of speaking is much like that of wrapping. You can make it bigger, smaller, longer, etc. You can do it with colorful paper, ribbons, bows, or plain paper. Do it your way, and nobody knows what's inside you. Let's start with this. What's another way to call a prison cell?"

Dongfang rolled his eyes and said, "Jail room?" Gusha corrected him. "A sheltered refuge." Dongfang found it amusing and laughed.

Gusha continued, "How about a container?"

Dongfang offered no words.

Gusha said, "A restraining framework."

Afterward, Dongfang became engrossed in this art of speaking and continued to practice with his tutor. Later, he even created some new terms for himself and used them. When his father and brothers asked for help, he told them that his hands needed more days to grow longer to pick fruits.

At first, his excuse worked. But after once or twice coming across Dongfang's ruse, his older brother, Adeel, became familiar with the same old trick, so he told him, "You know why hogs always raise a laugh. Because they are too idle to care about sex, they need help from someone else to hold their penis and insert it into the female hog's genitalia while another hand propped behind its backside and gives it a good push."

Adeel finished the story in smug self-satisfaction with a slight bob of his head. Upon hearing that, Dongfang drew a scowling face at this unexpected rejoinder. Afterward, the boy took it as an insult and felt affronted.

One day, as Dongfang practiced Chinese calligraphy, Gusha said, "People are prejudiced; they judge people by their handwriting. Once deemed unworthy, you never get back. It is like being condemned for who you are, not for what you did."

From there, Gusha, now tutor-turned-mentor, imparted a lengthy discourse in his accustomed didactic fashion. "Do you know why? Because the masses have a knack for judging people and distorting facts. They are selfish. They are reactionary. They demand. They grouse. They moan. They whine. That's all they can do. If you give them an inch, they will want a mile. Besides being greedy and bigotry, they don't amount to anything. If you heed these commoners, you will soon lose control of everything.

"It turns out that the greatest threat we Chinese face is the people themselves, not foreigners. They are a bunch of loose rabbles whose values and usefulness are designated expired. You'd better not reason with them; they are intractable, recalcitrant, and wayward. You cannot be candid with them, for they like being tempted and coaxed. That is what they are.

"For that reason, you need to stop them; you supervise them. But physical control is not enough. You know that the things that drive them to such bad behaviors are the stuff that swirls inside their heads. Because of that, we have to teach them how to think,

re-educate them, and turn them into a resource to generate a beneficial outcome. We have to drum them into knowing who they are. When their thinking aligns with ours, they will do it exactly how we want. That is when we have an orderly society. That is our socialist order."

At this moment, Gusha dropped his voice. He glanced over his shoulder with theatrical caution, leaned closer to Dongfang, and flicked his eyes toward Taafeef and his two sons standing at a distance. He quietly said, "Watch out for those religious devotees too."

Dongfang looked puzzled, but before he could figure out what his tutor was implying, Gusha straightened his back and stressed: "Either too much or a lack of education makes them intelligently incapable of making the right decisions or sound judgments. Our members know better than the masses. We are the ones to decide what is good or bad, what is right or wrong."

Gusha appended. "Only when we have total control of the masses can we unite with all our brothers against outsiders."

At this time, Dongfang broke his silence and inquired, "Brothers?"

Gusha nodded and said, "All people of Asian countries: Japanese, Koreans, Indians, Melanesians, etc."

"I don't understand."

After a moment of silent contemplation, Gusha gestured to Dongfang to get an egg, a spoon, and a bowl.

After a short while, the boy came out with what his tutor asked for. Gusha then took the egg, slightly tapped it on the rim, and broke the contents into the bowl.

While resting his left forearm on the table, he brought Dongfang's attention by pointing his right hand at the egg in the bowl and explaining, "The yolk in the middle is us - we and all our brothers. You see how the whites surround us? But how are you going to set all of us free, then?"

The boy just rolled his eyes. Gusha said, "Look!"

He then picked up the spoon and, holding the bowl with his left hand, began beating the egg.

Afterward, he placed the bowl on the table and said, "Now, it is completely blended, and the White is gone."

After a brief pause, he continued, "If Rome was to be built by a mob for the Republic in one day, we use that combined mob for our collectivism end."

As Gusha delivered his extensive critique aimed at the masses, he was unsure how well Dongfang would absorb his street-smart insights. Only time could tell.

Like many others, Dongfang needed years of experience and conflicts to develop a network of complex thinking. Without it, he would struggle. Otherwise, he needed to learn to focus on one subject at a time. From there, he could grasp how issues were interrelated and interconnected using his reasoning and understanding of cause and effect built over the years. Only then would he be able to evaluate the situation.

Yet, Dongfang was abandoned and raised in a rural environment. Because of that, the sophistication of his thinking bonded to the simplification of rural life. Unlike others with an established thinking framework, his was a primary juncture of simplicity, comprising only a few isolated nodes that connected one verity to another. Without facts, experiences, or knowledge, he might accept anything without questioning.

For Dongfang, his tutor's elaborate explanations of unforeseen circumstances only made the subject too difficult to comprehend. This precipitated Dongfang's departure from normality. Without being exposed to other unique sets of fundamental ideas, he became radicalized in one particular direction.

Unbeknownst to Dongfang, his tutor was also manipulating terminology to his advantage. By steering away from any words that might carry a negative connotation, such as 'communism,' he substituted them with other terms like 'collectivism' or 'socialism' for the same meaning.

Owing to that, Dongfang found himself unable to do much more than compile a collection of disassociated facts and statements, including terms like "the need to control," "the power of re-education," and "egg yolk," among others.

Dongfang also appeared to embrace his Chinese identity, mainly when Gusha occasionally referred to them as "we Chinese" during their conversations.

Over time, he also associated himself with a political group whenever Gusha used phrases like "we," "our," "our members," "our thinking," or "our principles."

Artfully, his tutor occasionally directed Dongfang's attention to seemingly unrelated objects or designs to immerse him in a more profound socialist conviction. These included symbols such as pandas, the Olympic Games, the Great Wall, and movies like "Wolf Warrior."

Time was slowly slipping away. With each passing day, Gusha's influence on the boy became more pronounced.

Six months toward a later point in time, the tutor arrived with three volumes of illustrated history books. They comprised many palm-size books, each containing a sequence of sketches presented in narrative format.

As they were easy to hold and to read, these full-length, independent stories reel off many interesting anecdotes and historical accounts of China's pre-dynasty periods and classic romanticized novels.

When Dongfang laid his hands on these books, he got so hung up on reading that he paid no heed to people talking to him. Captivated by the stories, he spent hours flipping through the pages, often forgetting to eat, which baffled everyone. They all had difficulty understanding how the boy could have suddenly transmuted into such an attentive egghead.

Through these graphic books, Dongfang learned about many notable figures from Chinese history, including famous writers, scholars, poets, political leaders, and strategists.

Without these palm-size books, it would take the average person years to make sense of the chaotic mix of confusing words and complex historical accounts, with a hefty dictionary sitting nearby. And through this bare-bones version of history presented in graphic format, not long after, Dongfang's overall knowledge of the Chinese historical past came on in leaps and bounds.

His tutor also gave the boy a book of philosophy made-simple, which mainly contained topics aimed at colorizing socialist ideologies. In it, not only did it dwell on a great deal of socialist unconventional mindsets; it also offered many bizarre deviate evaluations, such as likening Robinson Crusoe to 'a vagabond' and described being 'impractical,' or how Western liberal philosophers retreated in shame with 'tails between their legs' or labeled them as 'stray dogs.'

As Dongfang learned more, the effects on him became more apparent. The boy felt more worthy and lofty as he gained a new language and developed ideas that set him apart from others.

Unbeknownst to Dongfang himself or others, that was a significant shift: the boy was more open under Cemile and Baahir's guidance. However, he became more withdrawn and melancholy under Gusha.

Even though Taafeef was the first to notice, he attributed it to the fact that young people changed as they aged; they became mature over time, and thus, they wanted more independence.

However, Dongfang's mother suggested that Taafeef take the children to a city interlude to cheer them up. Taafeef thought that was a good idea.

A couple of days later, Taafeef took the children on an excursion to a nearby city. For Dongfang, this was the first time he had ever set foot in a place brimming with colors and grittiness.

As they wandered from window to window down a series of shops, his eyes fell on many jaw-dropping displays of items. Almost every object drew his covetous look, from a bicycle to computer games, from an enormous TV set to a sofa. The boy, wearing a face mask, stood there gawking at the displays as if falling under their spells, and he could not take his eyes off them until his brothers hustled him along.

Along the way, Dongfang remembered the roundabout trick with words he had learned from his tutor. Unable to resist the temptation, he made a lame insinuation that the family would benefit from owning a bicycle.

Little did he know, his attempt at humor fell flat. Taafeef, who fell in with his humor and took it as an enlightening discussion, told him, 'We should think of putting something by for a rainy day.'

Surprised by an unexpected turn of phrase, Dongfang grimaced with bewilderment. He glanced upward at the blue sky. Rain? What rain? He did not remember having seen a real rain here.

Halfway through the excursion, they finally stopped by a fast-food restaurant for drinks and snacks. Seeing Dongfang eat his fries with a plastic fork, his brothers teased him for being too classy and suggested he use his hands or chopsticks instead.

"Chopsticks?" Dongfang instantly felt offended by the remark, interpreting it as an attack on his culture.

Yet, he and his brothers were only sometimes familiar with the culture they were referencing, aside from some vague impressions gained from kung fu movies.

He ignored their teasing and continued to use his fork while his brothers continued giggling with their sally.

Unlike his two brothers, who were bubbly and thrilled to see a completely different lifestyle, Dongfang was cheerless on the way back. The more he saw what people had in a city, the more things he did not have haunted him. Instead, he felt ill-suited and inferior and became depressed at seeing that densely settled place.

After that trip, Dongfang wanted to avoid setting foot there again.

* * * * *

Months flew by as Dongfang continued to learn under Gusha's guidance. However, Gusha must still fulfill his promise to Taafeef.

During the remaining six months, his tutor-turned-mentor mainly used Hollywood movies to illustrate and exemplify Western mentality and attitudes. Taking advantage of this approach, the boy relished watching movies depicting the Trojan War and Roman gladiators with absorbed attention. He also enjoyed listening to dirt or sensational stories his mentor dug out from some tabloids, to his delight.

From there, Gusha exposed the boy, mostly, to popular socialist narratives and current affairs. The parts that covered the periods from the dust of antiquity to the early

20th-century turmoils were so negligible that his mentor treated the subjects like fairy tales, often interweaving historical accounts with a fair amount of romanticism.

Ultimately, only the well-liked version of history would form the backdrop of Dongfang's basic understanding of Chinese political reality. From that foundation, his imagination took off, taking him far beyond the simplicities of a rustic setting into a different realm.

One day, Gusha and Dongfang played chess outside the house. As they played, Gusha occasionally reflected on random past topics. At that point, Dongfang raised some questions about Chinese politics. At first, Gusha seemed reluctant to discuss, telling him he would learn more. Only after Dongfang kept hounding him did Gusha open up to his inner thoughts.

Gusha began by telling him, "Most nations, especially Western nations, have different policies in wartime and peacetime. They maintain a cooperation policy during peacetime and emergency acts during wartime. But we..."

Gusha's voice suddenly dropped away after the reference 'we.' He stopped short while tilting his head, wavering over what to say and what not to say. After pausing momentarily, he raised his head and continued, steering the subject differently.

Gusha continued, "OK, you know. As I explained earlier, western ideas and values are never compatible with our ideologies. Right? Because of that, can you maintain friendly cooperation with them? If you see someone you dislike hanging by the cliff, will you give him a hand or shove him off? It's as clear as day. What happens if you let Western ideas and values take control of our people? Just think about it. Will you let some spoiled brats tell us what to do then? And what about the masses? I told you something about the masses before, didn't I? If we let the rabble do whatever they want, they will overrun us. Would you want to let that happen?"

"So, for us, there is no such thing as wartime and peacetime. Is that what you are saying?"

He dismissed Dongfang's inquiry, saying, "You don't need to know its exact nature. I am just giving you a general idea."

"What then?"

On and off, Gusha had been snacking on some dried melon seeds left on the table. At that moment, he casually grasped one between his thumb and forefinger, placed the tip of it vertically between his teeth, and bit it until it cracked. Then, he said, "Well. Because of that, you must adhere to conflict engagement policies in wartime and peacetime.

Right? That is how we sustain, inside out. It will always remind you that human nature, either foreigners or mainlanders, is inherently bad. Therefore, they should be subjected to constant punishment, self-criticism, and re-education to align with the masses."

"Foreigners as well?"

Gusha continued, "Yes. But the disciplines are not always the same." "What does that mean?"

Gusha turned away from the chessboard and spat a piece of dried melon seed shell onto the ground. He turned back, nodded his head gratifyingly, and said faintly in a whisper, "Don't tell anyone! OK!"

He then glanced his eye around with theatrical caution and continued, "Yes, foreigners, too. One thing you might not know: foreigners would never hesitate to put their wives and grandmas on sale if there were some financial gains for them. Got that!"

At that point, Dongfang lifted his brows and raised a question, "But, alight them with the masses? I thought you said earlier that they don't trust the masses."

"The masses, collectively and ideally, are good. However, we have to punish those who stray from us."

That explanation sounded more complicated than Dongfang had thought. Thus, he kept hounding Gusha for clarification: "So, there are good masses, and there are bad?"

Gusha bobbed his head insouciantly and said, "That's right."

At this moment, Dongfang seemed eager to fill in the gap Gusha left off and asked, "But how can we tell the bad masses from the good?"

In a laid-back manner, without looking up while waving his hand, Gusha answered, "If we can't tell them apart, round them up and treat them all as bad."

"But if our forebears are not to be trusted, who can we trust?"

At this stage, Gusha grew irritated. As the discussion dragged on about all these distinct masses, Gusha worried that all these terms would entangle him in a hopeless mess. So, he gave a nonchalant shrug and concluded, "The Party always knows what they are doing. They know what is right and what is wrong."

"Really?"

Visibly running out of patience, Gusha raised his voice and lashed out, "Just stop asking me the good and bad masses for now and listen to what I want to tell you." "But are we telling people that, including the conflict theory?"

Gusha became even more agitated and snapped back, "Are you an imbecile or something? Are you deliberately obtuse? They don't have to know. We don't have to tell anybody anything. They are on their own. If it's their baby, they should hold it themselves."

After a brief pause, he fired another salvo. "It is not what the state can do for the people. Only the ruling class and elites can have the right to autonomy, privacy, and freedom. In contrast, all others are naturally subjected to dependence and to become instruments for the state. Thus, the state of equality, freedom, and dignity under our socialism is indefinite."

He then added, "That is the way it is. We don't have to tell anybody. Don't be stupid!" Afterward, Dongfang became quiet and asked no further.

After a brief pause, Gusha appended a note. "You will know more in the future."

At that point, Dongfang barged in with another question, "But I don't see how we maintain our trade relations with the West while maintaining conflict engagement policies both in wartime and peacetime?"

Gusha scoffed at the question. "Have you ever seen a theatrical setting composed of the front stage and the backstage? Remember? I told you Western ideas and values would undermine us. So what would you do if you were backstage?"

Instead of answering, Dongfang asked, "What are you doing backstage?"

Gusha gave Dongfang a scornful glare, shook his head, and said, "Don't be stupid to fancy yourself running a restaurant while preparing wonton soup in backstage to serve the customers in the front stage?"

Dongfang immediately reacted. "Oh! You are up to some mischief." Gusha, with a disdainful look, remained quiet.

Dongfang continued, "I see. The front stage presents a set of policies of peacetime, while the backstage embeds a set of guidelines for wartime. It is the primary engine powered by the mindset of permanent conflict to advance into the next phase of global totalitarianism, just as you said before."

With a sneer, Gusha mocked, "There are other functions too... Well, I don't have to go through this. Listen, Little Cabbage. Would you wait ten years or find a faster solution to get you into the next phase?"

Bizarrely, the remark 'Would you wait ten years' reminded Dongfang of what his foster parents once told him about finding him on a riverside. For years, Dongfang felt they had been living a lie all this time, never telling him the truth. Dongfang had also been simmering with resentment after being branded as an imbecile earlier.

Unsurprisingly, the unexpected epithet stung Dongfang to the quick. He shot back at once. "Something in a day? That was how your mom got you. And that is you? Slimy Noodle!"

Gusha meant to offer wise counsel, but his intention of serious discussions now strayed in the sauce of name-calling and derogating. Instead of anticipating positive responses, Gusha got flung back by Dongfang's sharp-tongued and rude comments. Dongfang also incensed him for having the nerve to question his mother and call him 'Slimy Noodle.'

Impulsively, he lashed out, "My mom? My mom has made more babies than any woman in this world."

The moment Dongfang made his outburst, he regretted his knee-jerk reaction. He thought he was the one who did not know who his actual parents were, let alone how many babies in the world.

Seeing Dongfang slump into complete silence, Gusha thought he had chastened him for good. He then gave him a blank look and looked away.

Afterward, both inclined their heads in different directions and remained unspeaking, as if reeling from the aftershock.

After a while, Dongfang raised doubts about what his mentor had related. "Based on what you have told me, could it drive home instead that America is the one who helps lift the multitudes out of poverty? Instead, as you said, the backstage is the inherited conflict mindset for both peacetime and wartime; are fake stamps part of hybrid warfare, then, or a Trojan Horse strategy?"

At first, Gusha thought they had cooled down, but it was time to discuss things with each other nicely and calmly. But when he heard what Dongfang said, it was like adding fuel to the fire and starting the spat all over again.

Gusha instantly flew off the handle, renewing his exasperation of old. "Are you stupid or something? Purely baseless and defamatory, that is a load of crap, I heard. This issue is not the thing you should say or ask... We are one friendly, peace-loving country!"

Dongfang rolled his eyes and said, "I am just asking. You told me to watch out for ones."

During his tutoring sessions, Gusha's street-smart talks encompassed a vast scope. His explanations needed clear boundaries, definitions, principles, or purposes. But when he randomly jumped from one unrelated subject to another, he presented bits and pieces of fragmented objects that swirled around chaotically. For Dongfang, attempts to reassemble these fragments without understanding their original context led to mismatched and distorted concepts. When Dongfang returned these new twist-out-of-shape propositions, the result might be chaotic.

Over time, Dongfang had also held some grudges against Gusha. His tutor repeatedly called him 'Ramen,' 'wonton,' and even once labeled him 'overnight spring roll.' The epithets irked him. When the teasing became persistent, it hit him as much an annoyance as mockery. The more the boy perceived himself as the underdog, the more he needed validation, and the more he became combative, aloof, and inclined to act out. Dongfang had always regarded Gusha with disdain, simmering with resentment. In silence, he waited for an opportunity to get even with this new tutor for being taunting and insulting.

Unbeknown to Gu, Dongfang's tendency was not entirely unexpected. When addressing challenges, Dongfang had nothing but obstinacy to fall back on. Gusha could not have missed it had he paid more attention to how Dongfang played chess. Whenever he got a piece of his own knocked out, he would seek even by eliminating one of his opponent's pieces, regardless of whether it was a wise move.

At that moment, Dongfang thought it was time to settle a score.

Dongfang attempted to clarify. "I am just curious. Because it somehow reminds me of Sun Tzu, who was captured and incarcerated by his adversary two thousand years ago. He devised a ruse, feigned insaneness, and ate feces. Subsequently, the captor released him on compassionate and humanitarian grounds. But he later turned back and blatantly sought vengeance for forcing him to eat excrement. I don't remember seeing Japan do that in the postwar era."

Predictably, Gusha was completely livid at being lectured by a kid, thinking Dongfang also had the cheek to badmouth an ancient figure.

In an unexpected move, he bent down and took off one of his Nike sneakers, grunting with the effort. Once straightening his back, he gave the table edge a fierce swat once, then twice. The bashing sent the melon seeds and chess pieces bouncing off one after another every which way, while the wooden chess board thumped and drummed against the tabletop.

Dongfang innately reacted by raising his right elbow to cover his face as if trying to dodge a blow.

In an ensuing manner, his tutor raised his voice in a fulmination, "Who do you think you are? You are just a kid from a rural, barely weaned off your pacifier."

After lowering his arm, Dongfang rolled his eyes and said, "I just retell you what you told me."

Gusha mocked, "Complimenting the Japanese? Even when you perm your hair or indulge yourself with daikon, you can not be white."

The tutor continued, "That is a silly riddle, totally rubbish, I heard. Who told you that? I don't know what the Americans fed them, but those overseas Chinese turn and bark at us like mad dogs. That explained why we have our 912..."

Dongfang followed, "9 what?"

Amid their uncontrollable rhubarbs, Gusha got so overexcited that he seemed to spill something accidentally. At once, he attempted to contain it. "I didn't say that."

"Yes, you did!"

"No, I didn't!" "You did!"

"I didn't!"

The mentor became ruffled at the dickering. He repeatedly banged the table with his shoe and interrupted, "Quiet!"

In a turnaround, he tossed his shoe back to the ground and justified, "If they were my kids, I would smother them. Not to waste my rice."

Gusha then stretched his eyeballs and harried, "Have you not seen what they did to George Floyd? Can you believe they did that to your grandpa?"

Dongfang looked disconcerted, eyes frowning. "Huh? Who the hell is George Floyd, my grandpa?"

At that point, Gusha just waved his insouciant wave with his hand and said, "You don't have to know."

Dongfang became even more bewildered. "Why did you tell me that, then?" Gusha got snappy and shot back, "Just listen! Don't give me any backtalk!"

After a moment, he continued by appending his resolve. "We will bury them. They don't have the time."

Dongfang became even more confused, arching his eyebrows. "Who? Grandpas?"

Gusha got agitated again. He jabbed his forefinger mid-air and shouted, "Of course, those American dogs."

Dongfang chipped in while rolling his eyes. "Yeah, Kanada."

Gusha, momentarily thrown by the words, sharply rebuked the boy. "What?"

But almost immediately, as if something dawned on him, the tutor amended and shouted. "Yeah, dogs of the free world."

Seeing Gusha erupt into fits of violent temper he had never seen before, Dongfang decided not to provoke any further. Instead, he just sat there, gazing at his mentor, who continued to pout and curse.

After a moment, Gusha cooled off a bit. Initially, he intended to show how thoughtful he was. But by now, the whole thing had fallen apart, and he was losing his zeal to continue the discussion.

At this time, Gusha cracked on some melon seeds again. He silently glanced at the boy, who was gathering some chess pieces from the ground and fiddling with one afterward. Gusha ended the conversation by suggesting Dongfang review the topics he had mentioned earlier and write some key points.

"Imagine a scenario where you offer a typical model of something; what message do you want to convey?"

But no sooner did Gusha make that suggestion than he clarified his proposition abruptly. "For all that, watch out for what you write. Our leaders mainly communicate with each other through their sixth sense, mind you. They can all make out beforehand what each other likes or dislikes. They don't record everything, got that?"

He then wrapped it up by offering his pearls of wisdom to back up his point. "Domestic disgraces shall never be allowed to drift beyond our doorstep. That is something you should reckon with. You hear?"

Yet, Dongfang waited to return his response. Behind his self-possessed countenance that seemed to emanate an air of serenity, a wisp of a smirk disguised.

That was the last main dialogue between Dongfang and his mentor.

* * * * *

After Gusha ended his tutoring, Dongfang had more time to conduct his daily routines the way he wanted. He would spend time with friends, pursue his hobbies, work in the field, or even dawdle around for amusement. More significantly, without Gusha, Dongfang felt intellectually unfettered.

Under Gusha's mentorship, the mentor constantly exposed his pupil to a different mindset and attitude, shifting him from life's simple milieu to a radical background. Because of that, whenever Gusha was around, the atmosphere abounded with tension and antagonism, with either party constantly looking for startling antitheses amid an otherwise tranquil life.

Since Gusha was the presenter of that outer frame of mind, he constantly cast himself as a representation of that mentality whenever he was around. Under the phantom of his tutor's influences, Dongfang's uncompromising attitude continued to rise and fall according to his tutor's mercurial temperament and guidance, encouraging himself further with extreme thinking and inclination.

However, the effects on Dongfang were only to wean off after the mentorship ended. Dongfang's mental tension returned to near the standard mark. Without the magnetism of Gusha, the boy adjusted back to the familiar groove with a more relaxed and calmer pose.

Yet, the immoderate cast of mind instilled in Dongfang was completed and consummated but would remain fallow until it rekindled itself six months later.

On a Monday afternoon, Dongfang wandered from the village and meandered into a nearby town. As he approached the town center, he heard a great commotion near a municipal building, and a tumult of shouting and screaming sprang up.

A sizeable crowd was gathering outside the building. The multitude consisted mainly of men wearing traditional white thobes, while others wore short-sleeved shirts and white trousers. Some held protest signs that read, "Down with America" and "Wake up Muslim World." Slogans and death threats bawled through the air amid the tumult in a disorderly fashion.

A large American flag as big as a car spread out on the ground where men were trampling on top of it. Some protesters took off one of their shoes and raised them high in defiance.

Dongfang, infected by the mass hysteria of the angry crowd, whipped into a frenzy and plunged into the thick of the action.

Little did he know what it was about or who the Americans were. Only once or twice did he come to hear of the word America or Americans from Gusha, when his mentor badmouthed them. Suddenly, Dongfang seemed to lose control and charged into the thick of the engagement by torching an effigy with faked American dollars.

Afterward, the crowd started throwing shoes, rocks, flaming clothing, and whatnot. Police responded in kind, with tear gas and rubber bullets.

Amid the anarchy, where no one gave a damn about any authority, the scene descended into utter mayhem and violence as yelling, screaming, and crying sprang up from all directions.

As distasteful clouds of smoke obscured the surroundings, Dongfang caught in the middle of the eddies. Overwhelmed by the environmentally unfriendly fumes, the boy did not see the police, who donned gas masks charged at the crowd.

As he was stumbling around, coughing and wheezing, a stranger grabbed the back of his collar and yanked him away in time, barely missing a baton that came his way.

As the man fled mad, he seemed to forget what he was dragging along. Being as small and spare as Dongfang was, the man dragged Dongfang like a plush bear, with his heels lugged against the ground.

Once the man realized he was still hauling the boy behind, he abruptly let go of Dongfang. The boy came crashing on his buttocks, and the force sent him rolling backward into a half somersault with both legs up in mid-air. A protester heeled them behind, tripped, and landed head over heels on Dongfang.

Both struggled and helped each other get back to their feet. They then took off in the direction the crowd madly fled while the riot police were hot on their heels.

Dongfang kept on running until he ran out of breath. Once out of harm's way, he breathed a sigh of relief, only to realize that he had lost both his flip-flops.

Stooping over while anchoring both hands on his knees, he looked back on the path running along the river but could not recall when he lost his sandals. With a slouching gait, he then slowly lumped his way home.

After he got home, the tear gas's sharp, irritating, pungent odor lingered. His eyes continued to stream tears while sweat dripped in his eyes, barely keeping them open. To make it worse, the burning sensation in his mouth and nose troubled him.

As he stumbled around, he found a washbasin and filled it with water. Slightly unsteady, he leaned over the basin and splashed his face until he felt better.

Only after the effects of the tear gas eased was Dongfang able to sit down and rest.

In silence and exhaustion, he was beside himself with his inner conflict. The boy brooded over the event, as the incident was not as revelrous as he first thought. Instead of sympathizing with the protesters, he reflected on the absurdity of the day, which made him feel inept at best and foolish at worst.

However, his feelings were not simply about the disorderly conduct of the unruly crowd.

Because the protest was about Americans, Dongfang attempted to relate his silliness and clumsiness to them. Subsequently, he came to assume Americans were the ones who brought on his silly behaviors.

Inadvertently, the whole anti-America sentiment formed amid this melee without direct contact.

Following that incident, Dongfang became quieter than the old. From that day on, at 11, he became more isolated.

Part III - The Dictates

The family had gone to the city before sunset to see some relatives.

Days earlier, strong winds and sandstorms had blanketed the region, followed by showers. The skies had remained cloudy, and dust hung in the air into the third day.

The day after the sandstorms, Dongfang was hanging out with his friends nearby in the morning, dilly-dallying back and forth through the neighborhood. They then spent quite some time with one of their favorite pastimes, blowing bubbles.

Afterward, as objects of their leisure were scarcely any, Dongfang was seen fiddling with some white powder by the side of a house with a stick. One of his friends told him it was rat poison and asked him to stop messing with it.

Thereupon, another friend suggested playing a Monopoly game in his house. The suggestion genuinely intrigued Dongfang, who strained at the leash excitedly to get started.

Despite his enthusiasm, Dongfang could have been a better contender for the games. Just as he had shown himself playing chess games with his mentor Gusha before, his mental strategy had always been one of the grand plans, pushing him into an extreme course of action. As a player who failed to achieve that, Dongfang would become wayward and reckless, bordering on destructive impulses and wilfully pushing toward lose-lose consequences. This impulsiveness had been a recurring pattern whenever he could not get what he wanted. When that happened, the boy would try to sabotage his opponent's progress; either he got what he wanted, or nobody would. He was as hard as nails, uncompromising.

Aimed always with this attitude, when Dongfang won a game, his manifestation of a self-satisfied smirk could hardly conceal his conceit, albeit his triumph never outlasted its ephemeral appeal. Instead, tragically, he lost a game most of the time. And when he lost a game, he would become sulky and resentful, lasting all day long.

When Dongfang played Monopoly with his friends, he employed the same mentality and attitude. He was particular about the properties he purchased and often dismissed the smaller ones. Eventually, he wound up owing fewer assets and losing to his opponents, forfeiting two 25-piaster coins to his friends.

After the game, much like when he lost in a chess match before, he was sulky and resentful, chewing over what those two coins could have brought him instead.

Afterward, Dongfang was morose and unspeaking when he got home. He put on his woeful face like nobody's business and silently stalled in a corner of the house. Nobody knew what had gotten into him this time, as he exchanged only two or three words. But as people were busy with their tasks, they left him undisturbed.

The next day, Dongfang declined to join the family excursion, citing his foot injury from playing games with his friend the day before.

After the family left, Dongfang was idling, first outside on the porch and then continuing inside the house. In time, as he grew tired of his monotonous pacing back and forth, he settled into a wooden chair and started flipping through the pages of a photo book. As his gaze fell on those pictures of old, they quietly sent him on a stroll down memory lane and evoked his acute nostalgia for many things of days gone by.

When he was around six, he remembered Yasmin brought him a kaleidoscope. The first time he looked into the viewer, various colorful objects, like beads and pebbles, captivated him. Every time he rotated the kaleidoscope, he saw a series of

spectacular-colored patterns shifting from one image to another. As years went by, however, his fascination waned, and it was left gathering dust. Someone must have put it away in the storage area afterward. On this day, Dongfang had the desire to see it again.

The storage area resembled an open closet. It was fashioned by installing a 3 foot by 8-foot wall positioned 3 feet from the far corner of the house next to where his foster parents slept. It comprised the upper shelf and lower storage space. A ladder leaned against the upper storage, where the family kept items for easy retrieval. To reach the lower rack, he had first to remove the ladder.

Dongfang was first searching the upper shelf, but needed help to find it. He then got down, hauled the ladder away, and leaned it against a wall. After removing a cover that protected the stored items from dust on the lower shelf, the boy found pillows, blankets, headscarves, sewing accessories, and whatnot piled up underneath. After removing the items individually, he spotted the kaleidoscope resting on a metal box. Curious about the box, he opened it. To his astonishment, it was full of cash, stacks of $100 US dollar bills. His eyes glittered while his heart throbbed. The needful would grant him many wishes - something he might only fulfill with.

Seeing that epic amount of money, the boy let his imagination run wild. Images of a bicycle, a game station, a plush sofa, among other things, drifted in and out of his mind excitably. He never thought it would be feasible to gain the things he wanted. Even the prospect of living in a city was now not unachievable.

As he stood there fantasizing about all the suggestions, he staked the find by hiding under his bed to have all the money. Yet another idea suggested he take the money and disappear.

But having seen that whopping sum of money, Dongfang was now dithering about how to handle it. What would happen if he got robbed or caught? At that point, thinking of the risks involved, the boy became see-sawed by all the suggestions.

As he emerged from the haze, he found a note on the stacks that said, "Our son is your son. Take good care of him, and we shall reward you." He read it again and still found the message more baffling than comprehensible. It showed an exchange.

Once, Gusha told him about abducted children in China, he remembered. Their captors sold them for hard cash, and they would punish them by cutting off their hands if they tried to escape.

The story of finding him on a riverbank now sounded too plain to believe. He felt something more sinister behind it, such as they made him work hard on the field. But when he suspected he was a victim of kidnapping, a chill ran down his spine. Even after the captors had received the payment, they had still not released him. He speculated. As he stood there contemplating the situation, various trivial details from the past and the grudges he had held onto for years kept resurfacing. The more he elaborated on the imagined details, the more he felt like a victim.

Early, Gusha started capitalizing on Dongfang's insecurity stemming from his background as an abandoned child by inciting suspicion and fear among the masses. The effect slowly brought on Dongfang's tense and defensive bearing. It gave him the dread that someone might pound on him anytime.

Later on, he would reinforce Dongfang's fear and anxiety by providing a rather graphic illustration of some disturbing accounts, such as a woman who held out the hand of a kidnapped screaming child while a man was holding a large meat cleaver and chopping it off for punishing him for escaping. The whole illustration created a mental projection of the external threats he saw in other people as what was fear within himself.

Last, Gusha reminded Dongfang to take the first initiative to subdue people before they might do anything to him. And so, as Dongfang continued to let his emotions roil inside him, Gusha's advice again flashed through his mind. "You can just sit and do nothing.

You can just wait until they come to get you. But if you act, you have to do it thoroughly and leave no trace. That's our socialist blueprint. Don't be weakling. Show yourself what a great husband among men you can be. Take them all out, be it three generations. Leave no trace, be it relate to friends, relatives, or associates. It's not about right or wrong. It's not about moral or immoral. It's about domination and authority. And that's how we gain the upper hand and remain superior."

Thereupon, taking a pre-emptive measure preconditioned by Gusha in Dongfang had become part of Dongfang's natural response.

At the moment, as he chewed over any abuses, real or imagined, anything negative or unhappy in the past, however inconsequential, became consequential. And when he looked at his own hands, they filled him with fear, trepidation, and vengeance.

For all that, an even more threatening thought entered his mind. What if the family took the money and never shared it with him?

This sneaking suspicion ultimately presented him with the primeval urge to act.

For a while, the boy seemed to freeze on the spot. Eventually, he came out of his daze, put the box back where it was, along with the kaleidoscope, and then heaped all the other things as before.

During the next two days, Dongfang seemed to have immersed himself in a fog. He was silent all the time. If he ever talked, he uttered only in a dull monotone. Nobody knew what got into him. None paid much attention to him as people felt lightheaded on the last days of Ramadan. But to Dongfang, his mood worsened when food was unavailable to ease his hunger. He became tired, irritable, and extreme. But as he was tilting toward extremes, he was overtly fixated on ensuring his safety and was hell-bent on reaping a reward.

One night before bed, Dongfang filled two large jars of water and hid them under his bed.

In the wee hours of the last day of Ramadan, Dongfang furtively crept out of the house and headed straight to the well. Amidst the darkness, he focused on something in his hands. For quite a while, drifts of dry powder constantly and briefly floated in the air before disappearing below.

Afterward, he returned and quietly slunk back into his bed. But Dongfang could not go back to sleep. His heart raced fast while images of the liminal space between past and present and between present and future flicked rapidly in his mind. He thought about the kaleidoscope and the money. Vivid images of mountains, sea, and a new life flicked on and off through his mind. He would remain at that stage and expect to see the first day of light. But the daylight failed to come. Under the canopy of his eyelids, he waited on and off. For the first time, it seemed like an eternal wait to see the darkness dissolve.

The city officials came. The minute they arrived, they appeared ill at ease. As the investigation endured, they became even more impatient, bickering endlessly about the causes that almost wiped out the entire village. They traded back and forth about their views, talked their talk, and rowed their row, but they seemed to have yet to heed their heed. Then, a junior official sparred with others about whether to conduct some tests.

"That is a waste of time," a man with a pockmarked face, who seemed eager to brandish his enduring chops on the field, shot back. "It happened from time to time when people gathered to celebrate the end of Ramadan and got poisoned by consuming fake alcohol."

Others were quick to confirm the fact that people showed signs of poisoning. "He could be right."

Chimed in another eagerly. "What else could that be?"

They then went to see Dongfang. Finding him lying in bed, officials followed up on his condition. Dongfang told them he did not feel well the night before and did not attend the gathering. However, he was feeling better now; he assured them. After a moment, the boy also told the visitors the water from the well seemed to taste bitter.

A middle-aged man with a sheet of white cloth wrapped around his head like a turban pointed his forefinger up and quipped, "You one chewy! You know how lucky you are! You almost end up there before your time."

After giving Dongfang instructions on how to look after himself and the things he needed to do, they took leave.

Together, they went to the other side of the village, where the residents gathered to have their meals that night. There, they devoted time to conducting surveys, gathering facts, collecting samples, questioning those who survived the ordeal, and examining anything that could aid their inspection.

The investigation dragged into the midday before they concluded their probe.

On their way to their waiting vehicles, they kept wrangling over this and that for quite some time. At one point, despite their differences, they all had this sneaking suspicion that the well might get contaminated in the aftermath. To free themselves from such doubts and any other responsibilities, they settled with each other by flushing the well once and for all.

That night was the loneliest moment since Dongfang was left alone in a kindergarten over a decade ago. Besieged by stillness, the boy endured as lonely as an apparition in an empty house. The tranquil silence was unbearable, the hush deafening. He paced back and forth, touching objects and belongings his brothers had left behind. He also looked at some of his foster parents' personal effects. Ironically, their absence only made his heart grow fonder. Only at this moment did the boy question what he did. As he grappled with his internal conflicts, his eyes fell on the storage, and the thought of the cash comforted him. In the ensuing moments, he justified he would not sympathize with or forgive those who wronged him.

The next day, to overcome his loneliness, Dongfang started digging out books left behind by his third and last mentor. He had been reading them occasionally but had never given them much thought. These books focused on communist ideology written by different authors and Chinese communist versions of history. On this day, he took the time to study and contemplate each topic. He felt more invigorated from afterward.

By the end of the second week, his loneliness recurred once evening fell upon him. At that moment, Dongfang thought of many things days outdated, such as what he went through, the things he learned, and the concepts he acquired. In these loneliest hours, images of his tutors and their teaching flipped through his mind one after another.

Amid random thoughts and memories, he then recalled his third tutor once saying, "We don't have to tell them anything." Immediately afterward, a flashback of the parabola he learned from his second tutor followed. Then, a sudden haphazard thought entered his mind that both seemed somehow related. The more he thought about it, the more he was interested in how they were associated.

Time ticked away as he sat there dabbling with the idea. At one point, he tried to convey the concepts by jotting them down on paper now and then. Not long after, he came up with one.

The most extreme side of human nature. Human nature mirrored the parabolic curve $f(x)=x^2$ in quadrants I and II, with rational thought on the right and sophistry on the left. Reasoning, or logic, combined positivity to yield positive results, on the right.

Conversely, the fallacies presented on the left, like disinformation and conspiracy theories, pushed people to act on information without analyzing it. Inevitably, each side would amass its momentum and expand in different directions.

Rendering by this understanding, ironically, Cemile's teaching became the only one that seemed unsubstantial. That was because he used and set the notion of her moral teaching only as a point to reflect the opposite extremes that he intended to go after.

As he continued to examine and absorb the extreme side of human nature, a sudden thought hit him about what his last tutor once told him, "Imagine a scenario... what do you want to tell?"

Amid this imparting, Dongfang suddenly craved an affiliation with a particular group. From that imagined associating came strength and succor. And from that mental sustenance came strategic thinking. He then started writing a set of principles called 'The Dictates.' This set of propositions was:

1. **System Of Equality Of Inequality.**

   A. First premise. We have long been heirs to our conflict mindset, seeing everything as a struggle over who is in control of people.

   B. Second premise. We can not balance equality or fairness while remaining dictatorial.

   C. Conclusion. Maintaining structural inequality is the only choice: the strongest gets the most, the healthiest survive, the poorest die.

2. **Conditioned Hostile Responses.**

   A. Foreign entities be responsible for past aggression,

   B. Shadow internal failures by shifting accountability to past aggression,

   C. External entities are the sole bearers of all things' fault.

3. The Parabola Divide. We can bring about people's subconscious minds by limiting or devoid of intelligence input. When people follow routines without conscious reasoning, they will come to take on stoic resignation and silent consent without questioning. Eventually, they also accept unfairness, indignity, injustice, inequality, and subjugation as part of their life.

4. The Evolution Threshold. Free thinking is a natural evolution process. However, we lack all the knowledge or experience required to handle human nature. If left unchecked, it will keep evolving and expanding beyond the threshold. To compensate, we evoke the opposite extreme measure by undertaking the mass psychology of fear as a deterrence.

5. Socialist x Indeterminacy. A statement can both be and not be simultaneously and in the same respect.

Subsequently, all actions and moral judgments are neither true nor false. Thus, there are no actions or ethical responsibilities.

6. Ideology Immersion. This is a process that relies on secondary focus as propaganda to affect people's opinions, emotions, attitudes, and behavior. Focus includes, but is not restricted to, pandas, the Great Wall, the Olympic Games, astronauts, etc. Half the propaganda worth is half the battle won.

7. The Chosin Pattern. This pattern sees the masses as a decisive factor in offsetting the balance of winning against losing at any cost in wartime and peacetime, even at significant losses—the siege of Changchun, land confiscation, the Korean War, the 'Natural' Disaster, the Great Culture Destabilization, the June Fourth Movement, coronavirus measures. Similar measures, with corresponding magnitudes and characteristics, will emerge again in ensuing campaigns, wars, or future trading won and lost.

8. Insurgent Diplomacy. What we can plead to others can instead be used to destroy them, and what we can inspire aspirants to annihilate others can help adversaries obliterate them.

9. Natural Selection. There are always some idiots who like doing stupid things. By not recognizing our communism as natural selection, they opt themselves out and have selective patriots, one less, to survive. For that reason, the Communist Awards salute the improvement of the socialist genome by honoring those who willingly eliminated themselves in a spectacular manner!

10. The Final Struggle. We will awaken millions worldwide to the issue of human rights and encourage them to fight for a life of justice, equality, freedom, and human dignity.

* * * * *

After Dongfang completed the rough draft of the Dictates, he daydreamed about a new life with all the money he had. He imagined himself living large and eating high off the hog. He saw himself riding a bicycle in a park, watching TV while sitting on a comfortable sofa, or eating a fancy meal in a restaurant. Suddenly, he felt free as air as all things were within grasp.

Toward one afternoon, as he fantasized hither and thither, he unexpectedly received a letter. Holding it, he gawked at the envelope he had never seen. It was a white envelope with short red and blue marks running along the edges. It had two stamps with Chinese characters. Puzzled about who might have sent it, he carefully tore open the envelope along the edge. Once removing the letter, he unfolded it. It read:

To our dear son, the light of our life,

I am your father, your legitimate father. Your mother and I have never ceased thinking of you all these years. We always asked each other whether they treated you all right, kept you warm, or fed you well. Every time I think of you, I cannot eat or sleep. I have endured all these years in agony.

It all happened on one ill-fated afternoon. Your mother wheeled you in a stroller long after birth to a nearby market. At one point, your mother turned to make a payment for items she had just purchased. But when she turned around, she was shocked to find you gone. She frantically rushed here and there, but there was no sight of you. As the place teemed with shoppers bustling about with their shopping, her search was in vain. Later, we got contacted by your captor, who demanded ransom money. We did pay and waited and waited. But you were not released to us. After that, the trail went cold.

We never stopped thinking about you after your abduction. But as much as we agonized, we were also angry when thinking about what people could do. Not a day passed without looking for you, high and low, far and wide, hoping to get you back again one day. We never gave up. You don't know how much we care about you.

Despite years of torment, we felt ecstatic the day we finally located you through reliable evidence and proof. But what surprised us was that while all these years we were looking for you nearby, you ended up in a place halfway around the globe. That shocked us. How did you ever end up that far?

We sent this letter immediately, especially after we had just learned what had happened over there. You are worthy of praise for taking such a bold step in setting yourself free. We could never believe you could have done it

single-handedly, and we applaud you. In any determinate or indeterminate circumstances, to preserve order and control, we socialists always reserve the right to take necessary steps, even over the loss of lives. We shall always adhere to our unique way, as we have always adhered to. You did it exactly the way we would do it. That is remarkable.

Your mother and I are doing fine. We are cared for in special housing because of our health problems. Therefore, there is no need to contact us, but in the coming days, we will eventually come to see you. So, please, do not worry about us.

In the days to come, there will be someone there to assist you in re-establishing your identity and speed up your safe return. But, closer than you might have realized, you're on the home straight now. Your dear Father

At first, Dongfang needed help to grasp what the letter tried to convey. It confused him, as it could have presented the entire event the way he envisioned. It did not mention how he ended that far or how his father found him. Poring over the letter, he reread it over and over. Left with no other resources, he connected the dots using what the letter disclosed with his imagination. Gradually, everything seemed more coherent.

The confirmation of the kidnapping brought great relief to Dongfang. It also justified what he did to the Eibrahem family. His father's endorsement of his actions comforted and braced him even further. The guilt he had been bearing with him in recent days faded away instantly.

Over the next few days, Dongfang immersed himself in moments of contentment and freedom. His father's comment that he was 'worthy of praise for taking a bold step in setting yourself free' kept replaying in his head, transporting him with immense pleasure.

As he continued to bask in his euphoric sense of freedom, he met two Chinese nationals who helped arrange a return trip. Only then was he brought back to reality.

In the early autumn of the following year, Dongfang was ready to leave. His departure that day was inconspicuous, quiet, and sad. There was no farewell party; no one turned out to bid him goodbye, and no one accompanied him. Carrying only a few belongings, a copy of the Dictates, and the metal box, he went away with a somber expression.

Sitting at the back of a car that slowly wended its way to a ferry terminal, Dongfang cast his last wistful glance at the place he had called home for more than a decade.

The seed he planted near the house had grown into a barely 4-foot-tall sapling. Beyond it, he caught a glimpse of the field where he had lazed away for many of his carefree years. Images of a bygone age - the colorful room of the kindergarten, the halcyon days of childhood, a photo of Taafeef and Yasmin with his brothers in an olive grove, feluccas unhurried through the flow of the meandering river, the languid days in the farm listening to the sound of the wind sighing through the field, and the winding dirt road that hoarded the memory of years gone by - flipped in and out of his mind.

These images and memories overcome him with profound sadness. Then a feeling of uncertainty swept over him. Has the Eibrahem ever mistreated him? Were they his captors? If not, how did the family get that hideaway trove of cash?

As conflicting accounts kept roiling inside him, he fixed his eyes upon a fleeting glimpse of the streets on that balmy afternoon one last time. In that instant, he was overwhelmed with an acute sense of loss as a melancholy thought briefly entered his mind. "This could have been a good life."

* * * * *

Dongfang's fate and whereabouts had long been subject to discussion at his ancestor's house since his departure. They saw his disappearance as the remediable way out to disburden his father's mind of anxiety and distress. Gossip thus flew around, and the servants and other members knew all too well the reasons for his departure.

It all began not long after Dongfang was born. Concerned about his son's future, Nin Yige sought a fortune-teller's advice in a temple, wishing to learn more about his destiny in the ever-changing nation.

After a brief ceremony, the fortune-teller took out a cylinder that contained many fortune sticks and started shaking it while tipping it downward. Once a stick dropped onto the floor, the fortune-teller picked it up and interpreted the corresponding message that came with it. It said, "Boundless azure skies, home from home.

Cast asunder those within reach, home away from home."

No sooner than the message was out into the open, the seer, Master Yon Situ, led his father to a corner. Once there, he pointed his finger at the infant while his eyes bulged and screeched, 'This child will take out whoever is close to him.'

Upon hearing that, Nin Yige felt a chill run through his veins. He was so frightened that he nearly dropped the infant. He took the term 'whoever is close' meant to imply him. He perceived it as the comeuppance of his misdeed that ultimately gave way to this negative karma, the retribution he was the one to bear, eventually.

Once Nin Yige returned home, he remained distressed for days and preoccupied with his safety and legitimate family. Lest the worst might betide him, he perceived his illegitimate son as the bearer of this karma. For that reason, he must move Dongfang to prevent that fate from befalling him.

However, his father, contradictory as he was, was vacillating whether Dongfang should be 'sent' just as predicted by the prophecy or to be 'kept' as that might affront the heavenly will, which would eventually put him and others in harm's way.

As he continued ensnared in his inner conflicts, a dream he had one night would settle the outcome. In that dream, he found his infant son with glaring red eyes. He awoke with a start, soaked in sweat.

Thereupon, he gave in. He came to accept that his son was to be 'guided by heavenly will, bounded to strive under the skyline, inestimable, to reach his potential. His destiny to be somebody or nobody does not rest on our decision; it was a divine volition we chose not to offend.'

As a man who held an important post as transportation secretary, Dongfang could be the death knell for Nin Yige. If their affair were to become public, he could lose everything he had worked for over the past two decades and left forlorn of hope. Therefore, he convinced Dongfang's mother that 'the best course of action was to act on Dongfang's behalf. By sending him away, we will allow him to learn foreign things like wisdom, customs, and moral fibers that help expand his views about humankind.'

Thereupon, his father sent Dongfang away on that fateful night.

But as a man long habituated to taking harsh measures throughout his life, he summoned his caretaker back to his study room, stressing that he shall only bequeath the infant in a 'vacuum' state.

After that, Yang traversed the Continent south, often thinking about what Nin Yige meant whenever he entered another country. Not until he reached Egypt did he realize that 'the vacuum state' was where no return or outreach was possible. Yang thus laid the infant into a vessel at this junction halfway home and let it flow north.

Over the years after Dongfang had expatriated, the word 'asunder' kept churning in the back of Nin Yige's mind time after time. As it repeated so often, it rhymed with other sounds, either willfully or unintentionally, until it lost significance. Thenceforth, the superstitious effect lost its grip on him as it became neutralized.

A decade later, he took to napping one afternoon not long after his wife met her untimely death at the age of 50. He then heard someone pass on an articulately clear message, 'Over yonder, home straight home.'

After Nin Yige awoke, he found the occurrence of something incredible. He subsequently took the unworldly message, amid an early spring, when the air was pleasant and permeated with a sense of renewal, life, and hope, as a sign to resolve an affliction resulting from human frailty that had beset him all these years.

Yet, it was not until years later the tutor sent him a picture that would change the outlook.

In that picture, he saw a boy dressed in a traditional thobe with a slightly swarthy complexion standing alone in a field. His face scrunched up while his eyes squinted under the glaring sun. He looked like a rustic, homely farm boy who endured undue hardship.

When Nin Yige saw this picture, his emotional anguish overcame him, and he cried. What have I done? He questioned himself. What he saw was the boy that he had sent away, the boy whom the father now felt so strange and distant that he could not recognize.

Not long after, Nin Yige summoned Yang, the caretaker, and confided in him one late evening that 'Yesteryear, I knew why I believed what I believed. But today, I am baffled why I did what I did. Nature is always bewildering, and so is our mind. But times change, and we with time. Once the hour to right from wrong reckoned with, let not that hour lost.'

As the man now in his late fifties who had become mellow over the years, Nin Yige could not pretend to be at peace with the world. As long as Dongfang was still dawdling somewhere afar, it filled him with remorse and shame.

Dongfang's tutor contacted and assured him a year earlier that 'the boy is getting along with the Eibrahem family very well.' Nothing seemed to suggest his son was anything out of the ordinary or the way foretold. But, out of prudence and fear, he spurred the tutor on 'to instill the boy with our socialist core values to make sure he knows who he is and how to coexist in harmony with others.'

Thus, the notion of 'right from wrong' and 'home straight home' emerged.

Still, his father's eagerness to get Dongfang back vexed him. He spent countless nights in contemplation, trying to figure out how to explain why his son ended up in that situation. He blamed that overzealous caretaker for having left the infant way too far.

Yet, as the one who had sent his son away, he found himself in an awkward position to find a satisfactory answer to vindicate himself, making it even more complicated.

As he drained over the vexed question, he unexpectedly received a message from Dongfang's tutor much later that 'that Little Baobèi! He has taken out the whole village.'

When this message reached Nin Yige, it perturbed him to no end, not by the blasphemy but by the surprised expression of shock about what the boy did. He now realized the seer's precise warning proved not to be misguided. What disturbed him even more was the realization that it took the village to raise his child, but he, who would turn his back on them, rejected and buried their shared values and beliefs that nurtured him.

Yet, as shocked as he was, the father grasped it was the best explanation he had been seeking: whatever drove Dongfang to do what he did justified his action to secure freedom.

After all, Nin Yige reassured himself that 'once my son has carried out and fulfilled an act foretold, it would cancel out and annul the spell.' Thus, his father acted on what his son did and came up with a scenario in a market one afternoon, as described in his letter to Dongfang.

However, the letter ended on an ambiguous note by mentioning his 'underlying health problems' and stating, 'No need to contact us.' That seemed to betray his father's fear and trepidation. Those like Nin Yige, who familiarized themselves with using threats against others, would find themselves equally vulnerable when they perceived similar threats played upon them. Besides, just as foretold, Dongfang could remain unpredictable and dangerous. After all, what the boy had done to Taafeef and his family was unforgettable. Even though his father wasn't entirely sure how to address this threat, he let some distant relatives and servants interact with Dongfang, providing him with help and support while he devised a personal excuse to keep his son away for the time being.

On this day, as soon as the servants learned about the homecoming, the atmosphere in the house had been fraught with uncertainties. All kinds of helpers, from old-timers to newcomers, huddled together. They whispered noisily to each other, occasionally erupting into a full clamor, like a small-scale vocal work of a symphony that raised and fell. They also grilled each other about what phrases like 'taking out' or 'anyone close to him' could mean.

At last, their hesitancy and suspicion finally gave way to an inauspicious omen. Then everyone in the room ran riot every which way. They pushed. They shoved. They dashed helter-skelter in a mad scramble for the exit. Outside, while those dogs and chickens, either sensing danger in the wind or seeing others rush pell-mell out of the courtyard, they too bolted headlong after them, leaving the house inside out all deserted.

The outcome came totally without warning. The only warm message Dongfang found was a note on the table at the main entrance. It contained scribbles almost illegible. "Welcome home."

Standing in the middle of the courtyard, a whirlpool of emotions seized him. The day he left, Dongfang was still a helpless newborn infant in his mother's arms. But the day he returned, on the cusp of adulthood, he was now a boy with broad shoulders. His thick, dark eyebrows and square jaw gave him a look of solemnity and composure.

For a moment, Dongfang felt lost in the sands of time. A bygone era seemed to slip through his mind in a great rush. He saw a simulation of life play out in front of him where his siblings frolicked in the courtyard with each other while his parents and other adults chattered on merrily or busied around. But this merry scenery of reenactment, imbued with warmth and happiness, had taken here in the bygone era without his presence. Instead, he was left alone, often gazing at the meandering river.

As he stood there wanting his parents, siblings, and others, a sense of great uncertainty and confusion swept through him, making his heart grow more bitter and resentful. In an ensuing moment, he questioned if the Eibrahems were his captors. But if they were not, those who deliberately excluded him from this picture should also shoulder a great wrong as that of his captors. And if the Eibrahems indeed were not his captors, he would make those who were responsible paid for what he did to Eibrahem and his family.

The first person who ever entered his mind was Gusha, his third and last tutor.

As questions and doubts continued to roil inside Dongfang's mind in great turmoil, groups of geese honked overhead as they flew south in a skein of V-shaped formation. It was getting windy outside, and the air was cutting. Dead leaves fluttered off the trees, but a flag in a distant field stuck in its post remained still. Aside from that, everything all over was eerily quiet.

A GREEN EXPANSE OF GRASSLAND

Shemshidin had no recollection of how he found himself confined in this place. He remembered being in his garden during springtime with his wife, Meryem. Both enjoyed watching the cherry blossoms in full bloom. Meryem was cheerful, moving in her blithe spirit while a smile spread across her face.

The next moment, Shemshidin saw his wife standing still, her head inclined. The cheerful expression she had earlier faded away instantly, replaced by a profound melancholia. Slowly, she turned to Shemshidin with sorrowful eyes and said, "The evanescence of life is much like the ephemeral beauty of cherry blossoms. We could only cherish each moment while it lasts." She then shed her tears and confided to Shemshidin, "Then while we live, in love let's so persevere, That when we live no more, we may live ever."

Upon hearing that, Shemshidin tried to approach his wife to offer her some tender and loving words. But his outreach remained distant, regardless of how hard he tried. Just as he was making another attempt, he suddenly found himself in a compound filled with endless corridors of cells where people lived in confinement. As he struggled to understand his surroundings, two guards led him to a large room and forced him to kneel among the other inmates.

Initially, Shemshidin fought back, explaining to the guards that he was looking for his wife when he suddenly found himself detained. He insisted that there had been a mistake and demanded they let him go.

But as he was rounded up with thousands of others in a vast concentration complex, he realized this was not a figment of imagination.

As Shemshidin became confused by things he could not comprehend, he found himself wandering down an unending corridor. At the next turn, he came in contact with an elder friend of his, Ehmet Dandan. Beloved by the townsfolk, Ehmet had been a teacher in his hometown for many decades.

When he saw someone he recognized, Shemshidin was overwhelmed with intense emotion and burst into tears.

Shemshidin told Ehmet he had gotten lost and wanted to see his wife. The panic-stricken Shemshidin rushed at Ehmet, grabbing and shaking his arms. "I don't know where I am. Why am I here? Where is my wife?"

Ehmet quietly led Shemshidin to a corner and said, "You must do your best to stay alive. If you die, no one will know you have ever existed."

With a grim expression, Ehmet said, "This whole thing has not come as a surprise."

After a brief silence, Ehmet ended the conversation by urging Shemshidin, "Be strong!"

By now, Shemshidin had to accept that what had happened to him was real. He must do whatever was necessary to free himself from this ordeal and reunite with his wife.

Shemshidin now realized that his fate was precarious. He reckoned that to secure his freedom, he would have to relinquish his dignity by stooping low and submitting to demands. That meant abandoning all efforts to uphold his human dignity and thus forfeiting the essential meaning of being human. Regrettably, that was a harsh reality he needed to come to terms with.

The thought that Shemshidin might not even exist perturbed him greatly. But if he was hoping for miracles to secure his release or praying for divine intervention, this unsettling possibility overshadowed everything. It meant that the chance of seeing his wife again might never occur.

After returning to his cell, he couldn't stop thinking about the upcoming review board. Initially, he had always struck a defiant attitude and followed instructions halfheartedly. But the longer he lingered there, the more pliable he became. He promised to study harder and memorize the party lines to impress the teacher. Deep down, he understood this was the only way to free himself.

The review board finally came, and Shemshidin was pinning all his hopes on this moment. When it was his turn, his heart beat fast with nervousness while his mouth was parched.

Mr. Shang, his interviewer, was a man in his late 40s with immature gray hair. He was an imperious man who was too condescending even to glance at Shemshidin when he entered. While being put off by his bourgeois hauteur, Shemshidin noticed that Mr.

Shang was wearing a black business suit with a Mao pin badge fastened to the upper part of the left lapel, striking a somewhat jarring image for a captor.

Shang started the interview by asking Shemshidin for his name. As he was jotting it down, his pen was not writing. He moved his pen and drew some scribbles on another paper. But the nib was still not writing. Frustrated, Shang sighed, "Umm," and briefly held the clogged ballpoint pen out to Shemshidin to look at it before taking it back to share the experience with him.

This behavior stuck with Shemshidin as odd as it was discordant with a man of extreme impassivity. Shemshidin also noticed that Mr. Shang maintained a cold, emotionless stare with his stone-cold face throughout, and there were little head movements when he spoke.

After going through Shemshidin's record, Shang asked without looking up, "How do you feel about being here?"

To please his captor, Shemshidin replied, "I am thankful to the Party for providing me with this education, which will offer me a promising future."

Shemshidin then replicated a passage from an inmate and repeated, "I grew up in the bosom of a blessed party, studied to my heart's content without worrying about anything in this world. There is more unknown love than known and accepted. I didn't know how to react to the happiness that surrounded me."

Shang remained emotionless and continued his interrogation. "How do you feel now compared to when you first arrived?"

With bated breath, Shemshidin mechanically recited tired clichés. "I used to be a bad person. It all has changed now. I have become a better person and pledge my loyalty to the Party."

Shang continued to comment with his quiet and staid comportment by giving a perfunctory nod with his somber expression. "I certainly believe this education will benefit you. The more you learn, the better person you become."

Shemshidin concurred. "I am a better person now. I have had no troubles here, as you can see. It has been so long since I last saw my wife. I hope to reunite her and restart our lives."

Shang nodded again without looking at Shemshidin. "I believe you will reunite with her eventually, only when you can prove to be an even better person."

Upon hearing this, Shemshidin felt a surge of panic.

Shang finally looked at Shemshidin and replied, "Your record shows your mark just above untrustworthy. If you can get that middle mark to be trustworthy, I'm happy to see you graduate."

In an instant, Shemshidin felt all hope had vanished. He would have to continue to endure his time. He suddenly felt lost and became disoriented. He attempted to reason, but only with an incoherent skein of words. "I... I have done everything... everything as best I could. I didn't... did nothing wrong."

Shang, speaking in a soothing voice, said, "Relax! You will do better. Trust me, earning the teacher's confidence will lead to better grades."

But wise counsel could no longer comfort a desperate man. At this moment, Shemshidin's anguish and despair awakened his deep anger. Suddenly, he became defiant and confronted. "What have I done? If I disappear or if I die, I want the world to hold you responsible."

The unexpected remark did not seem to infect Shang, who was used to indifference. Instead, it drew a snicker from him as he gazed at the table and tapped his fingers.

After a moment of dead silence, Shang surprised Shemshidin by saying, "OK. Come with me."

At that point, the sudden change in Shang's reaction confounded Shemshidin, but he silently followed Shang out of the room into a narrow passage.

They emerged into a long corridor before taking the stairs to the lower floor. Continuing forward, they navigated another long hall, passing many metal doors. Nearer to the end of the corridor, Shang instructed a nearby guard to unlock a large metal gate.

Once the door swung open, Shemshidin saw a green expanse of grassland where a long, winding road through green hills stretched endlessly into the blue sky.

Shemshidin, at this moment, seemed not to comprehend what he saw. What appeared in front of him was a green expanse in the middle of where the complex buildings were supposed to be. But seeing the stretch of open grassland before him, he felt immense joy and ran to the opening.

Boji the Canine was in a dream, dreaming of itself as a human called Shemshidin. The moment Boji saw the green expanse of grassland in his dream, he was roused from a deep sleep with an inexplicable joy. He hurled himself up from his slumber and dashed toward that opening in the night still.

But almost immediately, he smashed into an invisible object, sending Boji on one violent rebound. The impact left Boji lying on the ground, bruised.

It then dawned on him he was still confined within a large enclosure. Metal bars encircled the pound on three sides and vast concrete on the fourth. On that fourth side, a large mural adorned the entire concrete wall. It depicted a green expanse of grassland as scenery.

The Mother of All Antidotes

Tiantian Cao had just returned from Tongla after visiting her uncles and aunts before she was due to leave for overseas. Upon returning, her mother told her that something had happened to her grandfather during her absence. He now accommodated himself in a senior home in Jiexing, south of the Yangtze River. Her mother asked her to wait a week before giving him a visit. Tiantian thought she had time before leaving.

After his wife passed away, her grandfather moved in with them and had been living there for the past thirteen years. Known as Kanan Cao, he was initially a company manager. Amicable and approachable, he was well-liked among many people and workers. As a man who exhibited no pride and was always open and honest with people, his popularity grew beyond the company's threshold.

A gentle and even-tempered man, Kanan stood six feet tall with a slim figure that befitted an athlete. He walked unhurriedly, steady steps, giving him the composure of equanimity that cut a fine figure.

His dark hair was tinged with premature white, however. People said he gained his white hair after his wife's death, bleached by the sorrow of long, lonely hours.

Frequently, some well-connected circles invited him to attend promotional events and other social gatherings. His primary functions were to preserve the honor of his present or other companies, make connections, promote some product lines, or build greater trust among the public.

His relationship with the public and his akin affiliations unexpectedly brought him to new heights in his late 50s. A well-respected associate suggested Kanan take on the role of a security deputy. The suggestion quickly gained traction among people from all walks of life.

However, his daughter, Fan An, and her husband were dubious about this whole aggregation. She told her husband her father was not a proper choice for this post. But why would someone recommend him in the first place? Even though her father was a member of the Party, being a member was not as glorious as one might think, for China claimed to have more communist members than the total graduates of all the Western countries combined.

Yet, despite her questioning whether her father was fit and proper for the role, her skepticism soon grew remote. Eventually, it fell into oblivion after her father assumed that post. A year later, Tiantian was born.

On his last day as manager, the company staged a farewell party. Employees and friends alike attended. They shared many kind thoughts, followed by more tender words—You'll be sorely missed, Take care, Don't forget us, Come and see us —and mouthed more words of fond regard that comforted the hearts of those who cared.

Among the attendees at the party that day was a man known as Ahfa, who was a high school math teacher.

Ahfa was not very popular because of his rustic, unsophisticated manners. A man in his unfailing tacky outfits, along with his clumsy and awkward bearing, he often evoked an image of a country bumpkin. Despite that, Kanan liked his sincerity and his lack of pretension.

On this last day, Kanan and Ahfa sat outside at a table on that warm summer afternoon. In that idle hour, they chatted on a series of nothing topics, shared some tidbits here and there, or waxed lyrical about the old days.

At one point, Kanan talked about children. Ahfa then mentioned and recounted a conversation with a child the other day. He told Kanan, "This kid spoke as if he knew everything. At one point, he touched on a hoary tale of injustice in which British troops bayoneted many protestors and laughed at them in front of the monument to heroes." "Monument? Protestors?" Kanan interjected with a rising inflection.

Ahfa nodded and continued, "There was something wrong when I heard of that. He referred to the event in the twentieth century, but someone mixed it up with the one in the nineteenth century. It is treacherous. Can you believe what they do to them?"

Kanan was not sure whom Ahfa referred to as 'they.' He assumed he knew what Ahfa meant, so he grinned at his apologetic grin and protested, "No, no. I don't believe they did that. It comes down to a few bad elements, that's all."

Ahfa then offered a word of caution. "Maybe. But be careful. When someone alternates a term and uses it to cancel out one thing with another, it can also cancel you out. It can betray whoever falls for it, regardless of their side. When they can swap one thing with another indiscriminately, you can tell what that result could be. It is a method that is convenient, clean, and above reproach. You could call that 'impartial annulment.' Do you understand what I mean?"

Still, Kanan objected once more. "No, no. They don't do such a thing."

Yet, as he spoke, he had a presentiment that despite Ahfa being the one who put forth a supposition, Kanan would be the one to bear the onus of proof to the contrary himself.

Ahfa, at that point, thought he should not push Kanan too far. Kanan was no exception, much like other doctrinaire mules who preferred to rest on their stiff, unyielding ideology rather than on a comfortable pillow. He might strain one side of his neck by extracting it from him.

Ahfa shook his head and said, "That's fine. It's the luck of the draw."

He then cast a sideways glance, and on his lips, there spilled a word of warning. "Latish wisdom may one day come at a price."

Time flew by fast. It had been over ten years since they had held that conversation. Kanan afterward assumed his role without hesitation. Despite his boss being twenty years his junior, Kanan gave his greatest regard, heeded instructions, and worked days and nights without ebbing.

Unlike his daughter, who felt dubious, her father had been gliding through his days and had no challenges since then. Some attributed it to life being fair to Kanan. So blessed was Kanan, others said.

Yet, not all mundane roads would lead directly to their destination. One might wonder where that road beyond would lead. Around a corner, as it may, comes an open road through lush green fields and flowery meadows or to a high cliff where great ocean waves below crash and bounce.

At the east end of a quiet cul-de-sac, there stood a 10-story rectangular apartment block. All apartment units came with recessed balconies, which rendered an image of a gigantic pigeonhole cabinet. On the ground, metal fences surrounded the property on all four sides. At the back, it overlooked a broad river, which continued its passage east until it ended its journey on the open sea.

The street leading to the building was quiet. London plane trees, thick with green leaves, lined both sides. When the spring breeze gently sighed through the treetops, the soft whispering sounds exuded the tranquility and serenity of the surroundings even more noticeably. But that morning, that peacefulness did not last.

It was here, an unforeseen event of the day going to unfold.

On that morning in April, Kanan's boss informed him that a contagious arthropod was at large. He was concerned it might pose particular risks to the public and instructed Kanan to remain vigilant. Before ending the call, he advised Kanan to prepare for further instructions.

An hour had passed when Kanan's boss rang again. This time, he told Kanan the arthropod had slipped to an apartment block at the east end. He instructed him to implement and carry out "our precise and scientific spare-none enforcement" and to assist the enforcers of all three forces.

When Kanan heard of the terms' spare none' and 'all three forces,' he became utterly stiff. He realized how serious the situation was. He remembered having never encountered these terms since he held this post. Failing to complete his task was equivalent to being consigned to the back of the beyond. The message came through loud and clear.

At around 9 a.m., the wailing of police sirens broke the serenity of that area. Several police cruisers barreled down the street, followed by a column of black SUVs.

A military-like unit comprising some twenty members in black outfits sported an acronym, SWAT, arrived at the scene first. Immediately upon their arrival, they rushed toward the building and violently shoved anyone outside or near the entrance back into the building. One elderly woman fought back and yelled, "What's going on?" Without a word, the two officers grabbed her shoulders, one on each side, while the other grasped the back of her neck and pushed her head down. Together, they forced her back into the building and shouted, "Stay inside!"

They locked the front and back entrances and fastened the gate to the metal fence encircling the apartment building.

Next came three trucks transporting troops armed with rifles mounted with bayonets. Upon their disembarkment, they hurried and spread out the entire perimeter of the property to ensure that no one could leave.

A short while later, a helicopter was hovering above the building. Soldiers rappelled from the aircraft and landed on the roof, where they stood guard.

Amid an exceptional number of law enforcers and armed forces swarmed the cul-de-sac, encircling the entire perimeter, a soldier detected an ant trying to sneak to the other side. It prompted his attention, and he immediately stomped on the poor thing, completely flattening it. He then bawled, "We have total control."

Meanwhile, the apartment building residents went downstairs to investigate what had happened. They discovered that both the main entrance and the back exits were locked. After a brief commotion inside the building, people started making rackets and demanding to let them out.

Stern messages from a loudspeaker held them back outside: "Stay put and obey orders. Those who make disturbances will be prosecuted and punished harshly." Afterward, the protests died down.

As the troops and SWAT team quietly stood guard, a rumbling noise in the distance suddenly interrupted their pervasive silence. As onlookers turned their heads, they saw a column of tanks slowly coming into view, grumbling and rumbling toward the apartment complex through the city streets. Once the tanks took their positions, their turrets rotated, squeaking and groaning until the guns aimed at the building. After that, the guns slowly raised to an angle.

Almost at the same time as the tanks arrived, two warships were sailing past the estuary, slowly making their way to where the apartment block stood. Once they reached the vicinity, at a distance off the stretch of the coastline, they lowered their anchors and aimed their big guns at the building.

By now, the blockage had drawn a large crowd of onlookers who got accustomed to watching anything exceeding an ordinary experience. Any magnificent display, formation, or design would arouse their patriotism, much like the splendid Olympic opening ceremony, which gave them a sense of awe at the human exhibition.

As the situation unfolded, an elderly gardener, blithely working at the back of the building, was oblivious to his surroundings. Soon after, he wanted to return to the building, but he found it locked and demanded to be allowed in. He was given a short "No" in response.

The man clapped back, "Then let me out."

But the poor man was yet to be slapped with another 'No.'

Towards the afternoon, Kanan received a phone call from the seal-off area seeking permission to allow two residents to leave for health reasons. Afterward, Kanan called his boss, who instructed him not to permit anyone to exit, regardless of the circumstances.

His boss ended the call by giving him an earful. "We must resolutely strike hard against infiltration and sabotage activities by hostile forces—no compassion, no concession, no matter what. A revolution is not a dinner party, writing an essay, painting a picture, or embroidery. Got that?"

The lockdown dragged on into the night and continued into the second day. Then, from the second day, it extended to the third day.

Shortly after 2 p.m. on the third day, a great commotion erupted inside the building. People were screaming and yelling about the fire. They were banging on the main door. Some struggled to break the windows. But their attempts were futile as safety bars clasped firmly on all the windows on the main floor. Desperate, they screamed, yelled, and cursed while others implored others to let them out.

Shortly afterward, plumes of black smoke were billowing from the third floor on the right side of the building. Despite the desperate pleas, security forces remained unmoved. However, an official in the area called and informed Kanan about the fire.

Kanan immediately called his boss again. Without inquiring about the fire, his boss gave a pithy instruction: "Stay put."

Amid the looming threat of the fire and the safety of the people inside, out of nowhere, there descended a group of protestors who were holding a piece of paper challenging the inhuman treatment of people inside the building across the street.

Once it came to the attention of a group of security guards, they wasted no time. Immediately, they swarmed the protesters with their rifles fixed with bayonets, dispersed them, and arrested a score of ring leaders. But to their surprise, they also spotted another group of protesters down the streets.

At this dicey moment, the security guards faced an imminent threat - protestors on one side and the fire at their back, which engulfed the floors above it and spread fast. Amid this urgency, Kanan called again and informed his superior of the development. After some hesitation, his boss eventually instructed Kanan to let the people out.

He then summed it up. "The primary target has been located and impounded. I declare we have a total victory."

As the main entrance finally unlocked, residents rushed outside, pushing and shoving each other in a chaotic scramble. Some were coughing, gasping, wheezing, and crying. Others collapsed on the lawn, while those who succumbed to the smoke needed help to drag off the building.

At the moment of the evacuation, a Caucasian family of three emerged from the apartment block. As they were hobbling out, an official greeted them in Mandarin: "I am happy to see you all well. You Americans are lucky to live here. China is undoubtedly the safest country in the world."

Upon hearing this, the man presumed to be the father got the bilious look of someone having a piece of bitter food in his mouth that he could neither spit out nor swallow. His face flushed while his eyes emitted glints of hate and mistrust to a point where he seemed no longer able to hold on to the compression building up inside him. And then, like a shot, he blurted out one forceful interjection in a foreign language: "Stronzo!"

After the man let fly with his homemade insult, he turned and addressed his family,

"Continua a camminare. semplicemente ignoralo."

They then continued their way, paying no more attention to the man left standing there staring, staring with his emotionless expression.

The next day, family members and friends of those who perished in the lockdown arrived at the hospital to claim the remains. Unfortunately, some victims did not survive because of panic attacks or other underlying health conditions. Others succumbed to smoke inhalation. Still, some, caught in long dark corridors filled with black smoke on different floors, got disoriented and convinced themselves that the end was nigh, leading them to jump from windows high above.

There, relatives and friends gathered to place the bodies of their loved ones into coffins. Among them reposed the body of a young female teacher from South Africa. Afterward, they had the coffins brought to a large parking lot that led to the back entrance of a funeral home.

There, they hauled, wheeled, and dragged the coffins along, forming a long queue under a scorching sun in the afternoon.

* * * * *

The day after the lift of the lockdown, Kanan kept occupied with a steady stream of visitors, including friends, colleagues, and other officials. They all came to congratulate him on successfully resolving a crisis.

Amid the profuse compliments and lavish presents, the pleasure given on him was never barren. Swaddled in pride and complacency, Kanan was giddy all day with big compliments, from being labeled as 'talented' to 'a lantern of hope' to 'a beacon of social order.' Instinctively, those who came under the pretense of congratulating him on seeking favors offered even more glaring commendations.

The endless stream of visitations lasted all day in his office and continued at home until 5 p.m. Then, at long last, after dinner, he could relax and enjoy the tranquility in his study room.

Shortly after 7 p.m., his daughter told him Jian Gang was coming to see him. Kanan told her to send him in.

Jian Gang was a long-standing friend. They had known each other since their youth. After graduation, their paths diverged as they pursued different fields, yet their friendship remained fast.

As an accountant, Jian Gang was known for his honesty and did not mince words. He shot straight and would not put up with nonsense. Yet, not only did he seem too straightforward, but he also came across as clumsy and impulsive for Kanan's liking, who thought that might bring more harm than good.

Both were glad to see each other as they exchanged many traditional pleasantries. Jian Gang then broached the subject of the siege days before.

The choice of the word 'siege' surprised Kanan. Even more contrasting to others, Jian Gang had offered no congratulations from the very beginning.

Kanan's smile dropped as their cordial greeting when they met gave way to a sober topic. He explained, "There was an arthropod slipping into the building. We have to order a lockdown to ensure public safety."

"From outside?" Jian Gang quizzed him with a puzzled glance.

"Yes." came a flat voice.

Jian Gang nodded and said, "And about the news conference this afternoon..."

Kanan frowned, as if puzzled. But as a man who habitually showed his little humility, Kanan kindly replied, "Conference! Oh, that is flattering. I don't get used to all the praises..."

At that moment, feeling lightheaded and dizzy from the big compliments he had received that afternoon, Kanan appeared to perform an ancient ritual as he gazed at the ceiling.

While holding out his hands, he cupped his left palm over the fist of his right hand and chanted, "My good fortune could not have prevailed had it not been blessed by the Party."

Jian Gang immediately interrupted him with a wave of the hand. "No, no, not like that. Not like that. Put your hands down. Put your hands down."

Kanan seemed abruptly brought back to earth. Lowering his hands, he asked, "No? What then?"

Jian Gang replied bluntly, "Your boss said you overstepped the line." Kanan drew his face into a scowl. "What?"

Jian Gang looked intense and said, "They seemed to have trouble explaining what had happened."

Kanan's face grew darker. "And what?"

Jian Gang shook his head and said, "It is not good. Your boss said you did so without approval. He said that had he not intervened in time, the outcome could be even more inconceivable. He also quoted, 'We remain committed to peacefully resolving differences and disputes through dialog and consultation, and support all efforts conducive to the peaceful settlement of crises.'"

When Jian Gang filled Kanan in on what his boss did, Kanan's memories of previous generations' mistreatment instantly hit him as an execration.

The more Kanan listened, the more he seemed to hold up his breath. His complexion now turned purpled, now darkened. But if Jian Gang expected to see him red with rage, he did not. Instead, Kanan's face now became so pale, white as a bedsheet.

Suddenly, Kanan swung his right arm, grabbed his left shoulder, and let loose with a yelp. He slipped from his chair and slumped into a heap on the floor.

At that moment, Jian Gang could see Kanan's face contorted in great pain as he twisted and groaned, mouth gasping for air.

Jian Gang immediately leaped to his feet. While dashing here and there futilely, he stripped on a piece of rug on the floor, which sent him tumbling. Instinctively, he tried to cushion his fall with his right hand, which amassed half of his body weight and came pounding down on Kanan's chest. That gave Kanan a jolt and a yelp.

As Jian Gang tried clumsily to regain his footing, he noticed Kanan's appearance remained bloodlessly pale.

Without further delay, Jian Gang yelled at Kanan's daughter and her husband, who were in the next room. "Help! Help! Something is not right!"

* * * * *

The doctor said Kanan was extremely fortunate. The man suffered a massive heart attack but survived. The doctor said it was a miracle compared to a salted fish that came to life. Only

246

Heaven could have vouchsafed him. For that reason, he believed Kanan would thrive and prosper.

After two weeks of intensive care in the hospital, the doctor had him transferred to a nursing home, where he continued to recuperate. Two nurses were assigned to take care of him. But, much to their disappointment, Kanan paid little attention to them, for he was sitting at the edge of his bed, staring at the blank wall all day long.

At first, a nurse, out of concern, came to sit beside him and asked, "What's wrong?" Looking somewhat lost and confused, Kanan turned and replied, "I was sandbagged." A dotard he has become, they said.

Two weeks had passed, and people were surprised to see Kanan no longer sitting on the edge of his bed, staring at the blank wall. Instead, he paced back and forth in his room, occasionally smiling his bitter smile while bobbing his head as if he had hit on some revelations all day long.

The man has gone senile, a milder form of dotard, they said.

At the end of another two weeks, Tiantian finally swung by to see her grandfather. To her surprise, her grandfather looked cheerful and acted usually, which was not exactly how her mother described him, saying, 'Half his mind is forgetful while the other half is neglectful.'

After a brief exchange with Tiantian, Kanan inquired after everyone. At the mention of Tiantian's mother, Kanan seemed to grow nostalgic about the old days and said, "Your mom and I still talk a bit these days, but we used to talk a lot more."

He continued, his tone tinged with regret. "Life is always changing. I remember when you were born, I brought you a lot of gifts. Your mom and dad might remember that. But then time passed swiftly, and now you've grown into a teenager."

Kanan then descended into complete silence, and Tiantian could tell by the expression on her grandfather's face that he was miles away, thinking of days gone by.

After a moment, Kanan regained his attention and asked, "How old are you now?" "12."

"And where are you going to?" "Guo wai."

Kanan nodded rhythmically and murmured, "To wherever that will bring a different outlook on life, to wherever that a system can bring out the best in people."

Seeing her grandfather's rueful look, Tiantian assured him, "I will come back after I finish."

At first, Tiantian thought that would please her grandfather. But instead of looking well pleased, Kanan deflected, "Everyone, at a certain stage, must learn to release attachment to the outcome itself."

Tiantian, with a scowl on her face, replied, "I am sorry?"

"Did you know the ancestors of Polynesians hail from a different place, each bringing their contributions, honoring their natural rights, and developing a unique identity?"

Tiantian still looked puzzled. "What you are saying?"

Knowing his granddaughter was in her befuddled state, Kanan attempted to clarify. "If attachment is an evolutionary function, then the part that follows, or detachment, is also an evolutionary process. If they had done that, everyone could have done it."

"Detachment?" That was the only word Tiantian caught on to. It, subsequently, reminded her of what her mom had said earlier, 'Your grandfather being not in his right mind half the time.'

Her grandfather nodded gratifyingly.

Her grandfather continued. "What I say is that surviving under socialism is not for everybody. You see! Being cruel, unsympathetic, and manipulative are the elements of survival in this system. When you gain authority over people, you can exploit them as a conversion for your gains. Together, they form the typical model that decides who the socialist survival of the fittest is. But if you were given a choice at a crossroads, the decision is yours."

Tiantian still had a perplexed look. "Elements of survival?"

Kanan, who appeared to be immersing himself in his monologue, continued with a bob of his head and said, "How did it come about, and why did it happen that way? It is something that no one has ever explained to you. I will share it now, once and for all. But keep in mind that it will take time to understand. Even if that makes little sense, hold on to it quietly. One day, it will resonate with you."

Tiantian silently gave a slight bob of her head. After a brief pause, Kanan then carried on,

"A hundred years ago, when Bertrand Russell, a British mathematician, wrote an essay on whether science could bring happiness, a group of Chinese individuals pursued a different path in search of something completely different. Unlike Mr. Russell, these men were not seeking a source of happiness. Instead, they aimed to find something to bring about drastic changes and cure all problems and social ills.

"As they journeyed through the continent of Europe, they found a plant in Germany cultivated by a man who suffered from horrible diseases. In his quest to cure his frightening illness, this botanist sunk deeper and deeper into despair and was frenziedly looking for remedies not only to heal himself but also to manifest his self-hatred to ease his suffering.

"When the Chinese group met this botanist and explained their needs, the man advised them that the plants needed to be more sophisticated. The botanist suggested waiting, informing them he was cultivating the plants to produce an antidote. The group, however, having yet to acclimate to a foreign lifestyle, became impatient and reckless. They swiped one of his plants while the botanist was in deep slumber and fled under darkness.

"If they had known, they could have avoided fate. It is unclear if the horrible diseases caused the creation of the plant or if the belief in such a plant helped manifest his

self-hatred. However, it is beyond question that when the individual sought treatment with the plant, his mental condition only intensified as his disease worsened. As his conditions worsened, he further instilled his self-hatred into the plant, creating a vicious cycle. Thus, anyone who touched this plant would inherit a life-changing malady eternally.

"Even though chance favored the prepared mind, discovering the plant was hardly a serendipity. In truth, it was a curse in disguise - a precipice gamble for a desperate cure, a lethal quest for a mortal end, poison for poison.

"They brought it back to China, albeit knowing nothing about it. All they learned from this botanist was a theoretical, fanciful version of what this plant could do. Thus, they tinkered with it, dabbled with it, and even romanticized it with large swaths of humanity.

"As they experimented with the plant, at one stage, they thought they had eventually developed an antidote. To find a solution, they rushed headlong and administered it to their circles and members, hoping to create a better human prototype. Little did they know they had turned it into a poisonous plant. This cure, thought to be the mother of all antidotes, ended up poisoning them all.

"At that stage, they became psychotic and delusional, resulting from a plant-induced psychosis and losing all their identity. Like the precursor before them from whom they purloined the plant, they fell heir to the execration of self-hatred from that man. They resorted inwardly to extreme principles and cruel methods, growing into an obsession that borders on anal-retentive romanticism. Yet, being too obsessive, they are, at the same time, too cautious to state their ruthless desires. Ineluctably, not since the dawn of Chinese history has an entity evolved into a conflated artist by day, a radical by night.

"Like the precursor before them, they have distanced themselves from humanity. They have become vindictive, vicious, and brutal, deliquescing into the present embodiment of good with cruelty—the implementation of cruel practices to maintain good.

"They also rely on science and technology to strengthen their control. However, in contrast to Russell's belief that science is a source of happiness, they are bent on using science to enforce physical and mental restraints. Thus, the aftermath sees the culmination of moral turpitude and the making-up of a soulless counterfeit of humanity."

As Kanan finished, he bent over and rested his forearms on his thighs. He continued, "Deriving from facts and practices, what we inherit is a political system and theory that sees the end justifies humans as inferior by nature. Owing to that fact, you should also know another reality as strict directives implanted in your mind. The moment you came to this life, you entered a lease contract on terms you could not dictate; you became part of a socialist mechanism without consent, without free will. The person you see through the looking glass is a matching entity of the implant itself, not you. You might delusively think that you are in complete control of yourself. But that part of awareness is, in fact, a socialist consciousness that was forced into you in earlier times to ensure a smooth transition from formative years to adulthood and beyond. Your sense of control is the doctrinaire agency. Because of that, you can not tell right from wrong, moral from immoral."

At that moment, a female attendant entered the room and announced, "Mr. Cao, it's time for your checkup."

He turned toward the attendant and nodded his head.

Kanan continued, "Keep this in mind: one of the crucial characteristics of civilization is to foster the integrity of men and women. If a system, like apples on an apple tree, spoils from the outside, there's still a chance to save it. But if all the apples rot from the core outward, seeing branches heavy with comely red apples knowingly as they all rot is a tragic sight to behold. That's it. Hoping my rendering of the story will help you down the road. And, as my impartment desires, a person of integrity you will one day become."

At that moment, Tiantian seemed to look a bit stupefied after her grandfather's lengthy talk, but remained still and silent.

Kanan got up and walked Tiantian to the hallway. As Tiantian bid him farewell at the door, he whispered something into her ear and sent her away. He stood by the door watching Tiantian until she passed from sight into an elevator.

Two weeks later, Tiantian left.

As she crossed the border that day, she walked down a long, winding road through green hills that gracefully sloped into the vast blue sky. Patches of wildflowers swayed in the breeze across the fields, their blossoms scenting the air. Hither and yon, all life thrived, flourishing under the bright sun and blue sky.

Stepping into the openness of the free world comes all the possibilities and probabilities. Yet, away from institutionalized confinement comes a sense of emancipation and liberty.

Hoarded in her heart by the longing that finally brought deliverance, she carried on her journey down the road. At that moment, she recalled the day her grandpa mumbled something to her, and his words still reverberated in her thoughts.

"The minute you cross the border, you will shed your nymph. Only then will you be out of the cycle of malice. Only then will you be able to enter the real world and be genuine.

"You were nothing; you are everything.

"May your goodness be restored. May your righteousness be found. And let them guide your path to an open road. Be kind to yourself. Be kind to others. Take this high road to adulthood, and may you set your sights on your destiny."

ENDNOTES

The opinions expressed in this book are largely drawn from individuals of diverse backgrounds over the past decades.

Given its fictional nature, many quotes may not be enclosed in quotation marks. In addition to some footnotes, the quotes are taken from:

Unforgiven

"All persons are endowed with natural rights to life, liberty, and property." John Locke,

English philosopher and physician

"Men being, as has been said, by nature, all free, equal, and independent, no one can be put out of this estate, and subjected to the political power of another, without his own consent." Second Treatise, John Locke

"Let not any one pacify his conscience by the delusion that he can do no harm if he takes no part, and forms no opinion. Bad men need nothing more to compass their ends, than that good men should look on and do nothing." John Stuart Mill, English philosopher, political economist

"Power tends to corrupt and absolute power corrupts absolutely. Great men are almost always bad men." John Dalberg-Acton, English historian and writer

"A property that does not change after certain transformations." Invariance Principle

Event Horizon

"A relationship when one partner needs the other partner, who in turn, needs to be needed." Codependent Relationship, or Cycle Of Codependency, Medical News Today

"A system of anti-human nature, an anti-rational substance composed of ideologies that do not absorb, reflect, or honor human nature. Hence, it cannot be detected, conformed to, or ascertained by principles of humanity." A Dark Entity. Author note

"A human being who completely loses their moral compass exploits the benevolent role they assume and represent to bypass the welfare and security of tens of millions to emerge as a champion." Socialist Survivor Of The Fittest. Author note

The Winding Dirt Road

"A logical rule that states that contradictory propositions cannot be true at the same time and in the same sense." Law Of Non-Contradiction

"... action ensures the long-term survival of the species, by selectively allowing one less idiot to survive." Male Idiot Theory. Ben Alexander Daniel Lendrem, Dennis William Lendrem, Andy Gray, John Dudley Isaacs. The King Edward VI School, UK

"The principle or practice of subtly encouraging a behavior or belief by advocating its opposite." Reverse Psychology. Oxford Languages

A Green Expanse Of Grassland

To My Dear and Loving Husband, Anne Bradstreet, British American Poet

The Mother of All Antidotes

"In order to manifest our desires, we must release attachment to the outcome itself as well as the path we might take to get there." Law of Detachment. Mindbodygreen

"A political belief sees the end justifying humans as inferior by nature. Within this belief system's borders, humans are considered untamed, flawed, and untrustworthy. They must be suppressed, monitored, controlled, supervised, coerced, admit guilt, criticized, and denuded of dignity and respect. They are subjected to unconditional submission or incarceration, alteration of nature under reeducation programs, failure to reason, moralize, or rationalize, following strict directives, and possibly psychotic treatment.

Ultimately, they are expected to become inhumane, unfeeling, insensitive human beings in wartime and peacetime to assist the country whose ambitions override civil liberties and human values." Human Inferiority Supposition.

ACKNOWLEDGEMENT

I'd like to thank Dee Marley, Editor-in-Chief of Historium Press and her staff who made this book possible.

I'd also like to thank Dr Stephen Games, Editor, Booklaunch London, UK, for his comments that prompted a complete reexamination.

ABOUT THE AUTHOR

For years, Jiu Da has been intrigued by the question of whether the environment makes us who we are or whether we are the ones that shape our environment. For the good parts of early years, he stubbornly believed that motivation, talent, and effort could change the outcomes. It did not. It was not until the virus hit while finding himself perching at home that he came to accept that the environment is indeed the hand that shapes human behavior. It was during this time that he started spinning his first work. Yet, his work would only have formed with his interest in literature and history and endless bits and pieces of seemingly useless information hoarded in the depth of his mind in the past decades. Jiu Da lives and writes in Alberta.

www.historiumpress.com